PRAISE FOR
THE GISAWI CHRONICLES

*"With an **authentic and unique** voice, Voelz masterfully delivers a suspense-filled and highly entertaining sequel to* War Under the Mango Tree, *continuing* The Gisawi Chronicles. *The* **espionage tradecraft and geopolitical setup are spot on**, *leaving the reader to ponder where fact and fiction diverge. With* **intriguing characters and addictive dialog**, Operation Hermes *is* **a must-read!***"*

—Dave Edlund

USA Today bestselling author of *Valiant Savage*

"Voelz possesses **a wicked sense of humor that never disappoints**.*"*

—Robert Bruce Adolph

author of *Surviving the United Nations: The Unexpected Challenge*

"A **roller-coaster ride of international intrigue!** *. . . Filled with intriguing characters, a* **larger-than-life storyline, and back-stabbing politics**. *. . . This was a great read, and once started,* **hard to put down**. *[I]t has* **all the elements of a Fredrick Forsyth piece of work**.*"*

—Tom Wangler

author of *Nigeria - An Ancient Secret Becomes the Adventure of a Lifetime*

THE THIRD FORCE

GLENN VOELZ

A NOVEL

The Third Force, *The Gisawi Chronicles, Book 3*
by Glenn Voelz

Copyright © 2021 by Glenn Voelz
All rights reserved
First Edition © 2022

Published by

First Steps Publishing
PO Box 571
Gleneden Beach, OR 97388

The events, peoples, and incidents in this story are the sole product of the author's imagination. The story is fictitious, and any resemblance to individuals, living or dead, is purely coincidental.

Interior layout, cover design by Suzanne Parrott

Library of Congress Control Number: 2022932261
Genre: *dark humor, political satire, military fiction, war*

ISBN: 978-1-944072-65-0 (pb/Amazon)
        978-1-944072-63-6 (hb)
        978-1-944072-64-3 (pb)

10 9 8 7 6 5 4 3 2 1

Printed in the
United States of America.

DEDICATION

For Greg

*"No human being can really understand another,
and no one can arrange another's happiness.*

—Graham Greene

THE GISAWI CHRONICLES

War Under the Mango Tree

Operation Hermes

The Third Force

ACKNOWLEDGMENTS

Thank you to Jonathan for slogging through to the end and giving this far more of your time than it deserved. I'm grateful for your sound advice and friendship.

To Lara, thank you for your careful editing and sharp eye for catching my many errors and missteps.

Thank you to my mother for her willingness to read and reread galley proofs, always finding those last few overlooked mistakes.

Finally, thanks to Suzanne for supporting me along the way and being an endless source of good advice and encouragement.

*"The greatest victory
is that which requires no battle."*
—*Sun Tzu,* The Art of War

CHAPTER ONE

"I call this meeting to order," the chairman said, tapping his pencil against the microphone, scolding the room into silence. "Ladies and gentlemen, I welcome you to the House Armed Services Subcommittee Briefing on Intelligence and Emerging Threats. We are honored to have General A- with us here today, recently returned from his tour as the commander of Operation Brighter Dawn, the US advisory mission to the Democratic Republic of Gisawi.

"I remind everyone that this is a closed-door, classified briefing," he said before turning to the witness. "General A-, thank you for joining us and for your many years of tireless service to our nation."

The general sat ramrod-straight behind the table, a granite-jawed warrior, chest adorned with a collage of ribbons and badges. He took a sip of water and cleared his throat.

"Thank you, Mr. Chairman. I appreciate the opportunity to provide the committee with an update on our progress in DRoG. I trust that you received a copy of my prepared remarks?"

"Indeed, general. Thank you for the detailed overview. Perhaps we can start with your assessment of the ongoing counterinsurgency campaign," the chairman suggested.

General A- nodded and refilled his tumbler, hydrating for optimal performance. "As the committee members are aware, DRoG has been a vital US security partner since the days of the Cold War. More recently, it has become a critical hub in our fight against radical extremism by hosting our regional counterterrorism operating base."

"You're referring to the facility opened after Operation Brushfire?" the chairman asked.

"Correct. However, since the unexpected departure of former President Namono two years ago, DRoG has experienced a period of severe political and economic turmoil and the complete collapse of its internal defense apparatus. This situation created a security vacuum in the western region, which has become a breeding ground for the proliferation of adversarial non-state actors."

"I assume you're referring to the resurgence of the Gisawian Liberation Army?"

"Yes, Mr. Chairman." The general nodded grimly.

"For the committee's benefit, can you briefly characterize the nature of this threat to the American people?"

"After the fall of Green House and collapse of the Gisawian security forces, a group calling itself the new GLA emerged along the border region, gradually gaining strength and expanding its area of influence. We assess that this group now poses an existential threat to the viability of the PIG."

"PIG?" the chairman asked, losing track of the acronyms.

"The Gisawian Provisional Interim Government," the general explained.

"Objection!" a voice called out from the far end of the committee table.

The chairman winced as if jabbed in the side with a sharp stick, then turned to address the junior member of his committee. "Congressman Burke, need I remind you that this is not a legal proceeding? There are no objections to informational briefings. Do you have a question for the general?"

"Indeed I do!" Burke declared, puffing up in his chair. "General, can you please explain how the administration's bungling of the post-Namono transition enabled the GLA to regenerate so rapidly?"

The general's gaze drifted to his notes as he gathered his thoughts before speaking.

"Congressman Burke, those events occurred before the start of Operation Brighter Dawn. I was not privy to the decision-making process during that phase of the crisis."

"General, there's no need to beat around the bush," Burke pressed. "I think by now we're all familiar with what transpired. Before the Chinese-backed coup attempt, the CIA had identified a capable pro-American faction inside DRoG. This highly trained group of indigenous patriots was ready and able to stabilize the country after President Namono's departure."

"I assume you're referring to the Citizens Action Committee, led by the president's son, Fabrice Namono?" the general asked.

"Of course I am!" Burke spat in frustration. "But our feckless leadership in the White House deliberately yanked its support for the CAC at the critical moment of the crisis in a historic act of cowardice not seen since the Bay of Pigs!"

"As I said, congressman, I was not a party to those deliberations," the general said. "Therefore, it would be inappropriate for me to comment on the relative merits of the president's strategy."

"We're getting nowhere fast," Burke huffed. "General, let me be more specific with my question. In your professional military opinion, was the president of the United States derelict in his duty when he sold out a courageous band of freedom fighters in exchange for the lottery ticket of democratic elections?"

"Congressman Burke!" the chairman interrupted. "We only have a short time with the general. We're not here to relitigate Operation Hermes or debate the president's decision-making concerning US support for Fabrice Namono and the CAC. I ask that you please focus your questions on the current military situation in DRoG."

Burke slumped into his chair with his arms crossed and lips pursed into a pout.

"My apologies, general," the chairman said. "Please carry on."

"As I was saying. Over the last twelve months, we've made enormous progress in our effort to rebuild DRoG's army, helping them to contain and degrade the GLA."

"General, if I may," the chairman interrupted. "Can you provide us with some perspective on the apparent discrepancy between the Pentagon's view of the situation on the ground and the dire reports we're reading in the media?"

The general tensed in his chair, sensing an ambush. He waited, preferring to let the adversary reveal his position.

"I'm referring to a headline last week suggesting that the counterinsurgency campaign has stalled," the chairman continued. "The article claimed that the GLA has the initiative in the western region. Over the last two weeks, there have been multiple attacks against the forward operating base in Kiskow. How should we evaluate these events in light of your otherwise positive assessment?"

"Mr. Chairman, I can assure you that our strategy in DRoG is working," the general growled. "We are taking GLA fighters off the battlefield every day. We've reinforced the garrison in Kiskow and stepped up surveillance along the border. The GLA is largely contained in a remote, unpopulated part of the country. Despite what you're reading in the papers, our counterinsurgency campaign has turned a corner. We're on a glide path to victory."

"General, what about the GLA's sanctuary areas across the border? How do the Gisawians intend to defeat an enemy that enjoys a safe haven across an international boundary?"

"There is no safe haven for the GLA!" the general snapped. "We've degraded the GLA's command and control structure and strangled its logistic networks. Just last week, a precision strike operation against a high-value leadership target took out the GLA's number two operative."

"With all due respect, general, by my count, this is the third time this year that we've taken out the GLA's number two," the chairman noted.

The general's fingers tightened around his tumbler, threatening to shatter the glass in his bare hand. "Mr. Chairman, there will always be a number two," he snarled.

The room fell silent as the committee paused to ponder the irrefutable logic of warfare.

"Be that as it may, do we even know who's leading the GLA?" the chairman continued. "What do you make of these claims that the warlord Daniel Odoki has returned to take charge of his rebel army?”

“It’s a hoax!” Burke blurted out from the end of the table, waving his hands wildly in the air. “We killed him! I was there!”

The chairman’s microphone captured a deep sigh. “Congressman Burke, the committee is well aware of your record in DRoG. And we thank you, *again*, for your service. However, we’re here today for the general’s assessment. Sir, my apologies for the interruption. Please continue.”

“The insurgents are using Daniel Odoki’s legend as a pro-paganda tool,” the general insisted. “It’s nothing more than a psychological tactic intended to frighten and intimidate the local population.”

“So, you’re saying that it doesn’t matter whether Odoki is dead or alive?”

“We’re confident that he’s dead. However, we are en-gaged in a war of perception. All that matters is what the people believe.”

“Are you suggesting that we may need to kill him again?”

“Yes, Mr. Chairman. If the opportunity presents itself, we will exercise that option.”

“I have a question for the general,” Burke interrupted.

The chairman glanced at this watch and nodded re-luctantly, ceding the floor to the junior congressman from Pennsylvania.

“General, I think it’s obvious to everyone in this room that our strategy in DRoG is failing,” Burke stated. “We’re never going to win unless we take the fight directly to the GLA on their home turf.”

"Congressman Burke, as you know, we are operationally constrained by the complexities of the regional security environment," the general explained. "Given DRoG's history of adversarial relations with its neighbors, any ground incursion by the Gisawian forces across the international border risks triggering a major regional war."

"But what if it wasn't DRoG's army crossing the border?" Burke asked cryptically.

"I'm sorry, congressman, I don't take your meaning."

"I'm saying, what if there was a third force?"

"A third force?" The general looked nonplussed.

"A nonaligned entity, with the freedom to operate inside the GLA's sanctuary area. In your professional military opinion, could such an element have a decisive effect on the battlefield?"

"Congressman, an initiative like that is far above my pay grade."

"But hypothetically, could such a force, operating across the border, provide a distinct military advantage in the fight against the GLA?" Burke pressed. "That's a yes or no question, general. How do you respond?"

"Congressman Burke, we're not here to discuss hypotheticals!" the chairman interjected, glaring down the table at his colleague.

The general hesitated, caught in the crossfire and needing to move boldly. "Yes," he blurted out. "In my professional opinion, such a force would be militarily advantageous."

"Thank you, general," Burke said with satisfaction. "I have no further questions."

+++

Anna glanced at her watch, trying to decide whether to give Louie ten more minutes before ordering. Fortunately, the wait wasn't particularly unpleasant; she was passing time in the garden patio of her favorite restaurant. It was a cozy bungalow on a quiet street, far removed from the city's hustle and bustle. The usual clientele occupied the tables around her: a mix of diplomatic staff, expat businesspeople, and affluent Gisawians. Occasionally, a savvy tourist would discover the place based on a tip, but mostly it was a well-kept local secret.

Anna's visits there were a guilty pleasure, considering that the price of a dinner salad cost nearly the daily wage for the average local worker. She rationalized the occasional indulgence, telling herself that cooking dinner at home every night wouldn't solve the world's problems.

She read through the menu a third time, deciding what to order for Louie if he didn't show up soon. The offerings were vaguely continental, peppered with a few local dishes for adventurous customers wanting something authentic without the risk of intestinal distress from a roadside food stall. Anna felt her stomach growling and was on the verge of ordering when Louie walked into the garden.

"Sorry I'm late," he said, kissing her on the cheek and slipping into his seat. "I was stuck in meetings all day over at the American base."

"When do you get work done if you spend all day in meetings?"

"Good question. I suppose the meetings are the work," Louie answered, realizing the absurdity of what he was saying.

"Sounds fulfilling," Anna deadpanned.

"Mind-numbing would be more accurate," Louie sighed, delving into the menu.

"Are they still arguing over the security plan for the election?"

"Among other things. We're less than four months away and still don't have any idea how it's going to work. After the attacks last week in Kiskow, the Americans are getting nervous. The last thing they want is for the GLA to make a mess of the election and embarrass the Provisional Interim Government."

Anna frowned. "Is that likely?"

"I wouldn't bet against it. There will be hundreds of polling places scattered around the country. Even with the entire army deployed, we still don't have nearly enough soldiers to protect all the locations," Louie admitted.

"Are the Americans aware of the risk?"

"Of course they are, but no one wants to say it out loud. Every time the GLA launches another attack, it undermines the rosy story they've been telling back in DC. They've finally realized that an election isn't an exit strategy. I think they'd prefer to declare victory and move on to the next thing."

"We are not known as a people of long attention spans," Anna said with a helpless shrug.

Louie chuckled but left the comment alone. He caught the eye of the waitress and waved her over to the table.

"How were classes today?" he asked after they placed their orders.

"The usual, I suppose," Anna sighed. "I'm afraid that the life of an adjunct professor isn't much more exciting than nation-building by PowerPoint. In either case, one can't have a burning need for immediate gratification. The best we can hope for is that we're both planting seeds that will someday bear fruit."

"Next week will be the first anniversary since the university reopened. Are things finally getting back to normal?"

"Define normal," Anna requested.

"Hmmm. Administrative dysfunction, poisonous bureaucratic politics, and entitled students?" Louie said, winking playfully at her across the table.

"Ha! I grant you that the first two haven't changed, but my students deserve more credit than you give them. Don't forget, they did their part to get President Namono out of Green House. We wouldn't be sitting here talking about elections right now if they hadn't been willing to take that risk."

Louie looked dubious. "I'm not sure that sending the country into chaos and fueling an armed insurgency is something they should put on their resumes."

"You know what I mean!" Anna scolded him. "At least they didn't sit around complacently, waiting for someone else to make a change."

"Fair enough. However, they should know that dismantling a government is easier than putting one back together. No matter who wins the election, the hard part begins the day it's over."

"Speaking of elections," Anna said, ready to change the subject, "I'm going to see Didier and Nesi later this week."

"How have they been?"

"The same as always: burning the candle at both ends. A few months ago, they were unpaid volunteers on Francois Akua's campaign. Now, they're nearly running the entire show. I honestly don't know how they keep up with classes. They've been spending every free moment over at Akua party headquarters."

"Plotting the socialist revolution, I presume," Louie quipped.

"Please, Louie!" Anna groaned. "You sound like one of those attack ads on the radio."

"It's all the same to me," he shrugged. "I'm a simple soldier. I will follow the lawful orders of whoever ends up in Green House."

"I don't believe that for a second," Anna shot back.

"What part don't you believe? That I'll follow my orders? Or that I don't care who wins?"

"You know what I mean," she said, frustrated at his stubbornness. "You've got as much invested in the outcome of this election as anyone. Probably more. You expect me to believe that you don't care who wins?"

"Sure, I have an opinion. Just not one that I'm willing to share."

"Even with your wife?" Anna exclaimed, unable to hide her annoyance. "While I admire your adherence to principle, I think you're taking it to an extreme."

Louie feigned indifference and sidestepped her question. "The Americans aren't nearly as discrete about their preference," he said. "It's obvious that Francois Akua is not their first choice for Green House."

"But they aren't saying that publicly," Anna noted.

"No, of course not. They're under strict orders not to play favorites. But it's not difficult to read between the lines."

"Exactly what part of Francois' platform does my government find problematic?" Anna asked sarcastically. "He's running on a good governance agenda: anti-corruption, gender equality, jobs, and education. How on earth are those things threatening to America's geopolitical interests?"

"None of them are per se. However, the Americans seem concerned that he'll be overly friendly toward the Chinese or even reopen negotiations on the status of the counterterrorism operating base."

"They'd rather see Emanuel Sekibo or Fabrice Namono sitting in Green House instead?" Anna exclaimed. "That's completely crazy! Either one of them would be like a return to the old regime. They might as well put President Namono back in charge."

"I didn't say it made sense," Louie insisted. "I'm just telling you the rumors I hear around the American camp. I don't think anyone wants Fabrice Namono to come back and claim his father's seat. But for some reason, the Americans seem to think that Emanuel Sekibo is a safer bet."

"Safer for who? Sekibo was notorious for torturing people during all those years he was in charge of Police Intelligence."

Louie threw up his hands, unable to provide a reasonable answer. "I can only assume that the Americans believe that he's more likely to keep fighting the GLA. They want out and would prefer to walk away with something resembling a victory. Washington is worried that Francois Akua isn't committed to winning."

"Winning what?" Anna asked incredulously. "I've been living here almost four years and don't have the slightest idea of how the world is a safer place for having American soldiers here. It doesn't make any sense."

"The internal logic of empire, I suppose," Louie sighed with resignation.

"Speak of the devil," Anna whispered. She nodded across the room as a group of off-duty American soldiers barged into the cafe. They appeared slightly drunk, likely from an early evening pub crawl. The other patrons tried to ignore the disruption as the waitress steered the tipsy GIs to a table in the far corner of the garden.

"Do you know them?" Anna whispered.

Louie shook his head.

"They're probably from the counterterrorism operating base. I don't deal much with them."

Anna nodded, eyeing the men suspiciously as they stumbled to their seats and promptly ordered a round of drinks. When the waitress arrived with their meals, Anna and Louie ate quickly, reluctant to linger, as the soldiers had spoiled the ambiance.

"Have they told you anything about your next assignment?" Anna asked, trying to ignore the inebriated banter from across the garden.

"My career progression is the least of anyone's concerns right now. I doubt I'll hear anything until after the new administration gets settled into Green House. No matter who wins, I expect there will be a major reshuffling at the top of the ministry. Until that plays out, things won't get sorted down at my level."

"It's a bit surreal to realize your future—*our* future depends on what happens with the election."

"Anna, you knew that would be the case when we decided to stay," Louie reminded her. "I hope you aren't regretting it."

"No. It's just that it's becoming somewhat less abstract now that we're closer to the end. Or I should say, the beginning." Anna poked at the remains of her food, having lost her appetite. "Has your mother said anything more about moving back here after the election?"

Louie shook his head. "She's just like everyone else: waiting to see what happens before making any big decisions. I know she loves being around her grandchildren, but she can't live at my brother's house forever. Besides, New Jersey is a long way from home. I think she misses her friends back here."

"Would it be hard for her to come back after everything that happened with your uncle?" Anna asked.

"She's tried to put it out of her mind. We all know that he's still out there somewhere. I suppose if he wanted to contact my mother, he could do it."

"I don't think Mugaba would ever take that chance," Anna speculated. "He's on every watchlist in the world. If he tried to get on a plane or call your mom, it wouldn't stay a secret for very long."

"I'm sure my uncle is aware of the risks. That's why we haven't seen or heard anything from him in almost two years."

Louie saw the waitress delivering another round of drinks to the soldiers. When she passed by their table, he asked for the check.

"No coffee tonight?" Anna asked.

"I'm exhausted, and I have a long day tomorrow. We have our first meeting with the new American general in the morning. I need to go in early to prepare."

They paid the check and left the restaurant as the sun dipped below the horizon. Louie took Anna's hand and led her across the street to where he'd left the car. Just as his foot touched the gravel on the far side of the asphalt, Louie was lifted into the air by the force of a blast from behind them and lost his grip on Anna's hand. They tumbled into a shallow ditch beyond the edge of the pavement. Bits of debris fell around them.

Louie called out Anna's name but couldn't hear her reply, if there was one, over the sound of bleating car alarms. He rose unsteadily to his knees and glanced over his shoulder. The street was carpeted with shards of broken glass, shimmering in the fading sunlight. Smoke billowed from the restaurant, pouring through the broken windows. A few customers stumbled out the door, gasping for air.

Louie spun around, frantically searching for Anna, and spotted her lying face down in the ditch. Her clothes were covered in dust, and bits of debris were tangled in her hair. Louie scrambled to her side and reached for her shoulder. He gasped with relief when she responded to his touch.

"What happened?" she asked weakly, straining to lift her head.

"I think it was a bomb somewhere in the cafe. Maybe near the garden. Are you all right?"

Anna hesitated, then nodded. Spots of blood dotted her blouse and the backs of her legs where flying debris had nicked her skin. Louie helped her sit up and checked her for other injuries. When he was satisfied there weren't any, Anna hugged her knees and rested her head on her forearms.

"I'm going back in to help," Louie blurted out.

Anna nodded without processing what he was saying. Louie was gone before she had time to argue, sprinting across the street, heading back into the burning cafe.

The following day, Louie was sitting in a conference room on the American base, the only Gisawian officer at the table. The rest of the seats were occupied by American staffers from a dozen different agencies with obscure acronyms that Louie could never keep straight. Collectively, they represented the senior staff of Operation Brighter Dawn, the American advisory mission to the Democratic Republic of Gisawi.

They were awaiting the arrival of the new commander, General B-. Stacks of briefing books and slides littered the table. Someone had brought in a tray of coffee and pastries, anticipating an extended meeting. Amid the flurry of last-minute preparations, no one had bothered asking Louie about the bandages covering his head.

Colonel Severs, the chief of staff, appeared in the doorway and called the room to attention. Everyone leaped to their feet as General B- marched through the door. He moved decisively for the table's head, having played this role before.

"Good morning, team!" he barked out, exuding the aggressive enthusiasm of a high school football coach.

He scanned the roomful of white faces, stopping in confusion when his eyes fell upon Louie, the only Black man in the room, wearing a Gisawian military uniform, with his head wrapped in gauze.

"What the hell happened to you, soldier?" the general called out across the room.

Louie swayed unsteadily on his feet, feeling worse than when he'd arrived. Colonel Severs' jaw clenched with frustration when he spotted Louie, realizing that his carefully planned agenda for the general was already going off the rails. Severs scanned the room, looking for someone to blame for allowing Louie into the meeting looking as if he'd stumbled off some colonial-era battlefield.

Louie squinted under the glare of the fluorescent lights. He had a splitting headache and was having difficulty focusing on the general. Everyone around the table held their breath, waiting for him to speak or collapse onto the floor. It dawned upon Louie that he should have called in sick, but now he had no choice but to press on.

"I was involved in an incident last night but didn't want to miss the meeting," Louie mumbled, gripping the chair to keep upright.

"First, who are you? Second, why are you here?" General B- asked.

Colonel Severs jumped in, trying to regain control of the meeting. "General, this is Colonel Louie Bigombe of the Gisawian army. He's in charge of GAT MAP."

"GAT MAP? What the hell is that?"

"The Gisawian Army Training, Modernization, and Assistance Program. GAT MAP for short," Severs clarified. "It's our program for rebuilding DRoG's army. Colonel Bigombe works with us and coordinates everything on the Gisawian side."

"Got it," the general said, then turned back to Louie. "Colonel Bigombe, this incident you're referring to. Was that the bombing last night that got a few of our soldiers?"

"Yes, sir."

"General, we evacuated two men up to Germany this morning, both in stable condition," Colonel Severs interjected before anyone else had time to answer. "A few American civilians were also in the restaurant at the time. They were treated for minor injuries at a local hospital and released. Fortunately, we didn't take any other casualties."

General B- nodded and rubbed his chin. "Sounds like we got lucky this time."

"There were other casualties," Louie interrupted, contradicting Colonel Severs. "A waitress in the restaurant was killed. She was serving your soldiers when the bomb went off."

The room fell silent, waiting for General B- to respond.

"My condolences, Colonel Bigombe," he offered. "Of course, any death is a tragedy. Do we know who did it?"

"The GLA released a statement this morning claiming responsibility for the attack," Colonel Severs blurted out.

"Since when has the GLA been conducting attacks outside the western region?" the general asked, confused.

"They haven't, until last night," Severs answered. "We've assumed that retaking Kiskow was their top priority. Yesterday's attack was the first one here in the capital."

General B- turned his attention to Louie.

"Colonel Bigombe, what's your government saying about the bombing? Do they think the GLA is changing their strategy?"

"It's too soon to say for sure," Louie replied. "DSPO is investigating. I expect we'll know more soon."

"DSPO?"

"The Directorate for Security and Public Order. It was previously called Police Intelligence under the Namono government, but they changed the name. DSPO is responsible for internal security and counterterrorism. The bombing investigation falls under their jurisdiction."

The general nodded, eyes bright with interest. "If we're still assuming that the GLA's primary objective is taking back Kiskow, how does bombing a restaurant full of civilians help them achieve that?"

"I can't explain it, sir," Louie offered. "But that restaurant is popular with expats. Whoever did it must have known they were hitting a target filled with foreigners. That attack was intended to make headlines."

The general rapped his knuckles on the table, thinking over Louie's explanation. Colonel Severs seized upon the lull in the conversation. "General B-, we have a full schedule for your first day. Perhaps we can move on with our plan."

The general nodded and gave him a thumbs-up before turning back to Louie. "Colonel Bigombe, you look like you could use a day off. Don't feel like you need to be here for all these briefings. We'll have a chance to talk later." The general glanced over at Colonel Severs. "Let's get this thing started."

The lights dimmed, and slides appeared on the screen. Soon, everyone's attention was focused on the briefing. No one noticed Louie taking his seat and staying as the presentation began.

+++

Several hours later, the meeting adjourned for a short break. Louie went out into the courtyard for some fresh air. When he stepped into the sunlight, he felt his headache return. He had only gotten a few hours of fitful sleep after leaving the emergency room, then had come straight into the office. After the series of mind-numbing briefings, he wondered why he had even bothered. Louie closed his eyes and leaned against the building, debating whether to go back inside when the session resumed.

"Are you all right?" a voice called from the doorway.

Louie turned, squinting into the sun to see who was speaking. He vaguely recognized a young man who had been sitting in the back row of the conference room. Louie thought he was new on the staff, some kind of civilian advisor. He tried to recall the man's name but couldn't remember it.

"I'm fine," he replied.

The man walked over and stuck out his hand. "Owen Smith," he said. "I got here a few weeks ago. I don't think we've met yet."

Louie gave a weak handshake and studied the man more closely. He was generically all-American-looking. Louie guessed that he was in his late twenties, probably at the start of his career and eager to make a mark by coming to DRoG. His work attire consisted of a polo shirt stitched with the emblem of some obscure government agency, khaki pants, and beige combat boots, and he had a pair of wraparound sunglasses perched atop a tuft of close-cropped hair. The ensemble struck Louie as a uniquely American reinterpretation of the pith helmet and jodhpurs.

"Remind me again what you do here?" Louie asked. "There are so many people coming and going that I can't keep track anymore."

"I know what you mean," Owen said, grinning self-consciously. "I'm on the GET DRIP portfolio."

Louie stared at him blankly, his head pounding even more. "I'm sorry, but I don't have the slightest idea what that is," he admitted.

"Right. All these acronyms. They're a bit much, aren't they?" Owen said, chuckling. "It's the Gisawian Electoral Training and Democratic Reform Initiatives Program. GET DRIP. I'm on a short-term contract with the State Department, helping your government manage the election's technical aspects. Between you and me, it's pretty dry stuff. But critically important, of course."

"I suppose you must have run several elections, given that someone put you in charge of this one," Louie said dryly.

Owen cocked his head, vaguely aware of being trolled but uncertain how to respond.

"I'm sorry. That was rude," Louie muttered before Owen had a chance to reply. "I'm not feeling well. I didn't mean to take it out on you. I'm sure that whatever you're doing here is meant to help."

"Oh, I get it. No offense taken," Owen reassured him.

They stood for a moment in silence before Owen made another attempt at small talk.

"Can I ask about something you said during the meeting?"

Louie nodded but was struggling to remember what he had said just a few hours before.

"It was about the bombing at the restaurant," Owen clarified. "You didn't mention anything about the election. You don't think the bombing could be related?"

"I'm not discounting the possibility; however, I think it's too soon to say that for sure."

"Don't you think that the GLA would want to influence the election?" Owen speculated.

"Sure, I suppose anything's possible. But bombing a restaurant seems a rather blunt instrument for such a specific purpose. I'm not sure what they could hope to achieve by that."

"Good point," Owen agreed. "But we also shouldn't rule it out entirely."

"I suppose this is one of your areas of expertise?" Louie sighed, trying to think of a way to end the conversation.

"More of a side interest. I wrote a paper in grad school about affective influences on voting behavior, such as measuring electoral response to emotional states like fear and anxiety," Owen explained.

"I didn't realize that was a field of study."

"Oh, sure. Have you ever heard of Dr. Timothy Ziegler?"

"Should I have?"

"He's a scientist. A *political* scientist. Ziegler did some of the foundational research in the field. But now, he's mostly focused on the area of digital democracy. His most recent work is on a concept he calls virtual candidacy."

Louie glanced conspicuously at his watch, hoping Owen would take the hint. No such luck.

"That's one of the reasons I'm so excited to be here," Owen continued. "This election could offer a validation of Dr. Ziegler's central thesis, the VIVID model."

"VIVID?" Louie asked reflexively, immediately regretting it.

"Virtual Interactive Voter Integrated Democracy," Owen explained. "It's a new paradigm of political communication: hyper-personalized, digitally targeted campaigning that replaces formalized political discourse like speeches, rallies, and press conferences."

"What's the point?"

"Dr. Ziegler is predicting the total disintermediation of the political process whereby traditional media loses its status as king-maker and arbiter of truth," Owen enthused. "He sees digital democracy overturning the monopoly on the dissemination of political information. Instead, a candidate's success will be determined by their ability to capture a voter's imagination through one-on-one digital interactions."

"And…this is considered a positive development?" Louie asked.

"Dr. Ziegler isn't making a normative claim. He's simply describing the end-state of a path we're already on, a technology-enabled democratic process that's direct, visceral, and authentic. Why waste time kissing babies at rural campaign stops when you can energize thousands, maybe millions, of voters in seconds with individualized social media posts?"

"It sounds like chaos to me."

"Hardly," Owen scoffed. "We're already seeing the future of virtual candidacy right here in DRoG. Just look at Fabrice Namono. He's running his entire campaign remotely, appealing directly to voters through targeted digital interactions."

"Are you aware that Fabrice is in exile? If he stepped foot in this country, he'd be arrested."

"True. But that doesn't invalidate his clever use of technology. In many ways, Fabrice is proving everything that Dr. Ziegler has been describing for years. I can get you a copy of Ziegler's book if you're interested," Owen offered enthusiastically.

"Not really."

"Let me know if you change your mind," Owen urged. "I think you'd find it fascinating."

Louie nodded, hoping to drop the matter entirely and making a mental note to avoid sitting near Owen in the future. "I assume you'll be leaving once the election is over?" he asked hopefully.

"My contract is open-ended," Owen explained. "I'll stay as long as they need me."

Colonel Severs appeared in the doorway, signaling to everyone that the break was over. He turned to where Owen and Louie were standing.

"Colonel Bigombe, you don't need to stick around here for the afternoon session," Severs said. "We're briefing the general on the new DRoG 2035 development plan. It doesn't pertain to your portfolio, so you should go home and get some rest. You can check back in tomorrow."

"If it's all the same to you, I'd be curious to hear about this plan," Louie said. "Perhaps it might even be useful to have someone in the room with a Gisawian passport."

"Is that some kind of a joke?" Severs growled.

"Sadly, no."

"Suit yourself," Severs sneered. "But I don't want any more showboating in front of the general," he warned, squinting suspiciously at the bandages on Louie's head. Without waiting for Louie's reply, Severs turned on his heel and disappeared back into the building.

+++

Two days later, Louie was sitting outside a sundries shop near the city's bustling central market. The table offered a front-row seat for viewing the ecosystem of unrestrained capitalism. The road passing by the store was in a state of perpetual gridlock, no matter the time of day. Street hawkers maneuvered through snarled traffic, knocking on the windows of idled cars and offering drivers a selection of bottled water, snacks, and trinkets displayed in cardboard boxes. Small mountains of Chinese-made plastic goods overflowed from the shops, turning the sidewalk into an obstacle course. Between the storefronts, women merchants dressed in colorful, floral-patterned wraps sat behind plywood tables, selling fruits, vegetables, and sacks of dried spices.

Louie had been a regular customer at the shop for years. In addition to selling sundries, the owner served cups of cheap coffee and homemade pastries to patrons at a few tables set out on the sidewalk. The noise and chaos of the street made it the perfect place for sitting unnoticed. One could linger there for hours without attracting attention.

The shopkeeper appeared at the table, delivering Louie's milky tea, a cup of coffee, and a plate of fried dough. Louie nodded his thanks and slipped the man a few Gisawi banknotes. While he waited, an overcrowded minibus inched by, spewing sooty black smoke. Louie covered his nose with a handkerchief, trying not to breathe the fumes. When the exhaust cleared, Louie spotted a familiar face across the street. He watched the man working his way through traffic toward the shop. Louie smiled and rose from his chair to greet him.

"It's good to see you, Patrick," Louie said, pulling him in for a hug.

"Likewise," Patrick said. "You look terrible, my friend," he added, nodding at the cuts and bruises still visible on Louie's face.

"It looks worse than it is," Louie said.

"How's Anna?"

"Still shook up, but OK. She's taking the week off work," Louie explained.

"Was she injured badly?"

"Fortunately, no. We were lucky. She got a few stitches, but I think it was the business with the waitress that bothered her more. One second, the girl was giving us our change. The next moment, we were out the door, and she was dead. It all happened so quickly."

"I'm sorry for you both," Patrick said. "How goes the rebuilding of the army?"

Louie shrugged without enthusiasm. "How does that saying go? It's like trying to build an airplane in flight. As soon as we train the new soldiers, we send them right out into the fight. Some of them are seeing action within days of arriving in Kiskow."

"Will you move back to a field assignment once the election is over?"

"It's too far off to think about."

"What do you mean? The election is just a few months away."

Louie avoided Patrick's eyes and gazed into his tea. "To be honest, I'm not interested in a new position," he revealed. "Between you and me, I've been thinking about other opportunities."

"Other than the army?" Patrick gasped. "For as long as I've known you, that's all you ever wanted to do. When we were little boys, you always insisted on playing army. You told our teachers that you wanted to become a soldier, just like your father, even when they scolded you and said you should become a doctor instead."

"I know," Louie chuckled, thinking back on the elaborate military parades they had staged in the backyard as kids. "But eventually, one must move on from childhood fantasies. The grown-up version is never quite as we imagine."

"Have you told Anna?"

"Not yet. But I doubt she'll care. The decision to stay here hasn't been easy on her either. It's been a big sacrifice with little to show for it. What about you? How are things over at DSPO?"

Patrick chuckled and shook his head. "It still sounds funny to hear it called that, because on the inside, it's the same old Police Intelligence. Only the name has changed, not the way it does business."

Louie frowned. "That's not the story they're telling the Americans. It's all 'good governance' and 'the rule of law.' No more secret interrogation rooms and forced confessions."

"A leopard doesn't change its spots," Patrick warned. "Emanuel Sekibo may not be in charge anymore, but it's still his organization. Don't be fooled by the new name."

"I suppose I'm not surprised," Louie said. "Everyone said that when he left the government to start Sekibo Security Services, he was building a private version of Police Intelligence."

"That sounds about right," Patrick confirmed. "Sekibo built S3 Corp right out of his old office with help from his cronies. It's hard to tell where one organization ends and the other begins."

"Then I'm assuming everyone in DSPO will be voting for Sekibo in the election? Presumably, if their old boss gets into Green House, they won't need to worry about people poking into their business."

"I'd say that's a safe assumption," Patrick agreed.

"Speaking of DSPO, what have you heard about the bombing investigation? Do they have any leads yet?"

"I have no idea. I'm out of the loop."

"What do you mean?" Louie asked, surprised. "How's that possible? You're a section chief in the analytic bureau. Aren't terrorism investigations part of your portfolio?"

"They should be, but they've compartmentalized everything involving the GLA. It's all been moved into a separate fusion cell. They're handling all of the evidence relating to the bombing."

"Why would they do that?"

"Your guess is as good as mine." Patrick shrugged. "Anything involving the GLA goes straight to the fusion cell, then up to the director of DSPO. Access is on a strict need-to-know basis. And that doesn't include me."

"Strange," Louie murmured, sipping his tea, thinking through what Patrick had revealed. "Well, if you hear anything, please let me know."

"No problem. But do me a favor."

"Sure."

"Don't call me," Patrick said, without the hint of a smile.

"What you mean? I don't understand."

"We shouldn't be talking about this stuff on the phone. Meeting face-to-face is fine, but don't call or text my number.

In fact, it would be best if you just erased my contact information from your phone altogether."

"You can't be serious," Louie said. "Aren't you being a little paranoid?"

"You know what I do over at DSPO," Patrick said. "I'm in charge of the signals branch. My job is to keep tabs on what people do on their phones. Please trust me when I tell you that we shouldn't be having sensitive discussions on one of these." He held up his cell phone to emphasize the point.

Louie realized that Patrick was serious. He put down his tea and leaned across the table, lowering his voice. "We've been friends since we were boys. Over the years, you've put yourself in danger for me several times. I want you to know that I appreciate it."

Patrick waved his hands in the air, dismissing Louie's gratitude.

"I'm serious," Louie insisted. "I'd probably be in jail right now, or worse, if you hadn't helped me get that memory card from the drone wreckage after the attack on President Namono. And those interrogation reports during Operation Brushfire. What I'm saying is that you've done more than enough for me. I don't want you taking any more chances on my account. It's not worth it."

"You leave that for me to decide," Patrick said. "Don't think that I do these things just for you. I have my reasons for the risks I take."

"I know that, Patrick. But please, be careful," Louie begged.

Patrick finished his coffee in a quick gulp. "I'm sorry to rush off, but I've got a meeting back at headquarters."

Louie nodded and glanced at his watch. "I need to get back to the camp as well. Same time next week?"

Patrick nodded in turn and rose from the table. "Drinks are on me next time," he said. "And don't forget. No phone calls."

Louie waved goodbye as Patrick disappeared into the crowd. He took a last sip of the tea and grabbed his cell phone, making a mental note to be more careful about what he discussed on the phone with Anna.

CHAPTER TWO

Anna didn't leave the house for a week after the bombing. While Louie was at work, she kept herself busy catching up on household chores and puttering around the garden, listening inattentively to the news. Whenever she tried to do serious work, she found her thoughts too fragmented. While grading papers or composing an email, she got lost in the middle of the task, often needing to start over. No matter how hard she tried to distract herself, Anna's thoughts kept going back to that evening at the cafe, seeing the smiling waitress leave the check on the table moments before the bomb exploded.

After a week of self-imposed isolation, Anna finally ventured from the house, determined not to miss her appointment with Nesi and Didier. When she first got behind the wheel of the car, it felt good to be in control. But her anxiety returned as soon as she encountered heavy traffic near the city center. By the time she got to the cafe, Anna wasn't even sure if she could go inside.

She sat in the car and tried some mindfulness exercises that she'd found on the internet. Gradually, she gained control over her heart rate and breathing, enough that she felt able to continue with her plan. She paused outside the cafe door, took a deep breath, and stepped into the garden. The familiar surroundings had a calming effect, boosting her courage. Anna was relieved to see Nesi and Didier already waiting for her at a table; she was unsure if she would have stayed otherwise. When Nesi spotted her, she smiled and waved for Anna to join them.

"How are you?" Nesi asked, rising from her chair and holding Anna in a long embrace.

"I've been better," she replied, reluctantly letting go and sitting down.

"We couldn't believe it when we heard the news," Didier said. "You should have called us from the hospital. We would have come and picked you up."

"You know Louie," Anna said. "He would never want to trouble anyone by asking for help. He drove us home from the hospital, looking like a mummy with his head wrapped in bandages."

"Have you heard anything more about the investigation?" Nesi asked.

Anna shook her head. "Nothing more than what's already in the news. Louie met with his old friend from DSPO, but he didn't know anything either. It seems like they're keeping everything under wraps."

"Why are they so secretive?" Nesi asked. "The GLA already claimed responsibility. What more do they need to know?"

"I'm not sure. Maybe they think there's something else… to it…" Anna said, her voice trailing off.

She glanced around the cafe, realizing it had been a long time since she had been there. It was midday, and most of the tables were empty. A bored-looking waitress was slumped on a barstool, staring at her cell phone. The floor was unswept, and the plants in the garden were brown and withered from lack of care. Anna spotted some old artifacts from the original Sujah Bean Cafe, now dust-covered and faded from the sun.

"This place has seen better days," she said, feeling a sad nostalgia.

"Ever since Sammy left, the place has fallen apart," Nesi agreed. "I'm not even sure who owns it now."

"Do you ever hear from him?" Didier asked.

"Sammy?" Anna replied, awakened from her reverie. "Now that you mention it, no. The last time I saw him was when he delivered the final meal to the university during the sit-in. That must have been the night before Green House burned down. After that, he disappeared."

"You know about rumors, right?" Nesi asked.

Anna shook her head.

"People say that he was working for the CIA," Nesi whispered, even though they were all but alone in the cafe. "Supposedly, he's living somewhere in Virginia, but under a new identity."

"That seems far-fetched," Anna said skeptically. "But then again, crazier things happen around here all the time."

The bored server finally came over to take their orders. As she stood there with a notepad and pencil in hand, Anna froze, unable to speak. Her mind flashed back to the restaurant. Suddenly, she saw the dead waitress standing beside them.

"Are you all right?" Nesi asked, sensing something was wrong and reaching out for Anna's arm.

Anna felt her heart pounding in her chest, caught in a struggle with her imagination as it tried to hijack her emotions. She dug her fingers into the arms of her chair and took a deep breath, fighting her body's sympathetic response. Anna closed her eyes, willing the image of the dead waitress from her mind.

"I'm all right," she muttered. "It's just a headache." Anna looked up and managed a smile. "Just tea, please. Decaf," she whispered to the young woman.

The server gave her a strange look, then jotted down the order before moving on to Nesi and Didier. By the time the young woman had made it to the kitchen to relay their orders to the cook, Anna felt better and was determined to make it through lunch.

"How are things over at the Akua campaign headquarters?" she asked, trying to focus on the moment.

"It's been crazy!" Nesi exclaimed. "The election is three months away, but it feels like we're running out of time. There's so much to do between now and then."

"But it must be exciting, no? This is what you were hoping for all along. The student committee. The sit-in. The march on Green House. It feels like everything that you've been working for is finally coming together," Anna pointed out encouragingly.

"That's what worries us," Didier said. "We've come such a long way, but it still feels so fragile. Like it could all fall apart before we reach the finish line."

"What are people saying inside the campaign? Is the race close?" Anna asked.

"It's impossible to say," Nesi sighed. "This is all so new that nobody has any idea what will happen. We haven't had a real election here in almost thirty years. It's like we're starting from scratch. People have become so accustomed to sham elections. Now we need to convince them it matters. A lot of them still don't trust that their ballots will be counted. That's why so much is at stake. If this doesn't go well, people will lose faith in the system before we even get started."

"Do you think Francois has a chance?"

"Things seem to be moving in the right direction," Didier said. "But there are almost a dozen candidates registered in the first round. It's almost impossible to predict what will happen."

"But most of them aren't serious contenders," Anna offered, trying to stay positive.

"Who knows? I saw some polling numbers this morning that had Fabrice Namono running in double digits. He's in exile and not even living in the country!" Didier fumed.

"That can't be true!" Anna exclaimed. "He's a fugitive. There's no way he'll be elected."

"It's true enough," Nesi said. "Fabrice doesn't need to win to influence the outcome. If no one gets an absolute majority in the first round, the top three finishers go to a runoff. Whoever gets the most votes in the second round wins. Even if Fabrice only gets a few percent in the first round, that could still determine who moves forward and eventually wins."

"Where is Francois Akua polling?" Anna asked.

"That depends on which polls you believe," Didier explained. "Most say that we're in second place, just behind Emanuel Sekibo. But of course, a lot could change between now and then."

"It feels like we're gaining momentum," Nesi added hopefully.

"I hope so," Anna said, crossing her fingers in the air. "I know how hard you've worked for this."

"Speaking of hard work, how has Louie been?" Didier asked. "Is he still in charge of rebuilding the army?"

"Among other things. Right now, the focus is on the election. The Americans are worried that the GLA may try to disrupt the voting. The bombing last week didn't do much to lessen those concerns."

"What does Louie think about the elections?" Nesi asked. "Given his position, he must be anxious about who wins."

"If he is, he won't admit it," Anna said. "But confidentially, he did tell me that the Americans aren't excited about the prospect of Francois Akua getting into Green House."

Nesi glanced at Didier and shook her head in frustration. "They think he's a panda hugger," she blurted out.

"Is he?" Anna asked.

"No, of course not!" Nesi insisted. "He's not pro-China. He's not pro-America. He's pro-Gisawi. He wants what's best for this country. If that means working with China, then we work with China. If that means working with the US, then we work with the US. Why is that such a novel concept?"

"I don't think it is," Anna offered. "But given the climate right now, some people aren't satisfied with a sensible, middle-of-the-road position. The US wants everyone to pick a side."

Didier leaned forward. "But what if picking a side doesn't help us? For the US, everything is war. For China, everything is business. Who's going to look out for people's interests here?" he asked rhetorically.

"As Americans, we like to convince ourselves that what's best for us is best for the rest of the world," Anna offered. "We can't help it. It's our missionary spirit."

"God save us from that," Nesi muttered. "I'm not saying that Francois Akua has all the answers. But how can the Americans not see that Emanuel Sekibo is a far worse choice? If he gets into Green House, it'll be like going back to the old regime. Only worse."

"I suppose we'll hope for the best," Anna said, lacking a better answer.

"The first debate is two weeks away," Nesi reminded her. "Will you meet us here so we can watch it together?"

"Absolutely!" Anna said, happy to have something to look forward to.

+++

The following day, Louie arrived at work early, planning to attend the weekly Operation Brighter Dawn press conference. He walked into the briefing room and found a gaggle of local reporters already seated in front of an empty podium. Louie took a chair in the back of the room, far away from the crowd. He was busy working on his to-do list when Owen Smith entered the room. Louie buried his nose in his notebook, avoiding eye contact and hoping that Owen would find someone else to bother. Unfortunately, there were empty seats on either side of Louie's. Owen spotted the opportunity and made a beeline for one of the chairs.

"I didn't know that you came to the press briefings," Owen said, settling into his seat.

"I try to when I can," Louie mumbled, pretending to be immersed in his notes, hoping to avoid small talk.

"How's the local media around here?" Owen asked. "Are they as bad as back in the States?"

"I suppose that depends on what you mean by 'bad,'" Louie replied, resigned to socializing. "If anything, they're probably a bit too passive. I think they're still getting used to the new system."

"New system?"

"The one where they don't go to jail for asking the wrong question."

"Oh, right. I get it," Owen chuckled. "I guess things were a bit different under the old regime."

"You could say that. Everyone went through the motions, even though both sides knew it was a farce. The government would tell lies. The papers would report them. And both sides agreed to call it news."

"Is it better now?"

"It's not perfect, but at least there's accountability. People expect more from the government and the media. However, we still have a long way to go."

While they waited for the briefing to begin, a young Black woman walked into the room and sat in the front row, the only woman among the male reporters, dressed in Western attire.

"This should make things interesting," Louie said, nodding at the woman.

"Why? Who's that?"

"Janet Russell," he said, as if mentioning her name should have been sufficient to clarify things.

Owen looked blank. "Is she a Gisawian reporter or something?"

"No. She's one of yours, an American. She's a foreign correspondent for one of the wire services. You've probably read her stuff and didn't know it. She's been reporting over here for a while."

"Any good?"

"*Very*," Louie said without hesitation. "She doesn't let anyone get away with any nonsense. Just wait and see."

As he spoke, the American public affairs officer, Captain Howe, entered the room and made his way to the podium. When he spotted Janet Russell among the reporters' scrum, he winced and glanced at his watch, realizing that the briefing would go longer than expected.

Howe greeted the reporters, then launched into a dry recitation of the weekly press release covering the operational highlights; then he opened the floor to questions. After twenty minutes of softballs lobbed from the local press contingent, Janet Russell raised her hand. Captain Howe scanned the room, desperately looking for someone else to call on, before finally relenting.

"Yes, Ms. Russell," he said, smiling disingenuously.

"During your remarks, you didn't mention anything about the two mortar attacks last week in Kiskow," Janet said. "Can you fill us in on the details?"

"In the interest of time, we don't cover every single tactical action during the weekly roundup," Howe explained.

Janet ignored the dodge and pushed on. "My sources in

Kiskow reported that two Gisawian soldiers were killed and several others injured during the attack. Can you confirm those numbers?"

"Ms. Russell, I'm sure you're aware that we don't report on Gisawian casualty figures. You'll need to redirect that question to the Ministry of Defense."

"I understand that several American soldiers were also injured in the same attack. Perhaps you can comment on that?"

Captain Howe looked at his notes, pretending to search for the answer. "I can confirm that three American service members sustained minor, non-life-threatening injuries during an engagement in the area of Kiskow last week. They received medical attention at the camp and were returned to duty the next day."

Barely acknowledging his answer, Janet forged ahead. "Local media reported that another supply convoy was attacked this week on the road to Kiskow. Can you confirm whether this is being attributed to the GLA?"

"The incident remains under investigation. I'm unable to comment until we have all the facts."

Owen leaned over and whispered to Louie. "You're right. She's a bit more aggressive than the rest of them."

"She's just getting warmed up," Louie assured him as Janet continued peppering the captain with questions.

"According to my count, that's the sixth convoy this month attacked on the road to Kiskow," she said, referring to her notes.

"I can't confirm the precise number," Howe replied, staring down at the podium, avoiding eye contact with her.

"Do you have any idea why the group appears to be expanding its operations beyond the western region? Does General B- view last week's restaurant bombing as a sign that the GLA is gaining strength?"

"This command views any acts of violence directed against innocent civilians as a sign of weakness, not strength," the captain intoned, avoiding the question.

"What about the choice of the target?" Janet persisted. "That restaurant was an obvious landmark in the heart of the capital, a place frequented by foreigners. Was this an attempt to embarrass the Provisional Interim Government in advance of the upcoming election?"

"I would caution against drawing conclusions based on a single incident," the captain offered flatly.

Janet was unfazed. "Last week, the Chinese foreign ministry accused the US of mismanaging the counterinsurgency campaign against the GLA. Does the command have a response to that allegation?"

"Unfortunately, we only have time for one final question," the captain said, ignoring the bait. "Anyone?"

He scanned the room, looking for someone other than Janet. After an extended period of silence, he reluctantly nodded in her direction. "Ms. Russell, it seems that your colleagues have decided to give you the final word today," he said, appearing relieved to be nearing the end of the presser.

Janet closed her notebook, her final question already prepared.

"Can you please comment on the rumors about a so-called 'third force' conducting operations against the GLA across the border?"

Louie noticed Owen straighten in his seat. He stopped writing and looked up from his notepad, waiting for the captain's response.

"Our rules of engagement are clear," Howe said. "There is no authorization for any American or Gisawian ground forces to operate across the international border."

"That's not what I asked," Janet argued. "I want to know if this command has any knowledge of armed forces engaged in combat operations outside of DRoG against the GLA."

"Ms. Russell, I believe that my answer was clear. I can confidently say that no US or Gisawian military forces are presently operating across the border. I don't have any other information to offer. Thank you all for your attendance today. This concludes the Operation Brighter Dawn press conference."

Captain Howe quickly gathered his notes and left the podium.

"That was unexpected," Louie said to Owen as they waited for the reporters to leave the room.

"I agree," Owen sniffed. "I thought you said she was a pro. That sounded to me like some sort of amateurish fishing expedition."

"I don't know. Maybe," Louie said with a shrug. "It's not her style to throw out red herrings. I assume she had a good reason for asking that question."

"I'll take your word on that. Anyway, I'd like to stay and chat, but I've got some things to do before the afternoon meeting," Owen said, gathering up his things.

Louie watched Owen hurry off, heading out the same door Captain Howe had disappeared through. After he was gone, Louie stepped outside for some fresh air. He found a shady spot in the courtyard where he hoped no one would bother him. He was busy checking messages on his phone when he spotted Janet Russell walking purposefully in his direction.

"Colonel Bigombe, good morning," she said, smiling and reaching out for his hand.

"Ms. Russell." Louie nodded, hesitantly taking her hand.

"Haven't we known each other long enough to dispense with the formality?" she asked.

"It's nothing personal," Louie said. "I just prefer to keep things professional. People might draw the wrong conclusions otherwise."

"In that case, do I need to request permission before asking a personal question?"

Louie shrugged but said nothing, waiting for her to continue.

"How are you and your wife doing?"

Louie gave her a suspicious look.

"I'm not trying to pry," she added. "One of my stringers saw you coming out of the hospital after the bombing. He said you and your wife had been at the restaurant when it happened. I was just hoping that you both were all right."

"We're doing fine. Thanks for asking," Louie said curtly. "I suppose I should thank you for not putting our names in the paper."

"It didn't seem relevant to the story. Believe it or not, the job is not all about making headlines."

"In any case, I appreciate it. Anna was pretty shaken up," Louie revealed, starting to feel more at ease. "The young woman who died was our waitress. I think we may have been the last people she spoke to before she was killed."

"I'm sorry. That's an awful thing to experience." Janet paused for a moment, looking somber, then asked, "Do you have any thoughts about who was behind it?"

"Is that a personal or professional question?" Louie asked, suddenly back on guard.

"I suppose now we're moving into more of a professional discussion," Janet clarified. "Off the record, of course."

"The GLA claimed responsibility. What more is there to know?"

Janet cocked her head, seeming unconvinced. "Parts of that story don't add up," she challenged.

"Such as?"

"Such as, why would the GLA suddenly shift tactics? Until last week, they'd never conducted any operations outside the western region. Their objective is retaking Kiskow, but then they decide to blow up a restaurant in the capital? What are they trying to accomplish?"

"I don't know," Louie said. "That's not my area of specialty. You should ask the intelligence folks. Maybe with the election coming up, the GLA is trying to get attention for their cause. Isn't that the whole point of terrorism?"

"Perhaps. But the GLA isn't a major international terrorist group. It's a low-level insurgency with limited ambitions and somewhat ambiguous objectives."

"Are you assuming that acts of political violence are necessarily rational?" Louie argued.

"I'm not. But I tend to believe that things happen for a reason. That's what I'm trying to figure out. If it was the GLA, what are they trying to achieve by blowing up a restaurant?"

"There's nothing to be achieved from an innocent woman getting killed for doing her job. That's sickening to even think about," Louie muttered.

"I agree. However, I can think of one person who benefited from the attack. At least indirectly," Janet hinted.

"And who's that?"

"Emanuel Sekibo."

"That's ridiculous," Louie scoffed. "How does Emanuel Sekibo benefit from the GLA bombing a restaurant?"

"Don't get me wrong," Janet said. "I'm not saying that he or anybody in his campaign was glad to see it happen. But every time the GLA makes it into the headlines, Sekibo gets a bump in the polls."

Louie shrugged, unimpressed by Janet's theory. "Why is that surprising? He's running as the security candidate. Defeating the GLA is one of his campaign promises. If people feel their safety is threatened, then Sekibo is probably the candidate they want to see in Green House."

"True," Janet agreed. "But Emanuel Sekibo also happens to be the head of S3 Corp, the largest private security firm in the country. He stands to gain financially if the war against the GLA escalates. Don't you think that represents a potential conflict of interest?"

"Honestly, Ms. Russell, I haven't thought much about it," Louie said, looking to end the conversation. "I've got other things to worry about right now."

"So I've heard," she said cryptically.

"What's that supposed to mean?"

"Just that I've seen your name popping up recently in some social media chatter."

"I don't have the slightest idea what you're talking about," Louie said impatiently. "I'm not on social media."

"There's no need to be coy about it," Janet whispered as if they were sharing some secret. "It's understandable, given your family's history."

"I'm not being coy about anything!" Louie shot back, feeling his headache returning. "I don't have any idea what you're talking about."

Janet looked at Louie as if he was crazy. "You're honestly telling me that you haven't seen any of the stuff that people are posting about you?" she asked, incredulous. "About being a dark horse candidate in the election?"

Louie stared at her, dumbfounded. This unexpected twist in the conversation caused him to consider the possibility that his recent bouts of forgetfulness were due to something more severe than a minor concussion from the bombing.

"That's completely crazy," he said firmly, determined to assert his grasp on reality. "I can assure you, I'm not running for president. That's ridiculous."

"Is it really?" Janet asked. "You have a famous last name. A lot of the older generation still remembers your father. The younger ones know all about you pulling the trigger on the drone strike that killed Daniel Odoki. Not to mention your role in protecting those university students who marched on Green House before the fall of the Namono regime. I don't think anyone would be surprised to see your name on the ballot."

Louie shook his head. "I don't have any idea who these people are, but I can assure you, they're using my name without permission. I've got nothing to do with it. You can quote me on that if you like. For the record, I'm not a candidate for president. Dark horse or otherwise."

Janet put away her notebook, sensing that Louie wouldn't give her the scoop she was after.

"In that case, I'll have to take your word on it," she said. "But please let me know if the story changes. Here's my information." She handed Louie a business card. "There's an encrypted messaging option on the back if you ever feel the need to communicate confidentially."

"Thanks," Louie said, stuffing the card in his pocket. "However, I can't imagine a scenario where I'd need it."

"You don't until you do," she said, nodding at the card.

Louie looked at the card but said nothing more as Janet walked back across the courtyard and joined the other reporters lingering around the building.

Louie stood there staring at his phone, tempted to search through social media and find out who was writing about him. But he glanced at his watch and remembered how much work he had to do before the afternoon meeting. Reluctantly, he left the quiet spot in the courtyard and went back to his office.

+++

That evening, Louie and Anna were at home making dinner. They were listening to the news on the radio, content to let the announcer's voice fill the void of conversation. Once the food was on the table, they stared at each other over their plates.

"How was school today?" Louie asked, finally.

"The usual." Anna sighed, staring at her food but not feeling hungry.

"You seem tired. Are you still having problems sleeping?"

She half-nodded.

"It's been several weeks. Do you think you should see someone?"

Anna hesitated, then shook her head.

"It's OK to talk about it," Louie said gently. "It's perfectly normal to have trouble sleeping after a traumatic event."

"I'm fine," she insisted. "Let's talk about something else. How was your work today?"

Louie shrugged. "I'm not even sure what we're doing. It's just an endless series of ridiculous meetings. Everyone sits around the table, looking at slides on the screen, acting as if they bore some resemblance to the reality outside."

"What *is* happening outside?" she asked.

"I don't have the slightest idea," Louie said, drawing the hint of a smile from across the table.

"Are things going to get better?" Anna asked more seriously.

"I don't know. I guess it depends on how the election goes. The entire security plan is half-baked at best. We'll be lucky if we can keep the GLA from overrunning Kiskow between now and then."

"I'm sorry. Hopefully things will improve," Anna offered, trying to be encouraging.

They ate dinner in silence until Louie dramatically put down his utensils. "I spoke with my brother today," he announced out of the blue.

"That's nice. It's been a while. How is he?"

"Fine, but he thinks my mother is homesick."

"I'm not surprised. It's hard to imagine her being happy in New Jersey. Maybe she can come for a visit after the election," Anna suggested. "Did your brother have anything else to say?"

"He passed my resume along to the HR department at his bank," Louie said hesitantly. "He thinks they might be… interested."

"Interested in what?"

"Me," Louie said defensively.

"You working at a bank?" Anna said, trying not to act surprised. "I don't see you as the type. And please, take that as a compliment."

Louie shrugged, uncertain how to respond. After a few moments, he said, "I'm not actively looking. But if an opportunity came along, I'd certainly be willing to consider it."

"What kind of opportunity?"

"Research analyst, emerging markets. It would be entry-level, of course. But it might be a chance for a fresh start. Maybe you could start putting out resumes for some teaching jobs."

"Do you think you'd be happier living in New Jersey and working at a bank?"

"Would you?"

Anna didn't answer right away. She toyed with the edge of her napkin, thinking over the question. "Oh, I don't know…" she finally said, her voice trailing off.

Louie knew better than to push the issue. Anna was deliberative by nature, preferring to think over big decisions, exploring all the permutations before arriving at a solution.

While she was mulling over the idea, they heard a knock at the door.

"Were you expecting someone?" she asked.

"No. You?"

Anna shook her head.

"I'll get it," Louie said, getting up from the table while Anna cleared the dishes.

From the kitchen, she could hear him discussing something with whoever was at the door. Fragments of the conversation drifted through the house, but she couldn't make sense of the bits and pieces. Louie didn't invite the person inside, but the discussion lasted longer than it should have for a door-to-door salesperson.

Ten minutes later, Anna heard the door close, and Louie came into the kitchen. As soon as she saw his face, she could tell something was wrong. He was holding a stack of papers, staring at them and shaking his head.

"What was that all about?" she asked.

"Something weird is going on," he said.

Anna could sense his worry. "What do you mean? Who was at the door?"

"Some kid collecting signatures for an election campaign."

"Presumably, you informed him that your choice was a closely guarded state secret," Anna teased, making light of his reticence on the subject.

"He wanted me to sign a petition of support," Louie said, ignoring her comment.

"Who was the candidate?"

"Apparently, it's me," Louie answered.

Anna put down the dish she was drying and stared at her

husband. "That's ridiculous. Are you sure he had the right person? Maybe it's someone else with a similar-sounding name."

"No. There's no mistake. It was my name on the materials. There was even some bio information about me. But the kid didn't even realize that he was asking me to sign a petition in support of my own campaign. He had no idea who I was."

"Louie, you're not making any sense," Anna said.

She walked over to him and peered at the materials in his hand. Her eyes widened as she read through the pages.

"My god, you're serious. This *is* you. What did he say? Who is he working for?" she asked, now fully absorbed in the mystery.

"I don't think he knows who he's working for," Louie said, looking troubled. "When I started asking questions, he got nervous and clammed up. He said that he didn't know all the details and would have someone from the campaign get back to me."

"And you believed him?"

"Yeah. He seemed kind of clueless. He finally admitted that someone was paying him to walk around neighborhoods, passing out flyers and getting names on the list. He's just doing it for the money."

"But who's paying him? And why on earth would someone attach your name to a political campaign without even telling you? Maybe it's some kind of scam. Did he ask you for money?"

Louie shook his head.

"It's strange that this is the first you've heard about it," Anna pondered.

"Actually, it's not the first I've heard," Louie said, suddenly remembering his conversation that morning at the camp. "You know that African American reporter who covers DRoG? Janet Russell?"

"I don't know her personally, but I've read her stuff. Why?"

"I bumped into her today at the press conference. She mentioned something about seeing my name on some social media post about the election. It seemed so ridiculous that I didn't bother looking it up."

Anna frowned. "Maybe you should."

Louie went over to his desk and opened his laptop. He typed his name into the search engine, and the first link to appear on the page was a domain name for his supposed campaign. He opened the link and found a splash page with his picture and profile information, and some vaguely worded campaign promises.

"What the hell is this?" he mumbled, scrolling down through the webpage.

"Louie, is there something you want to tell me about your career plans?" Anna said, looking over his shoulder at the fake campaign site. "A few minutes ago, you told me that you wanted to move to New Jersey and become a banker. Now, I discover that you've secretly trying to become the next president of DRoG. What's next on the list? Astronaut?"

"Anna, this isn't a joke!" Louie said, taken aback by this new development. "Someone is using my name, but I have no idea who's doing it or why."

"Is there anything on the website about who's responsible?"

"No. But it all looks very professional. It's not the sloppy work of some internet con artist. This makes me look like I'm really running for president."

"Did Janet say anything else about it?"

"No. It was just an offhand comment at the end of our conversation. But now I understand why she was asking the question. If I didn't know any better, I'd believe I was running too."

"What are you going to do about it?" Anna asked, still more amused than concerned by the discovery. "Can you get into trouble for pretending to run for president?"

"Of course I can!" Louie said, becoming alarmed. "I'm an army officer. We're supposed to be apolitical. I could be fired, or worse. I need to figure out what's going on and shut it down before someone at the Ministry of Defense sees it. Otherwise, I'll have some explaining to do."

"Maybe it's a good thing you sent that resume to your brother," Anna said, trying to look on the bright side. "Should I start packing some things for New Jersey, just in case you get fired?"

"Not funny," Louie snapped, slamming closed his laptop. "I'm getting to the bottom of this tomorrow."

"How?"

"First thing in the morning, I'm going straight to the Electoral Commission office."

"To do what?"

"Get a letter stating that I'm not a registered candidate. At least I'll have that to show the ministry if they call me in to explain this website."

"I hope that works."

"Me too."

CHAPTER THREE

———

Early the following day, Louie was outside the Electoral Commission office, waiting for the doors to open. The entrance was locked and the lights were dim even though it was ten minutes after it was supposed to open. Louie peeked through the window and saw someone sitting at the reception desk, drinking tea and reading the newspaper. He knocked loudly on the door until the man had no choice but to acknowledge his presence. The clerk took another sip of tea, then slowly got up and made his way to the door.

"The sign says you open at eight-thirty," Louie said, pointing at the notice.

The man looked at the sign as if seeing it for the first time and nodded his agreement. Louie followed him back to the desk and waited until he was settled back into his seat.

"I need to speak with someone about candidate registration for the upcoming election," Louie explained.

"Do you have a number?"

"What do you mean, a number?"

The clerk nodded at a ticket machine hanging on the opposite wall. Next to the dispenser was a sign requesting that all customers obtain a number before receiving service.

"But I'm the only one here. Why do I need a number?"

Instead of answering, the man flipped a switch at his desk, activating an electronic counter mounted on the wall. Louie fought the urge to argue and went to the ticket machine to retrieve his number. He returned and presented the ticket. The clerk examined the number and set the counter to match, indicating that it was Louie's turn to be served.

"How may I help you?" he asked.

Louie took a deep, calming breath and dropped his ticket into the wastebasket. "As I was trying to explain, I need a letter indicating that I am not a registered candidate in the upcoming presidential election."

The man nodded thoughtfully, seeming to give the question his focused consideration before speaking. "I am sorry, sir, but we have no such letter among our forms. This would require a special request submitted through the Electoral Commission."

"Perhaps you misunderstand what I need," Louie continued, struggling to remain calm. "Someone created a fake campaign website using my name. I simply need a letter confirming that I'm not an official candidate. It's really quite a simple request."

"Did you register as a candidate for the election?" the clerk asked, confused.

"No! That's what I'm trying to tell you," Louie bristled. "I never registered. I'm not running for president. I just need a letter stating that fact. It shouldn't be a complicated matter."

"I see," the man said, jotting down a few lines in his notebook. "May I see your identification card?"

Louie handed his card across the desk. The clerk crossed the room to an old Xerox machine and waited while the relic warmed up. After making a photocopy of Louie's identification card, he returned to the desk. "Just one moment, please," he said, handing the card back to Louie and disappearing into a back office.

Ten minutes later, he reappeared, smiling apologetically.

"I'm very sorry, sir, but this office cannot accommodate your request."

"What?" Louie blurted out. "Perhaps you don't understand. I'm an officer in the army. I could be court-martialed for running a political campaign while in uniform. May I please speak to your supervisor?"

The man shook his head. "I'm very sorry, sir, but I've already spoken with the supervisor, and such a letter cannot be produced."

"If necessary, I will take this matter straight to the elections commissioner himself," Louie threatened, leaning over the desk to emphasize his point.

"As you wish, sir," the clerk said, smiling, unmoved by Louie's ultimatum.

Louie was on the verge of storming out of the office but, at the last moment, he thought better of it. "May I ask the reason your supervisor gave for not providing the letter?"

"Such a letter cannot be provided because you are, in fact, a registered candidate for the election. Therefore, it would violate our policy if we provided an inaccurate official document stating otherwise," the man said serenely.

Louie stepped back from the desk, feeling dizzy. His head was pounding, and he reached for the chair to steady himself. "That's impossible," he muttered. "I've never filled out any paperwork. There must be some mistake."

The clerk shook his head. "No, sir. All of the papers are in order. I reviewed the documents myself. Your name and national identification number are an exact match with those filed on the application form. I can say with complete certainty that you are a registered candidate for the presidential election."

"How is that possible? I've never been to this office before. How can I be a candidate if I didn't know anything about it?"

The man shrugged. "I'm sorry, sir. I can't answer that question. However, I can assure you an application was filed in your name, along with five thousand petition signatures, as required by law, and the application fee of twenty-five thousand Gisawi pounds."

"This is ridiculous! Someone is playing a game, and it's going to end right now," Louie insisted. "I am formally withdrawing my name from the ballot and demand that you provide me with written proof."

The clerk scribbled another note on his pad and got up from his chair. "I'm sorry, sir, but I'll need to look into this. It's the first time we've received a request for a candidate to be removed from a ballot. If you will excuse me, I must discuss this with my supervisor."

He disappeared into the back office again. Louie paced the waiting area, trying to imagine a plausible scenario that would explain the situation. By the time the clerk reappeared, Louie was determined to win him over with kindness.

The clerk looked cheerful. "Mr. Bigombe, I have reviewed the relevant regulations and discussed the matter with my supervisor. Unfortunately, there is no administrative guidance concerning a voluntary withdraw from the election ballot. However, I believe we have found a satisfactory solution."

"Great!" Louie said with relief. "I appreciate it. Can we do this right away?"

The man nodded and pushed a form across the desk. Louie quickly scanned the document and began filling in the blanks. He signed his name at the bottom and handed it back to the clerk.

"Do you mind giving me a copy so I have proof that I'm no longer registered?" Louie asked, happy to be finished with the ordeal.

"Ahhh, I'm very sorry, sir," the man said, sucking his teeth. "Unfortunately, this is just the first step. Our office will review the application to ensure that everything is in order. Then we will provide a recommendation to the commissioner for adjudication. However, before it can be finalized, we will require five thousand petition signatures and the application fee of twenty-five thousand Gisawi pounds."

Louie stared at him, dumbfounded. "Old pounds or new?" he finally asked.

"New," the clerk clarified.

"You've got to be kidding!" Louie exploded. "You expect me to pay twenty-five thousand new Gisawi pounds to get my name *off* a ballot for an election that I never entered?"

"Bank check or wire transfer is acceptable, sir," the clerk added helpfully.

"I don't have twenty-five thousand pounds!" Louie screamed.

The clerk's smile faded. He slowly rolled back his chair, putting distance between himself and Louie. "I'm sorry, sir, but the same process must be followed to leave the election as to enter it. That includes the full payment of the application fee and submission of the required petition signatures."

Louie stepped back from the desk, fearing that he might do something rash. He took a deep breath and forced a smile. "Thank you for your time," he said through clenched teeth. "Please inform your supervisor that I will be following up personally with the commissioner."

Louie turned and walked toward the door.

"Pardon me, sir!" the clerk called out as he was about to leave. "If you happen to change your mind, according to the election law, you are eligible for a full refund of your application fees if you obtain more than ten percent of the votes in the first round. Good luck, sir!"

Louie continued out the door without a word.

+++

The following week, General B- ordered the entire staff into the conference room for an impromptu meeting. He barged into the room, scowling as he took his seat at the head of the table. "Can someone please tell me what the hell happened yesterday afternoon in Kiskow?" he snarled.

"Sir, we're still gathering details," Colonel Severs replied. "Based on the initial reports, it appears that we lost another convoy, about fifteen kilometers outside of town."

"Damn it!" the general said, slamming his fist on the table. "How many trucks was it this time?"

"A total of five. Four were destroyed, and the attackers stole one," Severs explained, referring to his notes.

"What was in the convoy?"

"Mostly food and equipment," Severs said, then hesitated, reluctant to tell him the rest. "Uh…except for the truck that was stolen. It was carrying ammunition for the Gisawian units out in Kiskow."

"Jesus," the general muttered. "Could it have been a coincidence?"

Severs shook his head. "Unlikely. Several other convoys got through last week without any problem. But yesterday's was the only one moving sensitive equipment. The eyewitnesses said that the attackers went straight for that vehicle. They hogtied the drivers and set the rest of the trucks on fire."

"What do you make of it?" the general asked.

"We need to consider the possibility that the GLA is operating with inside information. It's the only explanation."

"Why didn't we get this report until this morning?" the general asked, pointing accusingly at Severs.

"There was a…a delay in deploying the quick reaction force from the garrison in Kiskow."

"A *delay?*"

Colonel Severs squirmed in his seat. "Sir, the Gisawian commander refused to send his troops out," he explained.

"What do you mean, refused? Are we talking mutiny?"

"The GLA has them running scared. Last week, the GLA took over a local radio station and started broadcasting recorded messages from someone claiming to be Daniel Odoki. The broadcast said that the GLA had surrounded the city and that there was no escape. Since then, the soldiers have refused to leave the base."

"You're telling me that half the goddamn Gisawian army

just surrendered to someone pretending to be Daniel Odoki on the radio?" General B— fumed. "They're going to give up Kiskow without a fight."

"Sir, may I speak?" Louie interrupted.

The general scanned the room and spotted Louie in the back row.

"There's more to the story," Louie explained, avoiding eye contact with Severs. "I spoke with the commander of the quick reaction force in Kiskow. It's true; he refused to send his soldiers out last night. But not because of the radio message."

"What's his version of the story?" the general demanded.

"Our battalion in Kiskow has been getting hit by GLA ambushes almost every time they leave the camp on patrol. They've lost so many soldiers that the unit is down to sixty percent strength," Louie informed him grimly. "The GLA seems to know their movements in advance. Even routine patrols are turning into suicide missions. That's the reason they didn't go out last night. They feel like sitting ducks out there."

"How the hell does the GLA know about our moves in advance?" the general demanded. "They must be getting their information from somewhere. They know when the convoys are coming and what's inside each truck. We've got a goddamn breach of security going on here!"

He turned back to Colonel Severs. "You need to get to the bottom of this ASAP! We're just over two months away from the election, and the GLA is running circles around us. We can't afford to lose Kiskow with the entire world watching."

"With all due respect, sir," Severs replied, "we can't hold the city with soldiers who aren't willing to fight. If the Gisawians won't leave the camp, there's not much we can do except wait for the GLA to overrun us."

"Damn it! I'm going out to Kiskow next week," General B- said, slamming his hand on the table. "We need to regain control over the narrative and show them that the GLA isn't ten feet tall. You tell the commander out there to get this thing unscrewed before we arrive. I want this turd polished until it shines. You got that?"

The general waited until he saw everyone around the table nodding in unison, then got up and stormed out of the room.

+++

After the meeting, Louie was crossing the courtyard, going back to his office, when he spotted Owen Smith moving in his direction.

"Interesting meeting this morning," Owen said, trotting to catch up.

Louie nodded but said nothing, continuing on his path.

"It seems like the GLA might be planning something big in Kiskow before the election," Owen said out of the blue. "That would be a major embarrassment for the Provisional Interim Government."

"And for the US, presumably," Louie noted, stopping in his tracks, unwilling to let the comment stand unchallenged.

"True. I suppose we're all in this together."

"Well, not literally, of course," Louie snapped. "If things go badly, you have somewhere else to go home to. But no one here has that option."

Owen nodded, conceding the point, then asked, "What's your take on this theory about the GLA having inside information about our operations?"

"It's the most logical explanation," Louie conceded. "And the most dangerous. I had an uncle who used to say, 'It's better to have fifty enemies outside the tent than one within.'"

"Is that your uncle who used to be the minister of defense?"

Louie stared at Owen, assuming he already knew the answer to the question. "You ask a lot of strange questions for someone whose job is running elections."

"Sorry. I didn't mean to pry into your business," Owen backpedaled.

"Since we're asking questions, I have one for you," Louie said. "I assume you're familiar with our campaign regulations?"

"I'm not an expert, but I know a bit," Owen offered.

"What about the process for registering candidates? Do you know much about that?"

"Some," Owen hedged. "Our team helped the Provisional Interim Government develop the draft election law. Why do you ask?"

"I'm wondering about how that works."

"It's easier than you might think," Owen explained. "That's by design. One of the problems under the old regime was how they wrote the rules to keep people out. President Namono made the process so restrictive that he virtually eliminated the possibility of any challengers getting on the ballot. In essence, he regulated the opposition out of existence."

"And your team changed that when they helped write the new election law?"

"Yes. The goal was to level the playing field. That's why you have so many candidates in the first round. That would never have happened under the old regime. All those names on the ballot are a feature, not a bug."

"But that list includes an indicted criminal," Louie pointed out.

"I assume you're referring to Fabrice Namono?" Owen said. "Of course, that was an unforeseen technical loophole. We hadn't considered the possibility of someone running a campaign from exile. But once you start limiting who can enter, then it becomes a slippery slope back to the ways of the old regime. In the end, we think DRoG will be better off with fewer election restrictions rather than more."

"What about a candidate getting put on the ballot without them knowing it? Would that be considered a feature or a bug?" Louie asked.

"I'm not sure what you're talking about," Owen muttered.

Louie decided the direct approach was best. "Did you know that my name is on the ballot?"

"Now that you mention it, I do recall seeing your name on the list of candidates," Owen said casually. "But of course, it's a big field. And given your family's history, I suppose I wasn't entirely surprised to see it there."

"It's funny that it never came up during our conversations," Louie observed.

"I didn't want to pry into your business. Besides, I'm not involved on the political side. My job is more focused on the technical aspects. Making the trains run on time, so to speak."

Owen paused, watching Louie's reaction. "Do you mind if I offer an opinion?"

Louie waited for him to continue.

"Your country could do much worse than having someone like you in the race," Owen offered.

"That's not the point. I didn't enter the race. Yet somehow, my name showed up on the ballot. That doesn't speak very well of this new system you're setting up."

"No system is perfect. But if you want, I'll talk to my contacts over at the Electoral Commission and try to figure out what happened. I'm sure there's a reasonable explanation. But it seems like a done deal now. What's the harm in seeing it through to the end?"

"I would hope that would be obvious," Louie said, unable to hide his frustration. "First of all, as an active military officer, I could go to jail for having my name on the ballot. But aside from that, this is the first real election we've had in almost thirty years, and someone is turning it into a farce. Doesn't that concern you?"

"I see your point. But then again, the real measure of success in a democratic system is what it produces in the end."

As Owen was speaking, his phone buzzed in his pocket. He pulled it out and glanced at the number. "I'm sorry, but I've got to take this," he said, waving goodbye over his shoulder as he walked away across the courtyard, chatting on the phone.

+++

The following week, Louie was back at the sundries shop near the central market. He had arrived early and found an empty table. He was expecting to meet Patrick, though he wasn't entirely sure about what. A few days earlier, Louie had gone out to his car after work and found a slip of rolled-up paper tucked under the windshield wiper. Written on it were a date and time, but nothing else. Louie stuffed it into his pocket, nervous that someone might be watching. At home that evening, he studied the handwriting more carefully and was fairly certain he recognized it as Patrick's tight script, virtually unchanged since their days in grammar school.

Louie went with his hunch and waited outside the shop at the time written on the note. It was a busy day at the market, and crowds of shoppers filled the sidewalks. Louie assumed that Patrick had selected the time precisely for that reason. Louie didn't see his friend until Patrick appeared at the table and slipped into the empty chair.

"I would have felt foolish coming here if that note wasn't from you after all," Louie said, smiling at his friend. "Are you testing me to see if I'll call you?"

"Laugh if you will, but I have good reasons to be paranoid," Patrick said.

"I think I'm starting to believe you."

Patrick had left his sunglasses on and was staring over Louie's shoulder, keeping an eye on the street. "How's Anna doing?"

"All right," Louie said. He hesitated, then changed his answer. "Actually, not that great. She's back at work but hasn't been herself. I think she should see someone. But whenever I mention it, she gets upset and insists that everything's fine."

"What about you?"

"Still having headaches," Louie admitted. "But I'm not sure if that's the concussion or frustration about work."

"More problems out in Kiskow?" Patrick guessed.

Louie nodded. "Between you and me, it's even worse than what they're saying in the papers. I wouldn't be surprised if the GLA tries to take the city before the election. All the signs are pointing in that direction."

"If that's their strategy, they may want to rethink it," Patrick said, taking a sip of his coffee.

Louie shook his head, not following his friend's logic.

"That would play right into Emanuel Sekibo's hand," Patrick explained. "His campaign is playing up the threat from the GLA every chance they get. There are rumors that he's considering a cross-border offensive into the sanctuary areas if he gets elected."

"He can't be serious!" Louie gasped. "That would only make matters worse. The last thing we need is a return of the border wars."

"Maybe you should say that as part of your campaign," Patrick said offhandedly, looking into the crowd, avoiding Louie's eyes.

Louie stared at his friend, trying to read his mind. "Patrick, it's a hoax. I hope you don't believe that stuff on social media."

"I don't know what to believe anymore."

"Come on!" Louie exclaimed. "We've been best friends since grammar school. Don't you think I'd tell you if I decided to run for president?"

"Would you?"

"Of course I would. The entire thing is a farce, I swear," Louie insisted, his voice cracking with emotion. "I just found out about it last week, and I don't have the slightest idea who's behind it."

Behind his sunglasses, Patrick revealed the hint of a smile. "Don't worry," he laughed. "As soon as I saw your name on the candidate list, I knew something strange was going on. Do you have any idea who's behind it or why they're doing it?"

"None," Louie said, relieved that someone believed him. "Last week, I went down to the Electoral Commission office and checked on the paperwork. It was all there and looked legitimate. Someone even went to the trouble of forging my signature on the registration forms. I can't explain it."

"What are you going to do?"

Louie sighed. "The only way to get my name off the ballot is by submitting five thousand signatures and a twenty-five-thousand-pound fee."

"Old or new pounds?"

"New."

"Ouch," Patrick said, shaking his head sympathetically. "Well…what's the harm in ignoring it? No one can force you to campaign. Sooner or later, people will forget about it and move on."

Louie shook his head. "If only it were that simple. What if someone over at the Ministry of Defense finds out? How will I convince them I had nothing to do with it?"

"I see the problem," Patrick agreed.

"There's also a chance that it could somehow influence the election, even if I did nothing at all."

Patrick rubbed his chin, considering the possibility. "There are so many candidates in the first round; anything could happen."

"But there's still the issue of who's behind it and why," Louie continued. "The clerk at the Electoral Commission couldn't remember who submitted the paperwork. And a kid who came by my house collecting signatures didn't know who was paying him to hand out the campaign flyers. Someone is doing a good job of making my campaign look legitimate but not leaving behind any fingerprints."

"What about the webpage and social media? Have you traced those back to a source?" Patrick asked.

"That's not my area of expertise. I was hoping you could help me with that."

Patrick thought for a moment. "We need to be careful," he said. "They monitor everything I do on the computers at work, so I can't look into it there. But I have some contacts with the technical skills to get the answer. I'll see what I can find out."

"Thanks, Patrick. I have one more question; then I promise to leave you alone. Have you heard anything more about bombing investigation?"

Patrick glanced around at the nearby tables, making sure no one was listening. He leaned closer and lowered his voice. "The fusion cell is still keeping everything closely-held. But my team picked up a few bits of information."

"Anything interesting?"

"Maybe. We know that the bomber detonated the device using a cell phone trigger. Based on that, we went back through the call logs on the cellular network and were able to identify the SIM cards used in the attack. One of them was attached to the bomb, and the other triggered the explosion."

Louie leaned forward intently. "Can that help you identify who did it?"

"Not directly," Patrick admitted. "Both of the SIM cards were prepaid and not registered by name on a mobile contract. But we figured out that they were purchased from a local kiosk a few days before the attack, in the same neighborhood as the restaurant. The cards had sequential serial numbers, so they were probably purchased at the same time."

"Then whoever did it may have been scouting the location before the bombing?"

"Possibly. The SIM cards weren't activated on the network until a few hours before the bombing. From the metadata, we could get the general location where the call was made that triggered the bomb. I can tell you that the person was somewhere very close to the restaurant when it went off."

"The American soldiers walked in just a few minutes before it went off. Maybe they were the target," Louie theorized.

"Maybe," Patrick said, not sounding convinced. "But from what I read in the incident report, those soldiers were out for a pub crawl. The bomber wouldn't have known in advance that they would be in that restaurant."

"Were you able to get any other information from the SIM cards?" Louie asked.

"No. They haven't been active again on the network since the attack. I had my team put a tracer on the number. If it goes hot again, we'll know right away."

"That's an impressive set of tools you've got over there in DSPO," Louie observed with a raised eyebrow. "Now I see why you warned me about talking on the phone."

"It was a package deal when the Chinese built our national telecom system. You can thank the old regime for that. President Namono liked listening in on private phone calls. Especially of his ex-wives and cabinet officials," Patrick said, chuckling to himself.

"I'll try to be more careful," Louie promised.

"Especially now that you're running for Green House," Patrick joked, giving his friend a playful wink.

"Don't remind me," Louie groaned.

Patrick took a last sip of coffee and got up from the table. "I'll be in touch if I find anything out about the website. But not over the phone. Keep an eye out for a note," he reminded Louie. "And please give my best to Anna." He tossed a few bills onto the table for the coffee and disappeared into the crowd.

+++

Several days later, Anna left her office on campus and made her way to the cafe for her rendezvous with Nesi and Didier. Once again, they were waiting at a table when she arrived, this time sitting in front of a large-screen television, ready to watch the presidential debate. Anna noted with disappointment that Sammy's old cafe was otherwise empty.

"Lucky you got here early for a good seat," Anna joked as she joined them. "I guess politics haven't yet become a spectator sport here."

"I'm not sure if that's good or bad," Didier observed, looking around at the empty tables. "But it's better watching it at home on my crappy TV."

Anna took a seat and looked up at the screen. The television showed the candidates milling around the stage, preparing for the start of the debate. Meanwhile, a newscaster provided commentary to fill up the time.

"Is Francois ready?" Anna asked.

"If not, then he never will be," Nesi said. "We've been preparing him for the last several days, even putting him through practice debates just like your candidates do back in the States."

"Did you have someone playing the part of Emanuel Sekibo?" Anna asked.

"We did; however, it turns out that wasn't necessary," Didier said, pointing at the screen. There were three empty podiums among the dozens of candidates on the stage.

"Sekibo isn't debating," Didier explained. "Officially, his team claimed that it was some kind of scheduling conflict."

"Is that believable?" Anna asked.

"No way!" Nesi jumped in. "It was planned. He's the front-runner, and his campaign doesn't think they have anything to gain by putting him on a stage with a bunch of minor candidates in the first round. They're worried it will lower his stature."

"That seems pretty cynical. Though I suppose it makes sense from a tactical standpoint," Anna said. "But it looks like he wasn't the only one who made that calculation," she added, nodding at the two other empty podiums on the stage.

Didier and Nesi glanced at each other, then back at Anna.

"You're kidding, right?" Nesi asked.

"What do you mean?"

"Anna, just because we're friends doesn't mean we're going to pretend like nothing's going on," Nesi insisted, frustration in her voice.

"Guys, I'm not kidding," Anna protested. "I don't have the slightest idea what you're talking about."

Didier was no longer able to hold back. "Anna, one of those empty podiums is for your husband. As a registered candidate, Louie is supposed to take part in this debate. You can't expect us to believe that you didn't know anything about it."

Anna stared at the television as the camera panned across the stage. When she saw Louie's name on one of the placards, she understood why Nesi and Didier doubted her story.

"Who else decided not to show up?" she asked, pointing at the third empty podium.

"Fabrice Namono," Nesi answered. "He's still running his campaign from exile."

Anna closed her eyes and shook her head.

"I'm so sorry," she whispered. "I swear to God, I didn't have the slightest idea. I'm sure Louie doesn't even know. They must have made a spot for him because he's on the ballot."

"Please, Anna!" Nesi begged. "Can we stop with the deception? Just be honest with us. This isn't a joke anymore."

"I know it seems unbelievable," Anna said. "I don't even believe it myself. But I swear, Louie never filled out the paperwork. We only found out about it when a reporter asked him about it at work. The next day, Louie went straight to the Electoral Commission and found out that someone had filled out all the campaign paperwork without telling him. They even submitted the application fee and signatures. But Louie doesn't have the slightest idea who's behind it. He tried to withdraw his name but didn't have enough money. I know this all seems crazy, but it's true. I swear."

Again, Didier and Nesi looked at each other, then back at Anna.

"Anna, can you blame us for being suspicious?" Nesi said. "Your husband is a senior military officer from a famous family. His father was a big war hero and his uncle the former minister of defense. It's only logical that Louie would have political ambitions. That's the way things work in our country. Politics has always been a family business."

"No, I don't blame you for not believing me," Anna sighed. "I probably wouldn't either if I was sitting on your side of the table. But it's the truth. Someone is playing a game, and Louie is the victim, not the perpetrator. He's terrified that he's going to get in trouble at work if anyone finds out."

"Well, if they didn't know before, they certainly do now," Didier said, staring at the screen. "Along with everyone else in the country."

"I promise, this is the last thing Louie wants to be part of," Anna said. "He's not a politician. It just isn't part of his DNA."

"But Anna, even if what you say is true, it doesn't matter," Didier pointed out. "Louie can claim this is some elaborate ruse, but no one's going to believe that story. The fact that he didn't show up for the debate makes it even more suspicious. He's playing like a front-runner. Just like Emanuel Sekibo."

"That's ridiculous," Anna snorted. "Once people realize that he hasn't given a single speech or interview, it will be obvious to everyone that the entire thing is a farce. His candidacy is nothing more than an elaborate meme. As soon as Louie finds out who's responsible, he'll go straight to the papers and expose the entire charade. He has no interest in letting it go on any longer."

"Anna, because we're friends, I want to believe you," Nesi said, a worried look on her face. "But have you considered the possibility that Louie isn't being honest about what's going on?"

"I think I know my husband!" she shot back.

"We're not saying you don't," Didier said, jumping to Nesi's defense. "But this is more serious than you think. According to the latest polling, Louie's now in a four-way race with Francois, Emanuel, and Fabrice. Even if what you say is true—that he doesn't want to be president—he's still going to influence the outcome just by being on the ballot. Like it or not, people know his name. They remember his father and his uncle. He might even be taking votes away from Francois. Has Louie considered the possibility that he could be inadvertently helping put Emanuel Sekibo into Green House?"

Anna slumped in her chair, unable to look at her friends. Uncertain what was real, she felt her world spinning out of control. A dozen times in the past week, Anna had thought she had seen the dead waitress passing her on the street. Now, for the first time in her marriage, she questioned whether she really knew her husband. She looked up at the television and the empty podium with his name on it, considering the possibility that she was a fool.

Nesi reached across the table and took Anna's hand. "I'm sorry if we upset you," she murmured. "We want to believe you. But it's hard to know who to trust right now. We've worked so hard to get Francois onto that stage. This was our one chance to make a difference. Now, it feels like someone is trying to take that away from us."

"I know," Anna sighed. "I don't blame you. I'd feel the same way. I hate so much that Louie is somehow involved in this. But please, give us some time to figure out what's going on. I know we can find a way to fix it."

"Don't feel like you need to stay here and watch this," Didier said, nodding at the screen as the moderator began introducing the candidates.

"Do you know where Louie is?" Nesi asked.

Anna shook her head. "I'm guessing he's still at work. I doubt he even knows there's a debate going on."

"Maybe you should go home and be there when he gets back," Nesi advised. "If what you say is true, it could be a long night for you guys."

Anna nodded and gathered her things. "I'm sorry about all of this," she said again. "I hope things go well for Francois tonight. No matter what happens, the two of you should be proud of what you've accomplished."

Nesi and Didier watched Anna leave, then turned back to the debate as the candidates began to make their opening remarks.

+++

When Anna arrived home, she found Louie sitting on the living room couch. The lights were off, and he was still in his uniform. The news was on TV with the sound turned down. Louie was staring at the screen, seeming catatonic.

His cell phone was cradled in his hands and buzzing intermittently with incoming messages. Anna turned on the light, waking Louie from his trance. He turned and looked at her as she stood in the doorway.

"I guess you heard about the debate?" she asked, nodding at his buzzing cell phone.

"I didn't even know until I started getting messages," he said. "I tried explaining the situation to the first few people who called to congratulate me, but no one believes my story. Everyone thinks I'm doing this on purpose. Even the fact that I wasn't on the stage tonight doesn't help. They think I was trolling Emanuel Sekibo by not showing up."

"I know," she said. "I was with Nesi and Didier at Sammy's old place. We were planning to watch the debate together. But when I saw your name on the podium, I couldn't stay. They had the same reaction as your friends. They refused to believe me when I told them it was all a farce and that you had no intention of running for president."

"I can't believe this is happening," Louie said, stuffing his cell phone under a pillow so they wouldn't hear it buzzing. "Were Nesi and Didier angry?" he asked. "I know how hard they've worked to help Francois get ready."

"Angry isn't the right word. I think they feel betrayed. But not because they think you're a bad person. It's just that they've poured their hearts and souls into the campaign. Now they're afraid that having your name on the ballot will pull votes from Francois. Most of all, I think they're frightened that Emanuel Sekibo will win the election."

"We should all be frightened of that," Louie confided. "If he wins, we'll be going back to the old days."

"In that case, we're leaving," Anna said unequivocally. "I'm not staying here if that's what we have to look forward to."

"It's not that simple. We can't just wake up on the morning after the election and decide to leave. There's more to it than that."

"Why not?" Anna challenged. "We're married. I'm a US citizen. You can apply for a visa, and we can leave anytime we want. Once we get to the States, I'll get a job teaching while you wait to hear back from your brother's bank."

"I think you're making it sound easier than it is. Although maybe if I move to New Jersey, people will believe that I don't want to be president."

Anna chuckled.

"What's so funny?" Louie asked.

'I'm just thinking about what you said. About how hard it is to convince people that you don't want to be president."

Louie shook his head, not seeing the humor.

"Not wanting the job," she explained. "That's probably your strongest qualification. The only person who can be trusted with power is someone who doesn't want it."

"That sounds like something you pulled out of a fortune cookie," Louie observed wryly.

"Do you trust any of the people running for president?" she asked, pointing at the television.

Louie pondered the question. "No. Not really," he finally answered.

"But unfortunately, leaving the country won't be enough to convince people that you don't want the job. Look at Fabrice. He's running his entire campaign from exile in Cyprus."

Louie sighed and turned back to the television.

"Have you heard anything more from Patrick?" Anna asked.

"Nothing yet. But I don't want to take a chance by contacting him. Now that my 'campaign' is out in the open, the last thing he needs is to be seen with me."

"What do you think will happen at work tomorrow?"

"That is the least of my worries right now."

Anna tried to hide her alarm at this statement. "What do you mean?"

"The Americans are panicked over the situation in Kiskow. They think the GLA is going to overrun the city before the election."

"Is that possible?"

"It's more than possible," Louie admitted. "We'd be hard-pressed to defend it if something happened tomorrow. The general wants to go out there next week and plans on turning it into a big production. He wants to take the press along to show them how well things are going."

"That seems like a risky strategy," Anna noted.

"That is an understatement."

"I assume he's dragging you out there as part of the performance?"

Louie nodded. "I have less than a week to make sure that everything in Kiskow looks good for when the media arrives. I've been put in charge of building the Potemkin village."

Anna grimaced. "Good luck."

"Thanks. I'll need it," Louie said.

He glared with annoyance at the pillow covering his buzzing phone.

"Can we both turn off our phones and watch something else on TV?" Anna asked. "My only request is no political dramas, war movies, or suspense thrillers. Nothing that could remind me of real life."

Louie smiled for the first time in days and reached under the pillow to turn off his phone.

CHAPTER FOUR

A trio of helicopters started their final approach to Kiskow's dirt airstrip. General B- was aboard the first aircraft. Louie and a delegation of Gisawian dignitaries from the Provisional Interim Government followed in the second. Crammed into the trailing helicopter was the press contingent and their handlers, invited along to witnesses the good news coming out of Kiskow.

An honor guard hoisting Gisawian and American flags lined the edge of the tarmac. Behind them, a military band dressed in formal parade uniforms suffered under the subtropical sun. As the helicopters touched down, the powerful downdraft from the rotor blades caught the receiving party by surprise. Hats, scarves, and sunglasses went flying in a vortex of dust and debris. A drum player and French hornist from the band toppled over and rolled across the yard like tumbleweeds while the color guard fought valiantly to hold its ground against the maelstrom.

As the official party exited the helicopters, the band recovered its fallen members and launched into a shaky rendition of the Gisawian national anthem. The press corps wandered the airstrip like lost sheep until they were corralled by their minders. Louie spotted Janet Russell among the flock, along with her stringer and a photographer. She appeared annoyed at the prospect of wasting her time reporting on a choreographed piece of performance art.

When the band finished its performance, the entourage boarded the buses to begin the official tour. An armada of armored vehicles and military police escorted the buses from the airstrip. The first stop was a walking tour of the newly rebuilt Kiskow city market. The press officer, Captain Howe, led the group and provided narration, citing a laundry list of accomplishments aimed at defeating the GLA by transforming the residents of Kiskow into aspiring free-market capitalists.

Louie scanned a copy of the day's schedule, speculating on the elements most likely to go awry. He was trailing behind the group, half-listening to the spiel, when Janet strolled up beside him.

"Long time, no see," she said.

"I've been busy," Louie mumbled, not in the mood for chatting.

"But not at the debate, I noticed."

"That's because I'm not a candidate, remember?" he said curtly.

"Right. But we both know that's not *precisely* true," Janet corrected him. "I went down to the Electoral Commission and requested a copy of your registration paperwork."

Louie shot her an annoyed glance.

"What?" she said defensively. "It was a legitimate document request. Fact-checking is part of my job, remember?

Besides, it's all a matter of public record. As far as the Electoral Commission is concerned, you are a registered candidate, just like everyone else in that debate."

"I'm surprised you're here today," Louie said, changing the subject.

Janet shrugged. "I go where the news is. And right now, Kiskow is the news."

"I just figured that a dog and pony show wouldn't be your scene," Louie said. "It's not exactly hard news."

"Don't be so sure. If you keep your eyes open, there's always a story to be found."

As they passed through the central market, Janet spotted a woman selling fruit from a wooden table. Louie watched Janet walk over and introduce herself. They chatted for several minutes before Janet bought a few apples. As she was walking away, Janet nodded at her photographer to get a picture of the woman standing proudly in front of her fruit stand. Then she caught up with Louie as the VIPs continued their tour through the market.

"Did you get a big scoop from the fruit lady?" Louie said in a somewhat mocking tone.

Janet smirked and gave Louie a wink. "In case you're wondering, there isn't an apple orchard within a thousand miles of this town. I thought it was strange that she'd be selling them way out here along with her local produce."

"And what was the explanation?" Louie asked, curious but also worried about what she was going to say.

"A truck arrived yesterday, out of the blue, filled with fruits and vegetables. The driver sold his entire load to the local merchants below cost, then drove away without explanation. I think someone wanted to make sure that the market looked busy today. The woman told me that most of the produce on her table couldn't be found here on a normal day. That's why the market is so packed. It's like Christmas has come to Kiskow."

Janet took a bite of an apple and offered one to Louie.

"Jesus," Louie muttered, shaking his head and declining the fruit.

They continued on the tour, with Captain Howe describing a new US-funded sewer system running underneath the town center and extolling the virtues of public sanitation as a precision-guided weapon of counterinsurgency.

"Any luck convincing people that you're not running for president?" Janet asked.

"Not particularly," Louie sighed. "Whoever was behind the social media posts has expanded to leaflets. I found one under my windshield wiper when I came out of work yesterday."

"You know, back in the States, candidates pay big money for that kind of thing."

"Apparently, here, one needs big money to stop it," Louie replied.

"At least you're keeping a sense of humor about it," Janet said. "It would make a great story if only you could give me some proof about who was behind it."

"Believe me, if I had that information, you'd be the first to get it," Louie assured her.

"Well, when you do, you know who to call," she reminded him.

As the tour continued, Janet stepped over one of the new utility hole covers, and something captured her attention.

She called over her stringer and photographer, instructing them to pry it up from the ground. They lifted the metal disk enough to see a layer of hard-packed dirt underneath it rather than a functioning sewer system.

"That's the oldest trick in the book," Janet said as her photographer snapped a quick photo of the ersatz sewer system. "I'm guessing that the local contractor made a nice margin on that project."

Louie shook his head. "I can't believe someone thought it was a good idea to bring you on this trip."

"General B- said he wanted to get out the real story about what's happening Kiskow. I'm just trying to give him what he asked for," Janet said with a look of satisfaction.

The tour continued past the old colonial-era railroad station, now fallen into disrepair. Janet gestured at its weathered, neo-classical facade. "I heard a rumor that some foreign visitors were out here last week looking at the old rail station," she said.

"I don't know anything about it," Louie said defensively, wary of another exposé dismantling the trip's choreographed propaganda.

"That's the real reason I wanted to be here today," Janet confided. "I don't have good sources out here in Kiskow, so I'm having trouble figuring out exactly what's going on."

"What's the rumor?"

"The word on the street is that some Chinese businessmen have been poking around the old station."

"That's not much of a scoop," Louie said. "There are Chinese investors all over the country. Maybe they want to turn it into a luxury hotel."

"Sure, I suppose that's possible. But they were also look-ing at the train tracks and the old trestle bridge over the river. That sounds like something besides a spa resort."

"That train line hasn't run since I was a kid," Louie said. "I remember taking it once with my father when I was young."

"That would be a big project, rebuilding it after all those years," Janet pondered as the tour left the market and contin-ued toward the garrison. "I presume that the Chinese aren't interested in using those trains to bring apples out to Kiskow. They must have something else in mind."

"Anyone investing in that would need a high tolerance for risk," Louie observed. "There are hundreds of miles of track between here and the capital."

"I agree. It's hard to imagine someone taking that risk. Unless they believe the government has a viable plan to finish off the GLA once and for all."

Janet glanced at Louie through her sunglasses, waiting to see his reaction. He ignored the bait and nodded up ahead to where the VIPs were heading through the main gate into the military camp.

"Time for the grand finale," he said.

"I think I've had my fill of whitewash for one day." she said.

They followed the official party toward the sprawling parade ground in front of the headquarters building. The VIPs moved to a reviewing stand, protected from the sun by a fabric canopy. Louie, Janet, and the rest of the non-VIPs were relegated to an unshaded gravel patch beside the parade ground.

Out on the field, several hundred Gisawian soldiers stood at attention, waiting for the main event. As the ceremony began, the sergeant major led the formation through a series of rifle drills, eliciting halfhearted applause from the crowd. Next was a martial arts demonstration performed by a group of soldiers clad in black ninja pajamas.

Once the mock fighting ended, the sergeant major ordered the units to march in review past the VIPs. At the same time, there was a roar of engines revving from a grove of trees behind the parade ground. Several brand-new armored personnel carriers raced onto the field and executed a series of high-speed maneuvers, to the crowd's delight. Machine gunners atop the vehicles fired off bursts of blank ammunition into the air, while pyrotechnics and smoke grenades gave it all the feel of a Hollywood movie set.

The armored vehicles raced in circles around the parade field before disappearing behind the headquarters building. Columns of soldiers marched past the reviewing stand as another set of armored vehicles emerged from the same grove of trees. They performed a similar routine as the other vehicles before disappearing into the smoke. When the third group of similar-looking vehicles appeared, Janet turned to Louie with a knowing smirk.

"How many of those things does your army have out here?" she asked.

"Three," Louie said flatly, realizing what was going on.

"Nice touch. I don't think I've seen that trick since the last May Day parade in Moscow before the Wall came down. But doesn't the enemy need to be watching for the charade to be effective?"

"I would assume so," Louie answered, staring straight ahead, silently praying that this farce would soon be over.

As the last formation passed the reviewing stand, Louie heard what sounded like a mortar round leaving its tube. When the first round exploded on the field, the crowd offered mild applause, assuming it was part of an elaborate grand finale. But seconds later, two more shells struck twenty meters from the first explosion.

As the field erupted into chaos, it became apparent that the explosions were not part of the show. Frightened band members flung their instruments to the ground and sprinted for the trees. The tight formations fell apart as soldiers broke ranks and scattered for cover while the VIPs in the reviewing stand tumbled over each other, trying to escape the mayhem.

Louie was lying flat on the ground when the fourth shell struck, listening for the distinctive sound of another round leaving the tube. Out on the parade field, he could see several soldiers lying wounded on the grass. One wasn't moving. Another was bleeding badly from his leg. Louie was frantically searching for a medic when a fifth shell exploded between him and the injured soldiers.

Before the dust settled, Louie leaped to his feet and dashed onto the field. He went first for the soldier who wasn't moving, sliding in beside him like a runner stealing second base. The man was unconscious but still breathing. Blood from a shrapnel wound on his lower leg soaked through the fabric of his pants, staining the grass.

Louie tore away the soldier's cravat and fashioned it into an improvised tourniquet. He secured it around the man's leg using his bayonet sheath and the decorative lanyard from his uniform. As he finished the field dressing, Louie heard the sound of another mortar leaving the tube. He threw himself over the man's body and held his breath. When the round exploded, Louie felt a hot sting in the back of his leg and winced in pain. When he touched the spot, he felt the sticky wetness of blood between his fingers.

Louie yelled for a medic, knowing he might not have another chance to get the wounded soldier to safety. Not seeing anyone coming to help, he struggled to his feet, hoisting the injured man into a fireman's carry. Louie took his first step, and his leg buckled. He could feel the shrapnel lodged in his muscle. He steadied himself against the pain and carried the soldier from the field, aided by a rush of adrenaline.

The closest protection was a concrete guard shack on the edge of the parade field. A medic was inside, treating another soldier. He took over caring for the injured man while Louie turned and sprinted back for the other two. With Louie's help, the next soldier was able to limp over to the protection of the guard shack.

Louie returned once more to the field. He had almost reached the last man when he heard the sound of another mortar leaving the tube. Louie yelled out a warning and threw himself to the ground seconds before the shell struck the empty bandstand, sending fragments of plywood flying into the air.

Before the dust settled, Louie was up and sprinting for the last soldier, pushing through the excruciating pain in his leg. The man was unconscious when Louie reached him, his face ashen and cold to the touch. Louie grabbed his uniform and tried to lift him, but his hands slipped away. Dark blood had soaked through the fabric and pooled on the grass underneath the man.

Louie fell to his knees, too exhausted to lift the injured soldier. He pressed his fingers to the man's neck, searching for a pulse, but couldn't feel anything besides the pounding of his own heart. The man's chest rose once, twice, then went still. Across the parade field, Louie heard the sound of engines revving. Two of the armored vehicles sped out the front gate toward where the mortars had been launched from.

Louie turned back to the man lying in the grass. With the last of his strength, he began giving him chest compressions until the medics arrived with a stretcher. After they took the solider away, Louie rose unsteadily to his feet. He looked over at where he had been standing at the start of the attack. Janet was there, unfazed, giving instructions to her photographer, making sure he was capturing everything happening on the field.

Louie took a step and felt lightheaded, the surge of adrenaline no longer masking his pain. Blood soaked through his pant leg where the shrapnel had torn into his skin. He dropped down to one knee, unable to leave the field without help.

+++

When Louie opened his eyes, he was in a hospital room. The last things he remembered were a medic loading him into a helicopter on the parade field and that before taking off, they had given him medication for the pain. His recollections after that were fragments of sounds and images aboard the aircraft. Sitting in the hospital bed, he wasn't sure if that had happened two hours or two days ago.

The lights in the room were off. The curtains had been drawn, but Louie noticed sunlight framing the edge of the windows. An IV line ran along the length of his arm, and his thigh was wrapped in bandages. He tried to sit up but felt lightheaded and collapsed back onto the pillow. He lay there listening to footsteps and voices out in the hallway. The door opened, and Anna poked her head into the room, smiling when she saw he was awake.

"How are you?" she whispered.

"All right, I guess," he answered, his voice dry and raspy.

She walked over to the bed and took his hand in hers.

"I came as soon as I heard the news. They wouldn't tell me anything until you got out of surgery."

"Is it bad?"

"Fortunately, no. The doctor took some shrapnel out of your leg. You lost a bit of blood, but he expects a full recovery. They said you were lucky, given how close you were to the explosion."

"What about the others?"

Anna shook her head. "The man you were with on the field didn't make it. The doctors said there was nothing anyone could have done."

"And the others?

"Both are alive, thanks to you. One man lost his leg but probably would have died if you hadn't got the tourniquet on when you did."

Louie knew that he should have felt happy, but he couldn't stop thinking about the last soldier he had tried to help.

"You did everything that you could," Anna said, reading his mind.

"Could you open the curtains?"

Anna drew them back, flooding the room with sunlight.

"How soon until I can leave?"

"Are you in a hurry?" she asked, a worried look on her face. "No one expects you back at work. The doctors want you to stay here for a day or two."

"I'd prefer to rest at home."

Anna shook her head ruefully. "You wouldn't say that if you saw our house this morning."

"Why? What happened?"

"There were about a dozen reporters outside our front door when I came out."

"What on earth for?"

Realization dawned on Anna. "I guess you haven't seen the papers yet," she said.

She reached into her bag and pulled out copies of the local dailies. She placed the stack of newspapers on Louie's lap so he could see the headlines. Above the folds were bold headlines covering the attack in Kiskow. Beneath the banners, several images showed Louie racing into the field and carrying away the wounded soldier over his shoulder. Another picture showed him crouching next to the dying man, trying to stop the bleeding as the medics arrived. A final image was of Louie lying on a stretcher in the back of a helicopter. The headlines all referred to him with the same terms: presidential contender; hero.

"I can't believe this is happening," he said, pushing the papers away in disgust.

"I hesitated to bring them. But it's better that you find out sooner rather than later."

"Has anyone told them that I'm not running?"

"I tried to, Louie. I swear. But nobody believes it. Even Nesi and Didier are now convinced that your denials are a charade. Everyone thinks you've planned the entire thing from the beginning. Who knows what people are going to say after seeing these pictures?" Anna said, nodding at the papers.

"I never asked for any of this," Louie whispered. He pressed his head into the pillow and stared up at the ceiling. "What should I do?"

"I don't know," Anna sighed. "I guess we need to endure it a little longer. Once the election is over, we'll leave as soon as we can. Then, hopefully, we'll never have to think about it again."

Louie tried to lift himself from bed, eliciting a dirty look from Anna. "You need to rest," she admonished. "Enjoy the peace while you can. This room is probably the last place where you'll get it."

"In that case, maybe I'll just stay here until the election is over."

"Only if I can stay with you," Anna said, smiling.

Louie nodded and closed his eyes. Within a few minutes, he had fallen back to sleep.

+++

A week later, Louie returned to work for the first time. From the moment he came through the gate, it was clear everything had changed. As he was walking across the courtyard to his office, a group of soldiers spotted him from a distance and snapped to attention, saluting him as if he were a general.

He got similar treatment outside his office, with the staff rising from their chairs and greeting him with applause when he came through the door. He obliged them with a few awkward handshakes, then quickly escaped into his office, closing the door behind him. They treated Louie like minor royalty for the rest of the day, with no need left unattended. He even had to insist on making his own cup of tea.

When news of his return spread around camp, Louie received a message requesting his presence in the general's office. When he arrived, the secretary sent him straight inside. General B- rose from his chair and greeted Louie with a warm smile and firm handshake.

"Good to see on your feet, hero!" the general gushed, slapping Louie on the back.

"Thank you, sir. It's good to be back."

The general led him over to a pair of leather chairs in the corner of the office, usually reserved for VIP meetings.

"Can I get you a coffee or a soda?" he asked.

"No, thank you, sir."

"How are you feeling?"

"A bit sore, but otherwise, fine," Louie said, downplaying the lingering pain in his leg.

"Good. Glad to hear it. That stuff you did out on the parade field was quite a story. Unfortunately, it was the only bit of good news from that goddamn trip to Kiskow. What a fucking debacle!" he fumed. "Did you see the front page of yesterday's *Tribune*?"

"I haven't been following the news," Louie admitted.

The general handed him a copy of the paper.

"Take a look at what that lady reporter had to say about it," he said, pointing at the offending story.

Just above Janet Russell's byline was the banner headline "US Puts Lipstick on a PIG."

"She didn't pull any punches," Louie observed. "Shall I read it, or does the headline capture the gist?"

"I'll give you the short version. It says that the Provisional Interim Government is grossly mismanaging the fight against the GLA. It's accusing us of throwing ill-prepared soldiers into an unwinnable quagmire. That attack in Kiskow couldn't have come at a worse time."

"What's the official response?" Louie asked as he skimmed through the article.

"Right now, it's damage control. There's a press conference going on this morning. We're trying to regain control of the narrative, but frankly, your government isn't exactly helping." The general scowled. "They've been mostly quiet since the attack and didn't provide any official response when the article came out yesterday."

"I imagine they're stalling for time, hoping that it will blow over," Louie speculated. "The provisional council will be reluctant to weigh in this close to the election."

"This isn't going to blow over anytime soon," the general said. "The article just hit the news back in the States last night. The White House is furious. As if that isn't enough, some jerkoff congressman has been all over the TV this morning, calling for investigations on the president's handling of the crisis."

"His name doesn't happen to be Burke, does it?" Louie asked.

"Yeah, that's it! From somewhere in Pennsylvania. You've heard of him?"

"Believe it or not, our paths have crossed a few times," Louie revealed.

"Well, I guess that explains it."

"Explains what?"

The general chuckled. "You really haven't been watching the news, have you?"

Louie shook his head.

"Maybe you should start. This morning, Congressman Burke mentioned you by name during his press conference."

"What?" Louie gasped. "Because of what happened in Kiskow?"

"Not exactly. He came out and endorsed you for president of DRoG."

"For God's sake," Louie mumbled. "I can't believe this is happening."

The general cocked his head, confused at Louie's reaction. "You expect me to believe that you had no idea that was coming?"

"Of course not!" Louie yelled in frustration. "Why would I expect to receive an endorsement from an American politician? This entire thing is absurd."

The general rubbed his chin, trying to decide what to make of Louie's response. "Well, I *was* born on a Tuesday," he said. "But not *last* Tuesday. You expect me to believe that you're not in it to win it?"

"No! How many times do I need to say it?" Louie pleaded. "I am not running for president and never have been. This is some elaborate ruse, but not one designed by me."

General B— interrogated Louie with his eyes. "If that's the case, I'd say you've got a lot of people fooled."

"I don't know how to be any clearer about this. There is nothing in the world I want less than to become president of the Democratic Republic of Gisawi."

The general broke into a smile. "You know something, Louie?" he said. "Someone once told me that if I wanted to become a general, all I needed were three things: ambition, luck, and talent. But if you've got plenty of the first two, you can get by without much of the third. This is the first time I've ever heard of someone having plenty of the last two without any of the first. But who the hell knows, maybe you'll be the one to do it."

"I don't know whether to be offended or flattered," Louie replied.

"Consider it a compliment," the general said, giving him a friendly slap on the knee.

Louie winced in pain from the poorly aimed gesture.

"Your country would be lucky to have someone like you in charge," the general continued. "Hell, *our* country would be lucky to have someone like you in charge. Anyway, don't forget about us little guys when you're sitting over there in Green House."

"I don't think we need to worry about that," Louie said. "In the meantime, is there anything I can do to help with the blowback over the article?"

"Yes! Get more soldiers out to Kiskow ASAP," the general said. "The GLA must be feeling confident after that attack. I'm guessing we don't have much time before they try something bigger. We need to be ready."

"The only way we can get soldiers out there faster is by pulling people off the street, giving them a uniform, and sending them straight to Kiskow."

"If that's what it takes to keep from losing it, then so be it," said General B-, getting up from his chair, indicating that the meeting was over.

+++

Louie left his meeting with the general and walked back toward his office. Halfway across the courtyard, he saw a pack of reporters filing out of the press conference. Janet was walking alone, furiously tapping out a message on her phone. It was the first time Louie had seen her since the fiasco in Kiskow. He knew he should avoid her instead of giving in to emotion, but he couldn't let go of that headline. When he approached, Janet glanced up from her phone, surprised to see him.

"I didn't know you were back," she said.

"Today's my first day."

"How are you feeling?"

"Fine," Louie said dismissively, though he was walking with a limp. "I saw your headline in yesterday's paper. You must be proud of yourself for getting everyone's attention."

Janet squared up and stepped closer, letting him know that she wasn't intimidated.

"First of all, I write the stories, not the headlines. If you don't like it, call my editor," she said, jabbing her finger at Louie's chest. "Second, I stand behind every line of that story. If I got something wrong, then tell me what it is. But before you do, you should know that I've got multiple sources backing up everything in that article."

"A soldier died right in front of you on that field," Louie shot back accusingly. "What about him? What about his family? How do you think they felt when they read the story?"

"What the hell does that mean?" Janet pushed back.

"His death got one line, and you didn't even mention his name. He was nothing but a bit of dramatic filler."

"If that's what you think, then you missed the entire point of the story. It wasn't about the attack. I'm not a war reporter. But I'm curious to know why you think it's disrespectful to ask why he was there in the first place. Or if he died for a good reason. I think those are fair questions that we should all be asking."

"Judging from the article, your opinion on the matter is clear," Louie challenged.

"It has nothing to do with my opinion," Janet insisted. "I'm trying to figure this out, just like everyone else. But of all people, I would think you'd be interested in finding out the truth."

"What's that supposed to mean?"

"Do you even know who you're fighting out there and why?"

"Are you suggesting that the GLA isn't a real threat?" Louie said indignantly. "For your information, this isn't some imaginary war. The bullets are real. The bombs are real. People are dying."

"I'm not saying it isn't real," Janet argued. "But who's calling the shots, and why? Those fighters who attacked Kiskow last week weren't operating by themselves. Someone is telling them what to do. This nonsense about Daniel Odoki coming back from the dead is nothing but a smokescreen. I want to know who's really behind it and what they're trying to achieve."

"Looking for another dramatic headline?" Louie asked, unable to hide his disgust.

"Why do you think we're on different sides? I want the same thing you do."

"Really?" Louie said skeptically. "How do you know what I want?"

"Do you want to know the truth about who's behind this fake presidential campaign of yours?"

"That has nothing to do with the GLA or what happened last week in Kiskow."

"How do you know that?"

"Please!" Louie groaned. "Enough with the conspiracy theories."

Janet crossed her arms, ticked off at the insinuation. "For your information, I don't do conspiracy theories. Furthermore, it's worth considering the possibility that all these things are somehow connected. You remember before the attack when we were talking about the old railroad station?"

Louie nodded.

"I found out that a Chinese industrial firm submitted a bid to rebuild the old rail line," she confided.

"I told you, there's nothing surprising about that," Louie countered. "The Chinese are doing major infrastructure projects all over the country. I don't see how that's related to the GLA."

"There's more to it than a simple business deal. Have you heard about the Mining Reform Act?"

"No. Should I have?"

"It's a piece of draft legislation recently approved by the Provisional Interim Government," Janet explained. "If it becomes law, it permits direct investment in DRoG's mining sector by foreign-owned companies."

"That's not my line of work," Louie reminded her. "Anyway, I don't see why it's a big deal. Lots of foreign firms do business here."

"The devil is in the details. I got a copy of the draft legislation from one of my sources. It contains a provision requiring that all foreign-owned firms hire domestic security services to protect their operations. Like you said, anyone building a new railroad out to Kiskow would have a hard time keeping it safe. That would require a lot of men with guns. Do you have any guess where a foreign investor would find that kind of highly specialized service inside DRoG?" Janet asked rhetorically.

"Emanuel Sekibo," Louie sighed, seeing where Janet was going with her logic.

"Exactly. S3 Corp is the largest security firm in the country. It's essentially a private army that happens to be run by the presidential front-runner. If that draft legislation gets approved, it would be an enormous boon for Sekibo and S3 Corp."

"When does the legislation go into effect?"

"The bill won't go forward for a vote until after the election, which means that whoever is sitting in Green House will get the final say on whether it becomes law. If Sekibo wins, his first act in office could be approving legislation that will bring an enormous windfall for his company."

"I agree, it's an interesting story," Louie conceded. "But I still don't see how that's connected to me getting put on an election ballot. It doesn't make any sense. There's no obvious motive."

"I'm not saying it's necessarily connected. But you should stop to think about who stands to gain by having you in the election," Janet suggested.

"It doesn't matter. Even if I won, I'd never take the job," Louie insisted.

"I don't know if I believe that. But that's not the point. Maybe your winning isn't what matters. According to the latest polling, you're in third place—just ahead of Fabrice Namono and a little behind Francois Akua and Emanuel Sekibo. There's less than a month to go until the first round. Like it or not, you're already going to be a factor in the outcome."

Louie considered Janet's theory. Across the courtyard, he spotted Owen Smith walking out of the headquarters building. "That's the guy we should be asking about the election," Louie said, indicating Owen. "He's the expert."

"You're kidding, right?" Janet chuckled, looking at Louie as if he was naive.

"That's his job. He's some kind of election advisor," Louie explained.

"Is that what told you?"

Louie nodded hesitantly, feeling left out of some secret.

"I'll bet you a hundred dollars he's CIA," Janet announced confidently, sticking out her hand, daring Louie to take the offer. "That cover story has more holes in it than Swiss cheese."

"Come on," Louie said, ignoring her outstretched hand.

"Hey, I don't know that for sure," she hedged. "But I've seen his type before. Let me just give you some friendly advice: watch what you say around him."

"You're paranoid."

"Yes, I am," she admitted without hesitation. "It goes with the job."

Janet offered a friendly wave and began walking back to the other reporters, leaving Louie standing alone, pondering her advice.

+++

That evening, Louie was on the couch watching TV while Anna was cleaning up after dinner. He was flipping mindlessly through the channels, thinking about the conversation with Janet and her suspicions about Owen Smith. Louie found himself replaying all their previous interactions in his head, searching for clues to confirm or deny Janet's theory. He was lost in thought when Anna came into the room.

"You look tired," she said.

"It was a long day."

"Maybe you shouldn't have rushed back to work so soon. The doctors said it might be a few weeks until you're back to normal."

"Now's not a good time to be away," Louie murmured.

"The world will go on without you," Anna insisted. "There's only so much you can do. You need to think about your health first. It won't help anyone if you drive yourself to exhaustion."

"Everyone's under pressure. I need to do my part. That article in yesterday's paper isn't helping. Between now and the election, everything we do will be under a microscope."

"You've done your best, Louie," Anna said gently. "Nothing that happened out in Kiskow was your fault. You're fighting against a broken system. There's only so much you can do to fix it."

Louie reached for the remote and turned off the TV.

"Did anyone say anything more about the election?" Anna asked.

"A lawyer from the Ministry of Defense came by my office today. He told me the only reason that I'm not in jail is because I haven't made any campaign appearances in uniform."

"That's a relief," Anna said sarcastically. "Did you tell him that you never filled out the registration forms?"

Louie nodded.

"What was his reaction?"

"Same as everyone else. He didn't believe me. Instead, he wished me good luck and said that he planned on voting for me."

"I think it's gone too far for you to convince anyone now," Anna said, looking sympathetic. "I met with Nesi and Didier today for coffee. They said that your name comes up at every single strategy session over at Akua campaign headquarters. You're the only one moving in the polls, so everybody is watching you."

"Watching what?" Louie said, throwing up his hands in

exasperation. "There's nothing to see. There is no campaign. I haven't done a thing. Why can't people see that?"

Anna put her hand on his shoulder to calm him. "Maybe your denials are working against you," she suggested.

"How's that?"

"I know it seems crazy, but Nesi and Didier are convinced that your seeming disinterest is the thing that's generating the buzz."

"That's ridiculous."

"It may sound ridiculous, but apparently, it's driving the other campaigns crazy. They don't know how to run against an opponent who's playing an entirely different game."

"Francois Akua may not know how to do it, but Emanuel Sekibo certainly does," Louie said.

"What do you mean?"

Louie pulled out his phone and showed Anna a recent social media post from Sekibo's campaign. Her eyes widened as she read it.

"Wow. That's a low blow, even for Sekibo," she said. "He's suggesting that you knew about the attack on Kiskow in advance?"

"He didn't come right out and say it. But he insinuated enough to get people talking. It's all the more reason for us to leave as soon as possible. I've had enough," Louie said, stuffing his phone into his pocket.

Anna gave him a moment to calm down, then asked, "Have you thought any more about what you want to do?"

Louie nodded. "I was going to tell you earlier, but with everything going on, I forgot. The HR department at my brother's bank called yesterday."

"And?"

"They asked about my availability for an interview. They'd like to meet in person as soon as I can make it over to the States."

"What did you tell them?"

"I told them I needed a few weeks to arrange it. The army is on alert until after the election. There's no way I can ask for leave before then. I explained the situation and told them I'd be available right after the election."

"Is this what you want to do?"

Louie nodded halfheartedly.

"In that case, I'll start looking for open positions," Anna said.

Louie shrugged in agreement and reached for the remote. "Can we think about something else for a while?" he asked, turning on the TV.

"Sure. That sounds good," Anna agreed. She leaned her head on his shoulder, happy to wait until morning to start worrying about finding a new job.

CHAPTER FIVE

Early the following day, Janet was sitting in a trash dump on the edge of the international airport. An unmarked gray transport plane had just landed. Through a pair of binoculars, Janet watched it taxi toward the American military compound at the far end of the runway. Several cargo trucks were parked on the apron, waiting for the jet. A few technicians dressed in olive drab jumpsuits rushed out to meet the aircraft when it rolled to a stop. After the engines powered down, the plane's rear door opened, revealing the cavernous interior cargo bay filled with pallets of supplies and equipment.

Janet scanned the airport's perimeter through the binoculars, watching for security vehicles. She glanced at her watch. It was almost time for the morning shift change, giving her a few minutes before the next security patrol drove by. Janet got up and trotted through the trash dump, heading for a cluster of trees closer to the fence. The position was more exposed, but it gave her a better view of the aircraft.

Janet crouched next to the fence and slid the backpack from her shoulder. She pulled out a compact telephoto lens and attached it to her digital camera. Usually, she left that type of work to her photographer, except when an assignment involved a good chance of ending up in jail. Those risks, she only took herself.

Janet focused the zoom lens so she could see men's faces as they unloaded the cargo. Some local Gisawians were doing the heavy lifting, under the supervision of the mostly white aircrew. Janet presumed they were Americans, but it was impossible to tell since they didn't have insignia on their flight suits. Forklifts moved the heavy cargo onto the awaiting trucks while a member of the crew did inventory. As the men worked, Janet snapped pictures of the aircraft's tail number and the trucks' license plates.

She heard the sound of a jeep's engine revving in the distance, then spotted a dust cloud on the horizon. Janet looked at her watch, noting that it was time for the rotation of the airport security forces. A white Toyota Hilux truck with a mounted machine gun was driving along the perimeter fence, moving in her direction. Janet cursed the timing; she had hoped to get a few more minutes before having to retreat from the fence.

She snapped one last picture, then quickly disassembled the equipment and stowed it in her backpack. Meanwhile, the security patrol rounded the corner, closing in on her position. With seconds to spare, Janet calmly trotted back to the safety of the garbage dump. Once the patrol jeep was gone, she pulled out her phone and sent a text message to her taxi driver, praying that he was awake and ready to meet her on the road.

An hour later, she was sitting in the taxi, parked at an intersection about a mile down the road from the American compound. Her driver was listening to music on a portable radio and nodding off to sleep. Janet decided to let him rest, guessing that it would be a long day. The taxi's windows were rolled down, and she was getting queasy from the exhaust fumes of the traffic passing through the intersection. She looked impatiently at her watch, beginning to question her theory. Janet fought the urge to play with her phone, knowing she needed to conserve her batteries if her hunch was correct.

A half-hour later, she was on the verge of giving up when she spotted one of the trucks coming down the road. It was driving away from the American base, heading in her direction. Janet nudged the driver awake and told him to start the engine. As the truck came closer, she saw the others following closely behind. Janet pulled out the binoculars and double-checked the license plate numbers against the ones from her photos. After confirming the match, she nodded at the driver, letting him know that it was time to move.

"Remember, not too close," she warned.

She donned a pair of sunglasses and a floppy hat. Once the trucks passed by, the driver eased the taxi into traffic, following the convoy at a safe distance. The streets were busy at midday, and the taxi easily blended in with dozens of similar-looking cars on the road. Once they settled into position, Janet breathed a sigh of relief, hoping that the most challenging part of the day was over. The rest of it depended on her driver's skills.

The city's sprawl gradually thinned and eventually disappeared altogether. A road sign announced their departure from the capital region and listed the mileage to all the destinations large enough to appear on a map. Janet's gaze drifted to the last town on the sign: Kiskow.

The driver trailed the convoy for several more hours along the lonely highway. At one point, Janet drifted off to sleep and was jolted awake by a bump in the road. She opened her eyes and realized that they were dangerously close to the trucks.

"Hey! What did I tell you about getting too close?" she scolded the driver.

After that, she kept a close eye on him. Even more concerning was the loud knocking sound coming from the engine, causing Janet to worry that the taxi might break down in the middle of the low-speed pursuit, stranding them on a rural roadside.

They continued driving after the sun sank below the horizon. Finally, late in the evening, the convoy pulled into Kiskow. The exhausted taxi driver followed the trucks to the garrison's front gate. Janet told him to pull off the road and dim the headlights. She watched as the trucks entered the compound and the gate closed behind them.

In the darkness, the weary driver turned and looked at Janet in the back seat. "What now, boss?" he asked, his voice revealing hope that their journey was ending.

"Get comfortable," she said. "We wait here until morning."

The man sighed and glanced at his watch. "What are we waiting for?"

"To see where those trucks go when they come back out," Janet explained. She reached into her purse, pulled out some money, and handed it over to the driver. "I'll stay here and keep an eye on the camp. You go find us something to eat."

The man nodded and took the money. He got out of the

car and started walking. Janet whistled for his attention before he got too far away. "Keep to yourself," she reminded him. "Don't talk to any girls, and no beer tonight. Understand? Just get some food and come straight back to the car."

The man chuckled, amused that she had been reading his mind.

+++

When Janet opened her eyes, sunlight was gleaming through the windshield. She had a moment of panicked disorientation, trying to remember why she was sleeping in the back of a taxi in the middle of nowhere. Gradually, the details came back to her. She took a deep, calming breath, feeling relieved…until she heard the sound of the driver's snoring; then she panicked.

"Shit!" she screamed, slamming her fist against the headrest, jolting the driver from his slumber. "You were supposed to keep watch while I slept!"

"I *was* on watch!" he mumbled, still half asleep.

"Bullshit!" she shot back.

"Don't worry, boss. If the trucks came out, we would have heard them."

"You better hope so," she threatened.

The driver got out of the car and wandered into the trees to take a piss. When he returned, Janet was brushing her teeth with some toothpaste smeared on a finger. She rinsed her mouth with water from a plastic water bottle and tried to spit out the window without looking conspicuous.

"I'll go find some coffee," the man said as Janet continued her morning hygiene.

"Only if you give me the keys," she insisted while casually swiping a deodorant stick under her arms.

The driver shook his head, uneasy with the idea of turning over the keys to his taxi.

Janet sensed his reluctance. "Listen, if those trucks come
out the gate and you're not here, I'm not waiting around. Do
you think I spend my nights sleeping in taxis just for fun?"
she asked incredulously. "Either you give me the keys, or you
don't go for coffee. It's your choice."

The man shrugged and got back into the driver's seat,
unwilling to argue. They only waited a few minutes before the front gate opened. Janet tapped the driver on the
shoulder, warning him to get ready. They heard the sound of
engines rumbling, then saw the lead truck exit the gate, with
the others following closely behind.

"Same deal as yesterday," she told him. "Not too close.
There isn't much traffic on the roads out here, so it'll be easy
for them to spot us."

The driver nodded and turned on the engine. He was
getting ready to make a U-turn, expecting to follow the convoy back to the capital, but the lead truck turned in the opposite direction. The driver glanced back at Janet, uncertain
what to do. The trucks were heading away from the city on
the road leading to the border. Janet smiled with satisfaction.

"Do we follow?" the driver asked nervously.

"Stay with them as long as we can," she instructed. "Did
you remember to fill the extra gas cans last night?"

The driver nodded and sucked his teeth, now understanding why she had made him bring the extra fuel. They
followed behind the convoy for the rest of the day, stopping

a few times when the trucks pulled over for a break. By late afternoon, Janet's entire body was sore from two days of sitting in the cramped car. The road got progressively worse the closer they came to the border. After they passed through the last settlement on the map, the driver glanced back at Janet.

"There's nothing beyond here," he protested. "There's no use going on."

"We're almost there," Janet assured him.

"Almost where? I'm telling you, there's nothing out there."

"That's not true. The border is out there. It's less than an hour away."

"We can't cross the border," he insisted in a tone implying that there was no room for negotiation.

"I know that. But we'll take it as far as we can go."

The driver reluctantly went on, keeping the trucks in sight down the road. About an hour later, they arrived at a dismal frontier settlement that served as the official border crossing point. Janet ordered the driver to pull off the road, out of view. She watched as the lead driver left his truck and went into the customs office on the Gisawian side of the border.

"Wait here," Janet said, slipping out of the car.

The taxi driver watched her sneak behind a row of merchants' shacks selling fresh fruit, cheap Chinese radios, and secondhand car parts. Janet worked her way to a spot where she could see the action but remain unobserved. The lead driver was speaking to a man in uniform who seemed to be in charge of the border crossing. They shook hands and smiled, appearing familiar with one another. Janet slipped the camera from her backpack and began snapping pictures through the telephoto lens.

The men chatted for a few minutes; then the driver handed the customs agent a small package, roughly the size and thickness of a paving brick. They shook hands again, and the driver returned to his truck. He started his engine and waved for the other trucks to follow. Several Gisawian border guards armed with AK-47s trotted over and raised the gate. Janet continued taking photos as the trucks crossed the border, leaving DRoG behind.

Once they were gone, she returned to the taxi and climbed into the back seat. The driver looked over his shoulder, concerned that she might have some idea about trying to follow them across the border.

"There's no going on from here," he reminded her, hoping he was right.

"Unfortunately, you're correct. But I got what I needed."

"Now what?"

"Back to the capital," she said, pointing at the only road leading back. "Wake me up if you want me to drive," she offered. "We don't have time to stop along the way."

The driver nodded. As he pulled onto the road, he glanced in the rearview mirror. Janet had pulled her hat over her eyes and appeared to be taking a nap. The driver did a U-turn and began the long drive back to the capital.

+++

A few days later, General B- stormed into the conference room and threw a newspaper onto the table. Louie and the staff scrambled to their feet, anticipating the coming storm.

He glared around the room, looking for somewhere to direct his anger.

"Who the fuck wants to explain this?" he yelled, pointing at the offending paper.

On the front cover was a picture of cargo trucks parked on the runway next to an American-registered transport plane. A second photo showed the identical vehicles at the border post, with the lead driver passing a wrapped bundle to a customs officer. The boldfaced headline put the pictures into context: US-Backed 'Third Force' Fighting Shadow War across DRoG Border.

Captain Howe raised his hand. "Sir, the article is based on nothing but speculation and empty conjecture. Those pictures prove nothing. There are hundreds, maybe thousands of trucks in this country that look just like those."

"The license plates and drivers are the same in both photos," the general fumed. "How are you going to explain that when you walk into the press conference?"

"Sir, the story hasn't changed. It's no different than what we've been saying all along," Howe insisted. "We've never confirmed or denied any rumors about a so-called 'third force' operating across the border." He used air quotes around the operative words. "There's nothing in that article contradicting any of our previous statements."

"The pictures show cargo moving from a US-registered aircraft onto trucks, stopping in Kiskow, then crossing the border. That's not going to be easy to explain," the general argued.

"Sir, what I see is a lot of uninformed speculation," Howe said reassuringly. "Ms. Russell has no idea what's in those trucks. They could be moving rubber dogshit for all she knows. Furthermore, she has no idea what happened inside the camp during the night in Kiskow. Those could have been empty trucks crossing the border."

The general was not mollified. "Who the hell do you think people are going to believe—her or us?"

"Sir, I can't control what people think. But what I *can* do is make an airtight case that there's no real evidence here suggesting any relationship between the US government and irregular fighters operating across the border."

"I don't care what you do, but this story needs to end right now. We're three weeks away from the election. We don't need a scandal distracting us from the main event. Our number one priority right now is keeping the GLA from turning this election into a fucking disaster. Everybody got that?" the general demanded, scanning the room for hints of insufficient commitment.

"Good," he said after a moment. "Then let's get back to work. And I don't want to hear anybody saying a goddamn thing about this 'third force' bullshit between now and the election. Does everyone understand?"

The general got up from his chair without waiting for an answer, then stormed from the room like a bull charging out of a rodeo chute.

+++

Louie left the conference room, baffled by what had just happened. He wandered across the courtyard to his office, lost in thought. Halfway there, he heard a faint whistle coming from a cluster of trees. He spotted Janet hiding inside the grove, trying to get his attention.

"Are you sure it's a good idea to be showing your face around here today?" Louie asked.

"What are you talking about?" she said, batting her eyes in a show of faux innocence. "I heard there's going to be a press conference later. I didn't want to miss it."

Louie rolled his eyes, unamused with the charade but still impressed by her boldness. "You better not let the general see you. He blew his top this morning about your article. He'll probably pull your access credentials if he catches you in camp."

"Why would he be angry with me? I'm not the one telling lies. I'm just trying to get to the bottom of what's going on."

"The bottom of what? Your coverage caused a buzz, but what did it prove? Some trucks crossing the border aren't much of a conspiracy. I'm surprised your editor let you get away with running that story."

"Did you read the entire article? There's more to it than trucks crossing the border," Janet informed him. "I've got reliable sources saying that the GLA has been getting hit inside their sanctuary area. Yet both the US and the Gisawian governments insist that no forces are operating across the border. If that's true, then who's out there launching these raids against the GLA?"

"I don't have any idea what you're talking about," Louie insisted. "If somebody is fighting across the border, nobody told me about it."

"Maybe you should ask your buddy Owen Smith and see if he knows anything about it," Janet said sarcastically.

"Are you still insisting that he's CIA?"

"Have you asked him yet?" Janet challenged.

"What do you think?"

She shrugged. "Fine. Ignore my advice if you like. I'm just trying to help you get to the bottom of the mystery about your campaign."

"This conversation is over," Louie said, turning away in frustration.

He began walking toward his office, leaving Janet standing in the trees. Louie didn't get more than a few steps when he felt the reverberation from an explosion off in the distance. He spun around and looked back at Janet. Her eyes were fixed on the horizon, where a massive cloud of dust and smoke was billowing into the sky near the city center.

Janet pulled out her cell phone and began scanning through social media. It only took a few seconds before eyewitnesses were posting firsthand accounts.

"There was an explosion inside Francois Akua's campaign headquarters," Janet said, reading from her phone. "They're reporting multiple causalities."

"Jesus," Louie muttered, watching as the cloud of debris filled the sky. "My wife has some friends working on the campaign. I should call her." He pulled out his own phone and dialed Anna's number.

Janet was reading off incoming updates while Louie waited for Anna to pick up. "My stringer at Emanuel Sekibo's campaign headquarters says they've ordered an evacuation of the building due to a suspicious package," she said.

Anna's phone went straight to voicemail. Louie tried

once more with the same result, then stuffed the phone into his pocket without leaving a message.

"The networks must be overloaded," he said.

People were wandering outside their offices and gathering in the courtyard, trying to figure out what was happening. They could hear the sound of fire engines racing by in the street. Then, without warning, a second explosion shook the ground. It seemed to come from the same general direction as the first blast, but it was impossible to tell for sure. Seconds later, Janet received confirmation.

"There's been another bombing, this time at Sekibo's campaign headquarters," she announced.

"This is crazy," Louie said. "Why would someone do this? It achieves nothing."

"The third force took the fight to the GLA. Now the GLA is bringing it back," Janet said, staring at the sky.

Louie ignored her speculation and tried once more to call Anna. When the effort failed, he turned toward his office. "I need to find Anna," he said, and walked off.

Janet watched him leave, wondering how he intended to find Anna amid the chaos. Everyone else in the courtyard was standing around in a state of shock and confusion. Janet saw no point in waiting for the press conference and headed for the gate, preparing herself for another long day.

+++

The phone lines were down all afternoon. Louie had tried a dozen times and never gotten hold of Anna, so he breathed a sigh of relief when he pulled into their driveway and saw her car parked by the house. The feeling evaporated as soon as he walked through the door. Anna was sitting at the kitchen table, head in her hands. Louie could see that she'd been crying.

He walked over and hugged her, already suspecting what had happened. One look into her eyes confirmed his speculation.

"Nesi and Didier were in the building when it happened," she said, struggling to hold back tears.

"Have you heard from them?"

"No. They haven't answered their phones. Someone I know on the campaign texted me and said they were taken to the hospital."

"Any word on their condition?"

"Nothing specific. But the person said they weren't in the room when the bomb went off. Hopefully they're OK. I'll go to the hospital tomorrow morning and try to find out more."

Louie wanted to discourage her from going into town but knew that his warning would be wasted breath.

"Did you hear about Francois?" he asked.

"Have they confirmed it?" she asked, sensing what he was about to tell her.

Louie nodded. "There was nothing they could do. He was in a meeting with his staff when the bomb went off right outside the door. Only a few of the people in the room made it out."

"Why would someone do this?" Anna asked, struggling to maintain her composure. "It doesn't make any sense."

"When I was pulling into the driveway, someone on the radio said that the GLA had claimed responsibility," Louie explained.

"Do you believe it?"

"I don't know what to believe anymore. The statement said that it was in retaliation for attacks against their forces across the border."

"Then what your friend Janet reported in the paper must be true."

"I wouldn't call her a friend," Louie corrected.

"But why would the GLA retaliate by attacking Francois Akua?" Anna asked. "He was probably the only candidate in the field willing to talk with them. All that they've done is poke a stick into a hornets' nest. Emanuel Sekibo's campaign issued a statement right after the bombing vowing revenge. He promised that if he wins the election, he'll take the war across the border."

"He's speaking in the heat of the moment," Louie said. "Give it a few days. Cooler heads will prevail."

"Why do you think that?" Anna cried. "With Francois gone, Emanuel Sekibo is certain to win the election. Nothing is holding him back. The media is already predicting that he'll get a big jump in the polls because of the attacks."

"One man alone can't make a war," Louie said. "He'll need the support of the legislature and the general staff. It's not as simple as Sekibo just ordering the army across the border."

"Louie, listen to yourself!" Anna begged. "Have you already forgotten Operation Brushfire? Your uncle showed us what one man can do if he's determined. That was a war built on nothing but lies and deception. What makes you think things will be any different under Sekibo?"

"We still don't know for sure what happened during Operation Brushfire," Louie muttered.

Anna rolled her eyes at Louie's statement, unwilling to argue but leaving no uncertainty as to her opinion.

"What happens now?" she asked.

"The Provisional Interim Government will meet tonight to decide how to respond."

"What can they do?"

"Probably not much," Louie conceded. "We're three weeks away from the election. They won't take any drastic steps until a new executive is sitting in Green House."

"You mean Emanuel Sekibo?" Anna spat, venting her disgust at the thought of him occupying the presidential mansion.

"*Whoever*," Louie said impatiently. "The point is, until we have a president, the interim government doesn't have the power to take decisive action. They won't commit to anything until a new administration is in place. I'm guessing they'll deploy some additional police on the streets. But if the GLA is determined to set off more bombs, I don't think there's much that's going to stop them."

"What about you?"

"I doubt this changes anything," Louie speculated. "Everyone is still focused on Kiskow. The Americans are convinced that the GLA will try to take it before the election. Protecting the garrison is their number one priority."

"Could it happen?" Anna asked, surprised to hear Louie put it so bluntly.

"I don't know. After today, I don't want to make any predictions."

"Is that what this 'third force' thing is all about? Are the

Americans trying to stop the GLA on the other side of the border?"

"Honestly, I don't have the slightest idea. If you read Janet's article in the paper, then you know as much as I do."

Anna gave him a skeptical glance. "But even if you knew something, you couldn't tell me. Right?"

Louie thought for a moment. "I suppose not. But I *don't* know anything," he added with a shrug. "Maybe I'll find out more tomorrow."

"What do you mean?"

"I found a note under my car's windshield wiper after work. Patrick wants to meet tomorrow."

"About the bombings?"

"I don't know. But I'm guessing it's not a social call. He wouldn't ask to meet unless it was important. Especially after what happened today."

Anna pulled Louie closer, not wanting to let him go.

"You know, New Jersey sounds better all the time," she whispered.

"Funny. I was thinking the same thing," Louie said, squeezing her tight.

CHAPTER SIX

The day after the bombing, the mood in the city had changed dramatically. On his way downtown, Louie encountered police checkpoints at all the major intersections. Armored personnel carriers were parked in front of government buildings, with soldiers perched in the gun turrets, watching for danger. Traffic was almost nonexistent, and Louie had no problem finding a parking spot when he arrived downtown.

Walking through the central market, he was almost alone. A few shoppers were out on the street picking up necessities, but most of the vendors' stalls were locked up tight. A block from the cafe, Louie encountered a patrol of young soldiers walking down the sidewalk with automatic rifles slung across their chests. He wondered if the weapons were loaded and what purpose it would serve if they were, but he didn't stop to ask. The soldiers seemed as nervous as everyone else on the street, and Louie was wary of giving them any cause for overreaction.

Patrick was already waiting at the café when Louie arrived with their usual order: coffee and cream for Patrick, and tea for Louie. Patrick nodded in greeting but didn't get up from his chair, and Louie could see that his friend was exhausted. He sat expressionless behind his mirrored sunglasses, seeming distracted. Patrick's eyes remained fixed on the street; he was unwilling to let his guard down.

"Did you sleep last night?" Louie asked.

Patrick shook his head. "I came straight here from the office. My team was up all night working. The delegates from the PIG are screaming bloody hell and want answers."

"The politicians are always quick with demands when someone else is doing the work," Louie said sympathetically.

"At least this time they're asking the right questions. Something's not right about this."

"What do you mean?"

"DSPO is still stonewalling about everything relating to the GLA. Ever since the first bombing at the restaurant, they've been citing 'security concerns' for why they can't provide more details on the attacks," Patrick said, adding air quotes for emphasis.

"What's going on at the headquarters?"

"Everything we collect goes straight up to the fusion cell, but nothing ever comes back down," Patrick said, frustration evident in his voice. "We're not even supposed to talk about the investigation unless we're part of the inner circle."

"You're telling me that no one inside DSPO is allowed to discuss the bombings?" Louie asked, shocked by the revelation.

"Only behind closed doors. It's always been a paranoid organization, but this is taking it to an entirely new level."

"What about yesterday's bombings? Is your branch just pretending they didn't happen?"

"No, of course not. But we're not allowed to work on the case unless someone from the fusion cell is there supervising. They're constantly looking over our shoulders, making sure they know everything that we're doing. It's almost like they're worried about what we might find."

Louie thought about this for a moment, then asked, "Do you think they're questioning the GLA's claims of responsibility?"

"Maybe. But if so, no one's willing to say it out loud."

Patrick glanced over his shoulder, making sure no one was around, then leaned over the table and lowered his voice. "We found something interesting last night," he whispered. "Do you remember me telling you about the SIM card that triggered the first bombing at the restaurant?"

"Yes," Louie said. "You said the card hadn't been active on the network since the first attack."

"That was true," Patrick confirmed. "Until yesterday."

"Was the same SIM card used in the bombings against the campaigns?"

Patrick gave an expressionless nod. "Not only that, but we were able to get the call location from the metadata."

"What did you find?"

"Both bombs were triggered from the same location, very close to Emanuel Sekibo's campaign headquarters."

"I guess that's not surprising," Louie observed. "Wouldn't you expect the bomber to have his targets under surveillance?"

"Yes, that's true. But it also means the bomber would have known that Emanuel Sekibo wasn't in the building. They evacuated his headquarters a few minutes before the explosion, just after the first bomb went off at Francois Akua's headquarters."

"That doesn't make sense," Louie said, confused by the sequence of events.

"Or maybe it does," Patrick argued. "What if the bomber wasn't trying to kill Sekibo?"

As soon as he asked the question, Louie understood its significance. "Are you suggesting that the GLA wasn't responsible after all?"

"I don't think we can say that, based on the evidence. But it does make you wonder about the motive," Patrick mused. "Why would the GLA want to take out Francois Akua? He's the only candidate who expressed a willingness to talk with them. If anything, Emanuel Sekibo should be the one they want dead. He's threatening to send the army across the border into their sanctuary area. His number one campaign promise is that he'll destroy the GLA."

"Did you report the information about the SIM card to the fusion cell?"

"No," Patrick said, shaking his head. "Our minders from the fusion cell didn't know we were analyzing the telephone metadata. As soon as I spotted the connection, I told my analyst to quarantine the records so no one else could access them."

"Can you trust him?"

"He works for me, not the fusion cell. I told him that I would notify the appropriate authorities, then I gave him a few days off. I'm the only one left in the office who knows how to access the files."

Louie's heart was racing as he thought about the implications of Patrick's revelation. "If someone found out that you were withholding information, you could go to jail," he warned.

Patrick looked grim. "That's the least of my worries. I think the stakes are much higher. That's why I wanted to meet with you right away."

"I don't see how I can help. I don't know anything about police work or signals intelligence," Louie admitted. "That's way outside of my expertise."

Patrick discreetly pulled out a pack of cigarettes, placing it on the table between them.

Louie raised his eyebrows. "A new habit?"

"Take the pack when you leave. There's a thumb drive hidden in the space at the bottom. I uploaded the phone records showing the time and location of the bomber's calls. There's also an explanation of the data in layman's terms. You don't need to do anything with it now. But I want you to have it, just in case."

Louie tried to hide his concern. "In case of what?"

"I don't know. But something strange is going on. I don't know who I can trust anymore."

"Are you going to tell the fusion cell about the bomber's location outside of Sekibo's headquarters?"

"I haven't decided yet. But there's another reason I wanted to meet. I was able to track down some information on your fake campaign," Patrick revealed. "It's not much, but maybe it will help."

"What did you find?" Louie blurted out.

Patrick glanced nervously around the cafe and frowned at Louie. "Relax," he scolded his friend. "I told you, it's not much."

"Just tell me," Louie said impatiently.

"The social media for your campaign is being routed

through multiple virtual private networks located in several different countries. That made it difficult to trace it back to the original source, but eventually, my guy figured it out. He thinks it's coming from somewhere outside of Baltimore."

"You mean Maryland?" Louie asked, baffled. "How is that possible?"

"There's also a local connection. Whoever set this up is amplifying the social media through click farms located here in DRoG."

"I'm sorry, but I have no idea what a click farm is," Louie admitted sheepishly.

"In this case, it's just a roomful of kids getting paid to make you look more popular on social media. It's a very low-tech influence campaign," Patrick explained. "They get paid a few cents each time they repost something positive about your campaign or sign on new supporters to your social media channels. The entire thing was designed to make your campaign look legit, like it was operating from inside the country."

"How did your guy figure it out?

"Whoever set up the local operation didn't cover their tracks. He was able to figure out the locations of the click farms from their IP addresses. I sent someone there to check them out."

"Were they able to figure out who was behind it?"

"No." Patrick leaned forward confidingly. "The kids working at the houses were clueless, just like the one who came to your door. All they know is that someone deposits payments into their mobile money accounts each week in exchange for making you look like a winning candidate.

And also for trolling the other candidates with lies and misinformation. For the kids, it's easy money with no strings attached. I wouldn't be surprised if the other candidates are running similar operations."

"This is completely crazy!"

"I know," Patrick agreed. "It makes you wonder why we were waiting for democracy all those years. So far, it looks a lot like how things have always worked here. But at least back then, we knew who was pulling strings. Now, we don't have any idea who's behind the lies."

Louie stared into his tea, trying to process everything that Patrick had revealed. "I have an idea who to ask," he finally said.

"Be careful," Patrick warned. "This isn't a game. Those are real bombs going off out there."

"You don't need to remind me," Louie said, touching the scar on his forehead from the restaurant bombing.

+++

The next day, Louie escaped his office at lunchtime, hoping to find some solitude in a quiet corner of the courtyard. With his newfound notoriety, even short trips to the mess hall invited awkward interactions, particularly as the election drew closer. Louie had no taste for celebrity and preferred eating his lunch out of the spotlight.

He found an old plastic chair hidden in a grove of mango trees and opened the lunch that Anna had made for him that morning. Though he appreciated the gesture, he didn't feel hungry after rummaging through the contents.

Ever since his meeting with Patrick, Louie had been preoccupied with their discussion. That night, after Anna fell asleep, he snuck into the backyard with a gardening trowel and a glass jar. Inside the container were the data files and notes from Patrick explaining the significance of the information. Louie buried it in a shallow hole, topping it with a distinctive rock that he wouldn't forget. After returning to bed, he felt better knowing that the information wasn't inside the house where someone might come looking for it.

Louie was still mulling over his meeting with Patrick when Owen appeared at the edge of the mango grove.

"I thought I might find you here," he said. "I hope I'm not disturbing you."

"Isn't that exactly what you're doing?" Louie snapped.

Owen didn't reply. Instead, he bent over and picked up an unripe mango that had fallen from one of the trees. He tossed it playfully into the air, catching it in his opposite hand like a baseball pitcher warming up on the mound.

"The mangoes taste much better here than back in the States," Owen said. "Somehow, we've engineered the flavor right out of them. They look great on the store shelf, but it's not the same when you taste them. I suppose that must be a metaphor for something," he added, trying to draw Louie into the conversation.

Louie ignored him. He closed his eyes and tried to pretend Owen wasn't there.

"I've got a friend in Mumbai who sends me a few cases of mangoes every year for Christmas," Owen continued. "Those are the best I've ever had. No contest. But the ones you have here come pretty close." He studied the fruit in his hand.

Louie sighed and opened his eyes, accepting that Owen wouldn't leave him alone. "That person who sends you the mangoes from Mumbai. Is he one of your CIA buddies?" he asked sharply.

Owen's fist tightened around the fruit, then relaxed as he forced a smile. "That's a funny accusation," he said calmly.

"Is it?"

"You've read too many spy novels."

Louie reached into his pocket and pulled out an old, wrinkled business card. He flashed it at Owen so he could read the writing on it.

"A guy from your embassy gave me this on the day Green House burned to the ground. He said his name was Mike Jones. I have no idea if that was true, but I presume he's a colleague of yours."

"Never heard of him," Owen said with a shrug.

"He told me that my father was working for the CIA during the border wars. Then he said that he wanted to talk about elections. Is that why you're here now?"

"Louie, you're acting a little paranoid. I told you when we first met, I'm a technical advisor. I'm here on a short-term contract with the State Department, doing electoral reform work. Believe me, there's no James Bond stuff going on here."

"By advising the election, you mean interfering with it?" Louie snapped.

"Don't be silly. The United States only wants what's best for your country, and that's free and fair elections. The only reason I'm here is to help ensure that happens."

"What's free and fair about putting a fake candidate on the ballot?"

Owen dropped the mango onto the ground and stared at his shoes, considering his words carefully before responding. "Are you serious about moving to New Jersey?"

"I won't even ask how you know about that," Louie hissed. "But why do you care? If you're only worried about a fair election, then it shouldn't matter who wins. Right?"

"Well, in the abstract, that's true. However, one measure of a good election process is that it provides citizens with a reasonable choice of candidates. Wouldn't you agree?"

"That's not for you to decide."

Owen shrugged, suggesting that he might not share Louie's opinion on the matter. "A lot of people seem excited about having you in the race," he noted. "Why is that such a terrible thing?"

Louie sprang up from his chair and pointed angrily at Owen's chest. "I never entered this race, and you know it. Someone forged the registration paperwork at the Electoral Commission. The social media campaign is coming from somewhere in Maryland. The kids handing out flyers on the street don't have any idea who's paying them to do it. Is that part of your job here? Running a shadow campaign?"

Owen chuckled and shook his head. "Louie, that's quite an accusation. Not to mention very difficult to prove. I imagine that if we looked hard enough at any of the campaigns, we'd probably find lots of irregularities."

"You consider a forged candidate registration an *irregularity*?"

"No election is ever going to be perfect—especially the first time out of the gate. But you're crazy if you think that the others aren't playing games as well. A year ago, Fabrice

Namono was living in Cyprus and up to his neck in gambling debt. Now, he's running a very well-financed campaign from exile and has an outside shot of making it into the runoff. Tell me, how do you think Fabrice made that happen?"

Louie shrugged.

"You didn't hear this from me, but the Russians have been bankrolling his campaign," Owen confided. "The entire operation is being run out of a beachside condo in Limassol."

"That doesn't make it right for everyone else to bend the rules. If that's the case, then what's the point of all this?" Louie said, throwing up his hands in frustration.

"The point is making sure that good people have a fighting chance. There's too much at stake," Owen insisted.

"Is that what you guys told my father? That too much was at stake? Then he went off to his death fighting someone else's war."

"Listen to yourself," Owen implored. "What you're saying makes no sense. I was still in diapers during your country's border wars. I don't know a thing about your father or how he died. But what I do know is that things could go very badly for your country if this election turns out the wrong way. We could easily find ourselves back in another senseless war. A lot of good men could die. Men like your father. Do you understand?"

"I assume you're talking about Emanuel Sekibo winning?"

"You've heard him on the campaign trail," Owen said. "He's threatening to take the fight against the GLA across the border."

"Maybe he should!" Louie said in frustration. "They're blowing up restaurants and campaign offices, killing innocent people. We'll be lucky if they don't overrun Kiskow between now and next week."

Owen shook his head. "There are bigger issues at stake here than the GLA. Any move across the border could spark a major regional crisis. The last thing we need is a new border war. How would that help anyone?"

"That's rich," Louie said, spitting on the ground in disgust. "My father died fighting a pointless war that the CIA thought was important, until it wasn't. Now you're telling me that fixing an election is going to stop another one? Why should I believe anything you say?"

"Louie, I'm truly sorry about how all this has played out. I hope someday we can have an open and frank conversation about what's happening. I think if you understood the entire story, we would see eye to eye on this." Owen paused. "Unfortunately, I'm not at liberty to discuss all the details. For the time being, I just need you to trust me. Please believe me when I say that your country will not be well served by having Emanuel Sekibo sitting in Green House. There's more to this than meets the eye. It's much bigger than the GLA."

"Is that what this so-called third force is about? A proxy army keeping the GLA in check, so Sekibo doesn't have an excuse to cross the border?"

"I told you, I don't know anything about that," Owen insisted.

"If Sekibo's so dangerous, why doesn't the US just come out against him?"

"It's never that simple. If he wins, we'll still need to find a way to work with him. We can't afford to play our hand too early. You need to appreciate that this is a very delicate situation."

"That's not my problem," Louie shot back. "For your information, I'm leaving the country right after the election."

"Can I convince you to reconsider?"

"Reconsider what?"

"Just let things play out. There's no harm in seeing what happens. Once it's over, then you can decide about the future."

"What part of 'no' don't you understand?" Louie snarled. "I don't give a damn what the ballot says. I'm not taking part in this charade."

Owen nodded but said nothing more as Louie turned and marched back to his office.

+++

Louie and Anna stayed home on election night. They were awake long past their usual bedtime, but neither could have slept if they'd tried. Louie was flipping through the channels while trying to ignore his phone and the continuous buzzing of incoming texts from friends and well-wishers. Anna was in the kitchen, cleaning up from dinner, when she heard Louie grunting in the living room.

"What is it?" she yelled out.

When he didn't answer, she joined him in front of the TV. He was staring at the screen, listening to a newscaster announcing the early returns.

"What are they saying?" Anna asked, sitting on the couch, resting her head on his shoulder.

"Some of the polling places in the city are beginning to report."

"And?"

"Emanuel Sekibo seems to be well ahead, but it's too soon to tell. They say it could be days before all the ballots from the outlying regions are counted."

"You look worried," Anna said. "Is it because he's winning?"

"No. Because he's not winning by enough," Louie replied, staring at the screen and avoiding her eyes.

"I don't understand."

"If the numbers stay where they are now, Sekibo won't get an outright majority. The election will automatically go on to a second round."

Anna studied the numbers flashing across the bottom of the screen, now understanding what Louie was talking about. The early returns showed Louie trailing a distant second behind Sekibo, with Fabrice Namono coming in third.

"The bastard is going to get what he wanted," Louie mumbled.

"Who? Sekibo?"

"No," Louie said, shaking his head. "Owen Smith. The one who put my name on the ballot."

"You found out who did it!" Anna exclaimed. "Why didn't you tell me?"

"It doesn't matter. There's no way I could ever prove it. They made sure of that."

"Who's 'they'?"

"Your government. The CIA, I assume. The ones who forged my name on the application."

"Do you know that for sure?"

"I know enough," Louie insisted.

"OK, I believe you. But what can you do about it?"

"Probably nothing, except go on with our plan to leave here as soon as possible. I'll need to call my brother's bank in the morning and tell them that I can't come for the interview next week. If the election goes to a second round, the army won't approve my leave until it's over."

"But the security plan worked," Anna pointed out. "There weren't any attacks today anywhere in the country. Nothing happened in Kiskow. Isn't that what they wanted?"

"Yes. And they'll expect the same thing for the second round. But I can assure you, it wasn't because of anything we did. If the GLA wanted to blow up the election, they easily could have gotten through our security forces. But for some reason, they decided not to."

"What do you think that means?"

"I don't know. But there's no guarantee it will go the same way next time." Louie paused, thinking of something else. "I'll call my brother and let him know I'm not coming."

"I'll change the tickets in the morning," Anna offered.

"Why don't you just change mine?" Louie said. "You should go back as we planned. There's no reason for you to cancel your interviews just because I can't go. You can spend some time with your family. It will only be a few more weeks. I'll join you as soon as I can."

"No way," Anna said, her tone leaving no room for debate. "I'm staying here with you. We'll go together once this is over."

Louie turned off the TV and looked at Anna. "What can I say to change your mind?"

"Nothing."

He didn't try to argue, having learned long ago that there was no use doing that once she had made up her mind.

"I'm exhausted," Anna said, getting up from the couch. "Can we forgot about this for tonight and go to bed?"

Louie nodded and followed her back to the bedroom. He paused in the hallway and glanced at his phone when it buzzed with a text alert. He was about to turn it off but froze when he saw the message.

"What is it?" Anna asked, seeing from his expression that something was wrong.

"It's Patrick," Louie mumbled. "He wants to meet."

"I suppose I'm not surprised," Anna said. "He's probably watching the returns on TV. Maybe he wants to give you some advice about running against his old boss."

Louie was staring at the screen, shaking his head. "Patrick told me never to communicate by phone," he mumbled. "Something must be wrong."

"When does he want to meet?"

"First thing in the morning, at our usual place."

Anna felt uneasy, knowing that Patrick was not the type to take unnecessary chances.

"Please be careful," she said, reaching out for Louie's hand.

Her touch broke Louie out of his trance. They stood for a moment without a word, then Louie turned off his phone and followed her back to the bedroom.

CHAPTER SEVEN

Louie hardly slept that night, agonizing over what the day would bring. He awoke early and slipped quietly from the bed, trying not to disturb Anna. He crept to the kitchen and made a cup of tea while checking the news on his phone, searching for updates on the election. In his message queue were dozens of texts from friends and well-wishers congratulating him on his surprise showing in the first round. Louie left them unread, uneasy at the thought of replying. He glanced at his watch and realized he was running late for his meeting with Patrick.

Louie arrived downtown an hour later and found an empty table outside the cafe. He caught the shopkeeper's eye and signaled for their usual order. The man returned a few minutes later, giving Louie a playful wink as he set the drinks down on the table.

"Congratulations, sir," the man said, rocking on his heels and smiling, awaiting Louie's response.

Louie stared back, expressionless. "Oh, that," he mumbled, reaching for his wallet.

The shopkeeper waved away his money. "On the house!"

he insisted. "But you must promise that once you are president, you will always come here for your tea."

Louie smiled awkwardly. He hoped the man was joking but wasn't sure. He was about to explain again that he wasn't a candidate, then realized the futility of that. Instead, Louie put away his wallet and thanked the man for his generosity. Once the shopkeeper disappeared, Louie closed his eyes and sipped his milky tea, grateful for the dose of caffeine.

The street was filled with traffic, and the sidewalks were already bustling with early morning shoppers. Louie hoped to remain invisible amid the frantic activity, but it wasn't long before he began attracting attention. A few of the cafe regulars sitting nearby stared at him, exchanging whispers and nodding toward his table. Meanwhile, inside the shop, the owner was having an animated discussion with another customer, gesturing excitedly in Louie's direction, eager to capitalize on his famous guest.

Louie was horrified by his newfound celebrity. In desperation, he snatched a newspaper from a nearby table and buried his nose behind the pages. However, his attempt at evasion only drew a round of chuckles from the men at the other table. It took a moment before Louie realized that his picture was on the front page that he was using for camouflage. Humiliated, he tossed the paper aside and stared glumly into his tea. He was relieved when he spotted Patrick crossing the street, heading toward the cafe.

"You look as tired as I feel," Patrick said, taking a seat across the table.

"I didn't sleep at all last night."

"Me either. I came straight here from work," Patrick said, sipping gratefully at the coffee waiting for him on the table.

Louie glanced toward the shop, where the owner was now chatting with a different customer but still gesturing excitedly toward their table. "I should warn you that our meeting place is no longer a secret," he said.

"Get used to it," Patrick offered sympathetically. "As of this morning, you're the most famous person in the country."

"Don't be ridiculous," Louie scoffed.

"Have you seen the papers yet?"

"Just one," Louie said, scowling at the copy on the table.

"It's the same with all the others."

Louie sank into his chair, feeling sick to his stomach. "I don't see why it's a big deal. I wasn't even close to Sekibo."

"It doesn't matter. With Francois Akua out of the race, everyone expected Sekibo to win outright in the first round. It may not have been close, but you got enough votes to force it to a second round. You've just become the David to his Goliath."

"Patrick, this is crazy!" Louie blurted out.

As soon as he said the words, he saw that people at the surrounding tables had begun craning their necks, trying to eavesdrop on their conversation.

"This can't be happening," he whispered in frustration. He leaned across the table, closer to Patrick, so no one could hear them. "Do you realize how insane this is? I'm not even a real candidate."

"True," Patrick chuckled. "But you have an excellent campaign manager."

"Who? You mean the CIA?" Louie shot back.

"Whoever," his friend said with a shrug.

"I was surprised to get your text last night," Louie said, eager to change the subject. "Especially after you warned me not to communicate by phone."

"I'm sorry. I didn't have a choice. Given last night's events, I was worried that this might be the last time we could meet face to face. At least until this is all over, you won't be able to go anywhere without attracting attention. We can't risk meeting out in public again."

As he was speaking, two young women stopped in front of them on the sidewalk. They whispered conspiratorially, then one took out her cell phone and snapped a picture of Louie at the table. They continued on their way down the street without a word.

"See what I mean?" Patrick insisted.

Louie tried to pretend it hadn't happened, refusing to look at the women. "We've known each other since grammar school. I don't see what's wrong with two old friends getting together for a drink or a cup of coffee."

"That's not what people will see when they look at us," Patrick argued. "Like it or not, your name is on that ballot, and I still work for DSPO. Emmanuel Sekibo may not run the place anymore, but there are still plenty of people inside the organization who report back to him. We can't take the risk of being seen together anymore. It wouldn't turn out well for either of us."

As he spoke, Patrick turned his head and sneezed. He took some Kleenex out of his pocket and blew his nose, leaving the package on the table.

"Are you sick?" Louie asked.

"I'm fine," he said under his breath. "But there's something I need to give you. When we leave here, be sure to take that Kleenex package with you. There's a thumb drive tucked inside."

"What's on it?"

"Cell phone metadata from yesterday's election."

"I'm sorry," Louie said, confused. "You're speaking a foreign language. I don't have the slightest idea what that means or why you're giving it to me."

Patrick glanced over his shoulder, making sure no one at the nearby tables was listening.

"Before the election, we built geofences around all the polling places. It's a way of monitoring cell phones when they enter a predesignated area. It's similar to how advertisers do location tracking."

"Were you looking for the bomber's cell phone?" Louie guessed.

Patrick nodded. "We thought it might show up on the network if the GLA tried to attack the polling locations, but we never saw it. The bomber's SIM hasn't been active since the attacks against the campaign headquarters."

"Then why are you giving me this?"

"Something else came up in the data. When I was watching the election returns come in, I noticed a discrepancy between the number of people entering the polling stations and the vote counts being reported in the news."

"You've lost me again," Louie said. "Can you explain it in simple terms?"

"Our systems allow us to monitor the movement of individual cell phones across the entire national network,"

Patrick explained, looking pointedly at Louie's phone on the table. "Anytime you have that thing in your pocket, DSPO knows where you are and maybe even what you're doing."

Louie glanced suspiciously at his phone, trying to remember the last time he'd gone anywhere without it. "I still don't see what that has to do with the election."

"We were worried about the GLA attacking election sites, so my team was collecting metadata on every single cell phone that went near a polling station yesterday."

"And?" Louie prompted, still not seeing the point.

"While we were trying to catch the bomber, I think we inadvertently found evidence of massive voter fraud."

Louie's eyes widened with surprise, but he forced himself not to stare at the package of Kleenex. "Can you prove it?"

"Maybe. I didn't have time to go through the entire data set, but at several of the polling places where I did the analysis, I saw major discrepancies."

"What do you mean by discrepancies?"

"A big difference between the reported ballot counts and the number of cell phone signals passing through our geofence. Several locations in particular were reporting far more votes than they should have based on the cell phone metadata."

"But how can you know that for sure?" Louie asked. "Maybe some voters didn't have their cell phones with them."

Patrick waved his hand, dismissing Louie's suggestion. "How often do you leave your house without your phone?" he asked rhetorically. "Plus, we know the average rate of cell phone penetration by neighborhood. Based on the number of ballots cast at a particular location, we can predict within reasonable certainty how many signals should have passed through our geofence. But some of those polling stations were reporting numbers far outside that margin of error."

"There's no way it could just be a coincidence?" Louie asked hopefully.

"Unlikely. If it were, we would have seen the discrepancies randomly distributed across all polling places. But there was a distinct pattern to the irregularities. Can you guess what that might be?" Patrick asked.

"Big margins for Emanuel Sekibo?" Louie sighed, finally seeing the connection.

"Exactly. The discrepancies tended to be in areas where Sekibo wasn't expected to have much support. His cronies must have made up the difference by stuffing the ballot boxes after the polls closed. There's no other reasonable explanation for how Sekibo could have gotten such big numbers at places where we saw very few cell phone signals entering and leaving the polling stations."

"So, what does it all mean?"

"I think it means that you were much closer to beating him than anyone realizes."

"How much closer?"

"I don't know. There's no way of telling for sure. But the metadata clearly shows that something fishy was going on," Patrick said, nodding at the Kleenex.

"What am I supposed to do with that?" Louie asked, glancing at the package.

"For now, it's probably best not to do anything. Our cell phone monitoring program is highly classified. If word got out that DSPO has been tracking every cell phone in the country, it would be an even bigger scandal than the news about Sekibo stuffing ballot boxes."

"Then why are you giving me this?"

"It's too risky to keep on my computer at work. DSPO is filled with Sekibo loyalists. I don't know who else can access my database. I'll feel better knowing that someone else has a copy of the data."

"Patrick, do you see how crazy this is?" Louie pleaded with his friend. "You've just told me that Emanuel Sekibo rigged the election but I can't show anyone the evidence. What's the point?"

"I'm sorry for dumping all of this on you, but I need some time to figure out the next steps. The important thing is that someone besides me has the information." Patrick paused for a moment, then added, as if it were an afterthought, "Just in case something happens."

"What do you mean, in case something happens?" Louie repeated. "I don't like the sound of that."

Patrick shrugged. "Right now, you're the only person I can trust."

"This isn't worth putting yourself in danger," Louie insisted. "This entire election is a sham. I'm a fake candidate running against a real candidate who's stuffing ballot boxes. It just proves that our system is hopelessly corrupt and probably always will be. The only difference between the old regime and what's happening now is that we're calling it something different and pretending that the people get a say in the outcome. We might as well throw away that thumb drive and agree to never speak of it again. In the end, it won't make any difference."

Patrick shook his head. "I'm sorry, Lutalo, but it's too late for that. Hiding from the truth won't protect us. Don't forget, I've worked around these men for a long time. Trust me, Sekibo won't stop at stuffing ballot boxes. The fact that his plan didn't work will only make him more determined the next time."

"No. I'm done with this!" Louie blurted out, again attracting the attention of nearby tables. "This country is hopeless. But it's taken me too long to realize that. I should have done like my brothers and sister did and left a long time ago."

"I don't believe you," Patrick said flatly, crossing his arms.

"What do you mean, you don't believe me?" Louie shot back, aware that everyone in the cafe was watching them. "I told you, I'm leaving as soon as the election is over. I've got an interview with my brother's bank in New Jersey. Anna's applying for teaching jobs. I'm not kidding. We've had it. We're getting out of here as soon as we can."

"I wish you'd reconsider," Patrick sighed. "Now is when we need people like you."

"How can you say that?" Louie argued. "It's impossible to win here if you play by the rules. The only way to survive is to become like them. You should know that better than anyone. You've seen it all from the inside. First, it was Operation Brushfire and the lies about killing Odoki, then President Namono's backroom deals with the Chinese and my uncle plotting to take over Green House. It's just one thing after another. It never ends."

"Running away won't fix it," Patrick countered.

"Staying won't either. Don't tell me that you haven't thought about leaving too. This isn't a game anymore. I'm not going to endanger Anna's life just to prove a point. If Sekibo wants Green House so much, he can have it. The place will be a curse on whoever takes it."

Patrick knew there was no use trying to change Louie's mind. They stared into their drinks, saying nothing, until the silence was interrupted by the sound of Louie's cell phone buzzing with an incoming text.

"For god's sake," Louie said, grabbing the phone in frustration. "It's been going nonstop since last night." He was about to stuff the phone in his pocket when he glanced at the screen and paused.

Patrick could tell that something was wrong from the expression on his face. "What is it?"

"It's from Emanuel Sekibo. He wants to meet me later today."

"What?" Patrick gasped. "Are you going to go?"

"I don't know. What do you think? Should I?"

"Sekibo is not the kind of man you can ignore. At least, not if you want to keep your family safe," Patrick warned.

"Are you serious?"

Patrick nodded but didn't elaborate. Louie slipped the phone into his pocket and got up from the table. "I need to get to work," he announced.

"You didn't answer my question. Are you going to meet him?"

"Do I have a choice?"

Louie turned to leave, but before he could step away, Patrick clicked his tongue to get Louie's attention.

"Don't forget your Kleenex," Patrick reminded him. Louie glanced around to see if anyone was watching, then grabbed the package of tissue and slipped it into his pocket.

"Be careful," Patrick called out as Louie stepped into the street.

"You too," Louie said over his shoulder, heading for his car.

+++

An hour later, Louie was at his desk when a second text arrived from Emanuel Sekibo's office. The message said that a car would pick him up outside the front gate before lunch. Louie was waiting there at the appointed time. Less than a minute had passed when a black Mercedes sedan with tinted windows rolled to a stop in front of him. A burly bodyguard exited the passenger seat, looking as if he had just walked out of central casting. He wore a form-fitting business suit and dark sunglasses. The wire of a radio earpiece snaked above his collar and into his ear.

The man opened the back door of the sedan and gestured for Louie to get inside. Neither the driver nor the bodyguard spoke a word during the short drive to Emanuel Sekibo's campaign headquarters. As they approached the building, Louie noticed some lingering evidence of the recent bombing, but the broken windows had been replaced, and a coat of fresh paint covered the spots where fire had charred the walls. A well-armed security detail was posted behind a line of concrete blast barriers that circled the block.

The bodyguard instructed the driver to go around the building to avoid the gaggle of reporters mingling at the main entrance. The sedan rolled to stop at the service entrance in the back alleyway. The bodyguard got out and did a quick check of the area, ensuring everything was clear. Louie saw him speaking into a microphone hidden in the sleeve of his jacket; then he opened the rear door and motioned for Louie to get out.

Another guard was waiting outside the service entrance leading into the back of the building. He held open a heavy metal door and waved for Louie to follow him inside. They walked at a brisk pace through a maze of hallways, then into a large professional kitchen. The man stopped Louie at an unmarked door near the far end of the room and gestured at him to raise his hands for a body search.

"Seriously?" Louie said, staring him down and refusing to play along.

The guard glared back in what felt like a standoff, but to Louie's surprise, he relented and opened the door. Louie stepped into an ornate private dining room. At the far end of the room was a table with two place settings. One chair was empty. Emanuel Sekibo occupied the other.

The guard closed the door behind him, leaving Louie standing alone. Having no idea what was supposed to happen, he crossed the room to where Sekibo was sitting. The man rose from his seat and smiled as Louie approached the table.

"Colonel Bigombe, thank you for accepting my invitation," he said, reaching out for Louie's hand. "I apologize for the unusual reception. However, given last night's events, I thought it would be preferable for us to meet privately, without the media's attention. I hope this is acceptable?"

"As you wish," Louie said, shaking the man's hand without enthusiasm.

It was the first time they had met face to face. Sekibo was smaller than Louie had imagined from years of seeing him on TV. His hands were soft and his voice disarmingly genteel. It was a jarring contrast with the rumors about his persona in the interrogation room during his years at Police Intelligence.

"Please, sit," Sekibo offered, motioning to the table.

A waiter dressed in formal attire appeared beside the table. He uncorked a bottle of white wine and poured a sip for the host. Sekibo made a show of tasting it and nodding his approval, but before the waiter could fill Louie's glass, Louie waved him away.

"It's quite good," Sekibo encouraged, seeming disappointed by Louie's refusal.

"Water is fine, thank you," Louie said firmly.

The waiter nervously removed the wine glass from Louie's setting and disappeared into the kitchen.

"I should begin by congratulating you on your showing last night," Sekibo said. "I think everyone was surprised by the results."

"It was a surprise to me as well. I wasn't following the race very closely," Louie explained without elaboration.

Sekibo smiled and nodded, concealing any skepticism at Louie's assertion. "But of course, I shouldn't be surprised by anything you've achieved," he continued.

"Why is that?"

"Because I know where your talent comes from," Sekibo hinted, smiling as he sipped his wine. "Did you know that I was close to your father when we were young men?"

Louie felt a flash of cold sweat under his uniform. He

swallowed hard to calm his nerves, determined not to give Sekibo the satisfaction of drawing a reaction from him.

"I don't recall my father ever mentioning your name."

"I'm not surprised. You would have been very young at the time. We met as junior officers, back at the beginning of the border wars."

The waiter reappeared at the table with two salads and a basket of warm bread. Sekibo picked up his utensils and, with a gesture, urged Louie to eat.

"You remind me of your father," he continued. "That's why I should have known better than to underestimate your ambition."

"No one who knew my father ever described him as ambitious," Louie challenged.

"You're right!" Sekibo exclaimed, chuckling and shaking his head. "That was a poor choice of words. Indeed, your father was big enough to leave such things to lesser men. Even when we were young officers, it was obvious to everyone that he was destined for great things. Those who knew him always said that someday he would be president. So I suppose it's only natural that his son would desire to fulfill that unrealized promise. If your father was alive, I know he would be very proud of you."

Louie took a bite of the salad and put down his fork, having lost his appetite. "Is that why you called me here?" he asked, staring across the table. "To talk about my father?"

The smile faded from Sekibo's face as he saw that Louie would not be won over by shallow flattery and small talk.

"No," he said firmly. "I asked you here as a sign of respect. And to discuss your future."

"I have no future here."

Sekibo appeared perplexed by Louie's answer. "Because I knew your father, I know that can't be true. He loved this country and gave everything for it."

"Why do you care about my intentions? You were far ahead in yesterday's polling. Certainly, the second round will only be a formality."

"Believe it or not, the election is not my immediate concern," Sekibo insisted. "I'm confident that we'll do fine in the polls. However, I invited you here to discuss other opportunities." He paused, waiting for Louie's response, but received none. "People speak highly of your talents," he continued. "I was hoping that you might accept a position in my administration. We are beginning to develop a shortlist of candidates for the top jobs."

"I appreciate your consideration; however, I already have a job," Louie said, motioning at his uniform.

"Of course. You are a professional soldier, just like your father. That is why I want to offer you a position well suited to your talents. I want you to be my minister of defense," Sekibo revealed. "You will sit at your uncle's old desk."

Louie remained expressionless, trying to hide his surprise. Under the table, his fingers brushed against the pocket where he had stuffed the Kleenex packet from Patrick. Louie imagined how differently the conversation might proceed if Sekibo knew what was on the thumb drive inside that Kleenex packet.

"I'm certain there are many men in your organization who are highly qualified to take that job," he answered in a calm voice.

"Perhaps a few. However, most of them only want it for the sake of the title. And, of course, the fringe benefits that go along with it," Sekibo conceded. "But I'm afraid they have less interest in doing the hard work that will be required. I'm sure you're aware that my first order of business will be to destroy the GLA once and for all. To accomplish that, I need a strong leader as my minister of defense. Someone who understands how to manage and use the army."

"Why would you trust me with this task?"

"You worked closely with your uncle when he was the minister. You understand the army, and you know about fighting the GLA. You killed Daniel Odoki, after all," Sekibo said, a hint of cynicism in his voice.

Louie ignored the mention of Odoki's name, assuming that Sekibo must also have known the truth behind Operation Brushfire. If there was such a thing as the truth.

"My uncle fled this country as a traitor after the fall of Green House," he said. "I can't imagine that anyone would accept me sitting at his old desk."

"Nonsense," Sekibo said, dismissing Louie's concern with a wave of his hand. "When people look at you, they don't see your uncle's nephew. They see your father's son. In any case, you should view this opportunity as preparation for greater things. The experience will serve you well when your time comes."

"When my time comes?" Louie repeated. "You make it sound as if your journey to Green House is preordained."

Sekibo just smiled.

"I'm assuming that your offer comes with preconditions," Louie continued.

"I'm building my staff now. The GLA will not give us the luxury of a honeymoon. I intend to commence a major military offensive immediately after the inauguration. That's why I need a commitment from you now. Otherwise, I'll have to consider other candidates."

Louie took a sip of water, waiting to see if he had more to say.

"If I may give you a bit of advice," Sekibo continued. "Your father was killed before he realized his potential. He was a great man—the best of our generation. I considered him a friend, and it was a terrible loss when he was killed. I hope you see my offer as helping you to fulfill his promise. Perhaps someday, you will achieve what he was denied. Please, do not turn away from this chance."

"Should I assume that by accepting, you expect me to withdraw my name from the ballot?"

Sekibo gave the slightest nod, confirming Louie's suspicion without saying the words aloud.

"As much as I would like to withdraw from this election, I'm afraid that I am unable to do so," Louie said.

Sekibo put down his utensils and leaned forward in his seat, frustrated that the conversation was not going as expected.

"You're a fool to pass up my offer," he hissed across the table. "If you insist on staying in the race, you'll lose the election and walk away with nothing. I am offering you an opportunity of a lifetime."

"I don't doubt the value of your offer. I know that my uncle made the most of his time in the ministry," Louie said, hinting at the secrets they both knew.

"Then why do you not accept?" Sekibo pressed.

"I can't withdraw from an election that I never entered. I've told everyone who will listen that I'm not a candidate. I will say it one more time for your benefit. I'm not interested in Green House. It was never my intention to have my name on the ballot."

"Do you take me for a fool?" Sekibo exploded, slamming his fists on the table, spilling his wine.

"No, sir, I do not," Louie said, unruffled. "I understand why you may find my excuse improbable. I wouldn't believe either, was I not caught in the middle of it."

"I'm done playing games," Sekibo said impatiently. "This charade has gone on long enough. Even if what you say is true, that's no longer relevant. You've succeeded in forcing this election to a second round, but surely you realize that you have no chance of winning. If you insist on seeing this through to the end, you'll walk away with nothing."

Louie was unmoved. "With all due respect, there is nothing you can offer me that I want. Including my uncle's old job."

Sekibo tossed his napkin into his half-finished salad. "You're more like your father than I would have guessed," he spat.

"How's that?"

"He was a man of principle as well. And in the end, he paid a terrible price for something of so little value. I only hoped that you would not be so foolish as to follow in his footsteps."

The waiter appeared beside the table, delivering the main course. He hesitated when he saw the unfinished salads, trying to decide whether to leave the food or retreat quietly back into the kitchen. Louie spared him the dilemma by getting up from his seat.

"Mr. Sekibo, I appreciate the invitation to lunch and the offer of the job. However, I must get back to work," Louie said, dropping his napkin onto the table. "Please accept my congratulations on your showing last night."

Sekibo glared across the table. "The driver will take you back," he snarled.

Louie turned and headed for the door, leaving Sekibo alone at the table. By the time he got outside and into the alleyway, the sedan was waiting with the engine running. The bodyguard stood next to the open door, expressionless behind his sunglasses and seeming unsurprised by the abrupt end of lunch. Louie got into the car, and the guard closed the door behind him.

The sedan pulled out of the alleyway, and within minutes, they were mired in midday traffic. Louie tried making small talk with the driver but received only monosyllabic grunts in reply. As they crawled through the city, Louie contemplated getting out and walking back to camp, but they were still miles away. Instead, he read the news on his phone, trying to avoid any stories having to do with the election.

Louie was checking the scores of the latest soccer matches when he felt the car shudder. The driver slammed on the brakes while the bodyguard instinctively slipped a hand into his suit jacket, reaching for the weapon in his shoulder holster.

"What was that?" Louie blurted out.

"Stay here!" the bodyguard ordered.

The man bolted from the car with his weapon drawn, locking the doors behind him. Louie watched through the tinted glass as he cleared the area around the sedan, searching for threats. People were stopped on the sidewalk, pointing at a cloud of smoke rising on the horizon. From inside the car, Louie couldn't judge the distance, but it appeared to be coming from somewhere near the city center.

The bodyguard spoke to an unseen interlocutor through the microphone hidden up his sleeve, then got back inside the car.

"What's going on?" Louie asked as the bodyguard locked the doors behind him.

The man stared straight ahead, ignoring Louie's question. "We're making a detour," the guard told the driver. "Take the route away from the university."

"Why?" Louie stammered, alarmed. "What happened at the university?"

"There was a bombing. The roads around the campus are closed except for emergency vehicles," the guard revealed.

Louie checked his watch, trying to remember Anna's teaching schedule. One of her classes had just ended. Louie guessed she would have been walking back from the lecture hall to her office when the bomb went off. He dialed her cell number, his heart racing as he waited for her to answer. When the call went to voicemail, Louie felt like someone had kicked him in the stomach. He hung up and tried again with the same result.

"I need to get to the university *now*!" he yelled from the back seat.

The driver glanced nervously at the bodyguard, looking for guidance. The man kept his eyes focused through the windshield, shaking his head a single time as his answer.

"My wife works at the university," Louie pleaded, seeing that the driver wasn't changing course. "She's not answering her cell phone. I need to find her. Either you take me to the university, or I'm getting out and walking."

"Mr. Sekibo instructed us to take you directly back to your camp," the bodyguard said without looking back. "We're not authorized to deviate from those instructions."

They were stuck in heavy traffic again, and Louie realized that he had no choice. He reached slowly for the door handle, trying to conceal his intentions. Before the bodyguard could react, Louie had the door open and was out on the street, jogging in the direction of National University.

He arrived at the campus gate twenty-five minutes later and found a scene of complete chaos. Ambulances and fire trucks lined the street. Medics were conducting triage and treating stragglers wandering off of the campus. Louie spotted smoke billowing from the windows of a building that must have been the target.

The police had established a security perimeter around the scene, keeping bystanders away. Louie was still in uniform, and no one stopped him as he walked purposefully through the cordon. Once inside the campus, he tried again to call Anna, but with the same result. He headed for the building that housed her office.

When he arrived there, he found the building empty. He went straight to Anna's office and found that the door was wide open. Louie breathed a sigh of relief when he spotted her handbag on the desk, knowing that she always carried it with her to class. His head began spinning through possible scenarios. He imagined that she could have been walking back from class when the explosion happened. Perhaps she had dropped the bag on the desk and forgotten it in the excitement. Louie did a quick search through her purse and found everything except for her cell phone.

The discovery left him baffled about why she wouldn't be answering her phone. Having no idea what else to do, Louie remembered the triage station near the front gate. He grabbed Anna's bag and sprinted from her office, arriving breathless at the medic station. By then, the worst casualties had been evacuated to local hospitals. Some of the medics were still treating minor injuries and cleaning up the scene. Louie approached a man in uniform who was holding a clipboard and appeared to be in charge.

"My name is Colonel Bigombe of the Gisawian army," Louie said. "The Ministry of Defense sent me here to check on the status of any foreigners injured during the incident. Do you have the names of everyone that came through the triage station?"

"Not everyone, sir," the man said, too harried to question why Louie would need such information. "The first ambulances left before we identified all the victims."

Louie pulled Anna's passport from her purse and showed it to the man. "What about this woman? She's an American and works at the university. Do you have her name on your list?"

The man glanced at Anna's passport, then his clipboard. After going through two pages of names, he looked up and shook his head. "I'm sorry, sir. I don't see that name on the list. But if she was badly injured, she's probably already at the hospital. You would need to check with the emergency department to be sure."

Louie thanked him and hurried off, worried that his unusual line of questioning might attract suspicion. He spotted two plainclothes policemen interviewing witnesses on the street. He considered asking them about Anna and then realized that his bluff about being sent from the Defense Ministry wouldn't fool an undercover officer from DSPO.

He was just about to leave for the hospital when he spotted Janet Russell standing outside the main gate. She was talking to some witnesses while her photographer snapped pictures of the smoldering debris. Louie walked over and waited while Janet finished her interview.

"Are you here as a soldier or a presidential candidate?" she asked him when she was done.

"Neither!" Louie snapped, annoyed at her presumption. "My wife works at the university. I came as soon as I heard about the bombing."

Janet grimaced, regretting her flippancy. "I'm sorry. I should have remembered. Is she all right?"

"I don't know. I can't find her. I think she was teaching a class when the bomb went off, then went back to her office, but she's not answering her phone."

"I got here a few minutes after it happened," Janet said. "I haven't heard about any foreigners being among the casualties. Maybe she lost her cell phone when they were evacuating the campus. Or the battery went dead."

Louie was relieved to hear someone offer a perfectly

reasonable explanation. "You're probably right," he agreed, trying to convince himself. "But I'm going to check with the emergency room, just in case."

"I wouldn't recommend going right now. It's complete chaos over there," Janet warned. "One of my stringers is at the main hospital. He said it's filled with families looking for information. But they're not releasing any names until they've accounted for all the injured."

"I'm not doing any good standing around here," Louie sighed.

"I'm certain she's all right," Janet reassured him. "But if you want, I'll call my stringer and have him ask around the hospital. If she's there, he'll be able to find out. In the meantime, you can go home and wait for her there. I'll call you right away if I hear anything."

Her confidence felt reassuring, convincing Louie that there must be a good reason for Anna not answering his calls.

"All right," he agreed. "Please call if you hear anything."

Janet nodded, then hesitated, considering her words before speaking. "I suppose this is an odd time to offer congratulations," she said.

Louie stared at her with a blank look on his face.

"The election," she reminded him.

"Right. Sorry. It's been a long day," Louie muttered.

"I realize it's probably not your first priority right now, but it was still quite an achievement. I don't think many people expected it to go to a second round."

"Including Emanuel Sekibo," Louie said.

"Why do you think that?"

"We had lunch today," Louie revealed.

Janet's eyes widened, and she waited for him to continue.

"He offered me a job if I dropped out of the race."

Out of instinct, Janet reached for her notebook and pen, but Louie shook his head. "That's off the record."

"Don't do this to me," she begged. "That's the biggest news of the day."

"Bigger than the GLA bombing a university?"

"There haven't been any claims of responsibility," Janet said. "Why are you sure it's the GLA?"

"Who else would it be?"

Janet shrugged skeptically. "In my line of work, I try to avoid jumping to conclusions, especially when they don't pass the commonsense test. I can't think of a single reason the GLA would bomb the university. Can you?"

Louie thought for a moment, then shook his head. "No, you're right. It doesn't make any sense."

"Out of curiosity, what job did Sekibo offer you?" Janet asked, unwilling to let him change the topic.

"Off the record, right? If I see this in the papers tomorrow, I'm never speaking to you again."

"If I confirm it from another source, then it's mine. Otherwise, you have my word. I'll keep quiet."

"He offered me the Ministry of Defense."

"Your uncle's old job!" Janet gasped. "Did he say why?"

"He told me that he wanted someone strong in the job. To help him run the offensive against the GLA."

"That's not why he asked you," Janet argued. "There are dozens of his cronies he could put in that position. He's doing it because he's scared of you. You know the old saying: Keep your friends close and your enemies closer. That's the real reason he offered you the job. He's trying to neutralize you."

"It doesn't matter," Louie said. "I told him I wasn't interested."

"And he accepted your answer?"

"I'm not in a position to deliver my end of the deal," Louie reminded her. "How can I pull out of a race I never entered?"

Janet smiled at the absurdity of it all. "You're lucky you got out of there alive after saying that to his face. I don't think Emanuel Sekibo hears the word 'no' very often."

"I don't plan on being around here long enough to see him again."

"I'm not sure I believe that. More importantly, I'm certain that Sekibo doesn't believe it."

Louie turned, distracted by the sound of an approaching siren. The medics were helping a few last casualties into ambulances.

"Why don't you go home and wait for Anna there?" Janet suggested. "If my guy at the hospital hears anything, I'll call right away."

Louie hesitated, then nodded. "Thanks. I appreciate it."

"I'm sure she's fine," Janet added.

Louie stepped into the street, searching for a taxi to take him back to the camp so he could retrieve his car.

+++

Back at home that evening, Louie had fallen asleep on the couch after waiting all evening for Anna to call or walk through the door. Sometime after midnight, his buzzing phone woke him. His heart was racing as he grabbed it, but the screen showed an unknown number that wasn't on his contact list. Louie hesitated, fearing bad news, but realized that he had no choice but to answer it.

"Hello?"

"Lutalo. It's Patrick. I saw that you tried to call my cell phone earlier."

Louie was relieved to hear his friend's voice. "I didn't recognize the number. Are you calling from work?"

"No. A restaurant. I didn't want to take a chance of calling you from my cell phone."

"I'm sorry, Patrick. I know you said never to call, but it's an emergency. I didn't know what else to do."

"What happened? Is this about your meeting with Sekibo?"

"No. It's Anna. I think she's missing," Louie said, shuddering to hear himself say the words aloud.

"Missing? What do you mean?" Patrick asked sharply. "Was she at the university during the bombing?"

"I don't know, but I assume so. I was on my way back to work after lunch with Sekibo when I heard the bombing. I went straight to the university to see if she was all right. But when I got there, I couldn't find her. The police had already evacuated the campus, and she wasn't in her office."

"You checked the hospitals?"

"Yes. She wasn't at any of them. I also called the American embassy. They didn't have any reports of US citizens injured in the attack."

"Could she have gone to the hospital with someone else who was injured? Maybe a student or one of her colleagues?"

"I thought about that too, but it doesn't make sense that she wouldn't call and tell me that she was all right," Louie said. "The bombing was over ten hours ago. She would have called by now. When I went to her office, the door was open, and her purse was sitting on the desk. Everything was there except for her cell phone. It doesn't make any sense."

"You've been trying to call her?"

"Yes. But all my calls go straight to voicemail."

Patrick was quiet on the other end of the line, thinking through a list of possible scenarios. "Have you guys been cool lately?" he asked reluctantly after a time.

"What do you mean?"

"I mean, have you had any big arguments or anything? I'm sorry for asking this, but could there be a reason Anna might decide to leave without telling you?"

"No!" Louie said emphatically. "I mean, things have been a little tense with the election nonsense. But since we decided to go back to the States, things have been good."

Patrick took a deep breath. "Louie, if that's the case, then I think we need to consider the possibility that she was kidnapped."

"*What?* Wh- why?" Louie stammered. "She's a college professor! There's no reason anyone would kidnap her. We don't have enough money to make it worth the risk."

"I doubt this is about money," Patrick speculated. "I know you didn't ask for this, but like it or not, you've been attracting a lot of attention lately. Your name is in the news, and everyone knows your face. Whatever happened today, I'm guessing it's more about you than her."

Louie felt sick to his stomach when he considered the possibility that he bore some responsibility for Anna's disappearance. "Should I call the embassy again?"

"It couldn't hurt," Patrick said. "But they won't do anything yet. Anna's only been gone for ten hours. I'm guessing that they'll wait for at least a day or two before taking any action."

"I can't just sit here doing nothing. Can you help me?"

Patrick thought for a moment. "I can't make this an official investigation. It would attract too much attention."

"But you work for Police Intelligence. Why wouldn't you make it official?" Louie argued, not understanding Patrick's caution. "Isn't that standard procedure for a missing person?"

"If this is a kidnapping, then we're better off keeping it out of official channels," Patrick recommended. At least for now. I don't know who I would trust with something like this."

"Then what else can we do?"

"I have a few ideas. I can't promise you that it will lead to anything, but it's worth a try."

"I appreciate anything you can do," Louie said.

"I'll contact you if I find anything out. But just to be safe, don't call me directly. There are too many eyes and ears. From now on, nothing you do will be private. You need to remember that," Patrick warned.

"I'll try to be careful," Louie promised.

"By the way, how was lunch?"

"Interesting."

"That's all you're going to say?" Patrick asked incredulously. "Something must have happened."

"I don't think it's something we should be discussing on the phone," Louie said.

"Good point. Save it for next time."

"Right," Louie agreed.

"I'll be in touch if I get anything," Patrick said before hanging up.

CHAPTER EIGHT

When his alarm went off, Louie slapped the snooze button and stared at the ceiling. His mind was foggy from lack of sleep. For a brief instant, he entertained the possibility that yesterday's events had been nothing but a bad dream. That hope evaporated when he slid his hand over to Anna's side of the bed and found it empty. His heart sank, and he reached for his phone, hoping to find a message. But there was nothing new since he'd checked an hour earlier.

Louie lay there considering his strategy for the day. Before going to bed, he had spoken with a consular officer at the American embassy and explained the situation as best he could. The man had been sympathetic but lacked a sense of urgency. He promised to open a file and contact the Gisawian police in the morning but couldn't offer much else. He asked Louie to call back if Anna was still missing after forty-eight hours.

Louie couldn't stand the thought of sitting around the house, waiting for a phone call. It would only make the uncertainty more unbearable. Instead, he got out of bed and dressed for work. An hour later, he was sitting in his office, going through his inbox and trying to think about something other than Anna. His attempt at self-distraction was interrupted by a knock on the door and Owen poking his head inside the office.

"Are you busy?"

Louie reflexively picked up a sheet of paper. "Actually, yes," he said, waving it in the air, hoping to discourage him.

"I only need a minute," Owen insisted, making it clear that he was coming in regardless. He closed the door behind himself and claimed one of the chairs in front of Louie's desk.

"How can I help you?" Louie said impatiently, preempting small talk.

"I wanted to say congratulations on your showing the other day," Owen said, casually. "That's quite an accomplishment. I don't think anyone would have predicted it."

"Really?" Louie snapped, making it clear that he didn't share Owen's enthusiasm.

"What I mean is that Sekibo was heavily favored. Most everyone expected him to take the first round. Especially after Francois Akua dropped out of the race."

"Francois didn't exactly 'drop out' of the race," Louie said, making air quotes with his fingers. "He was killed by a bomb. Remember?"

"Of course, that's what I meant," Owen backpedaled. "I didn't want to dwell on the negatives. In any case, you've turned this thing into a real race, coming out of nowhere and challenging Sekibo like that."

"Do you expect me to be grateful? You and I both know that this entire thing is a farce. I never asked for any of this."

Owen sighed, appearing genuinely disappointed by Louie's reaction. "I wish you would stop staying that. You're just as much a candidate as anyone else in the race. Why can't you just accept the fact that a lot of people support you? That's not a farce. Those were real people who went to the polls and put a checkmark next to your name."

"You're acting like you've done us some great favor, but all you've done is poison the process!" Louie said, pointing accusingly at Owen. "Those people who voted waited a lifetime for that opportunity, and you've turned it into a charade."

"No one ever said democracy was a perfect system," Owen argued. "In the end, the important thing is that it produces better outcomes. People want a change. A lot of them seem to think that you're the one who can deliver it."

"I'm not doing it."

"You're not doing what?"

"Whatever it is you're trying to get me to do," Louie said, crossing his arms defiantly over this chest.

Owen shook his head. "Louie, I think you're confused about what's going on here. I'm not trying to get you to do anything. That's not what this is about. I told you the first day we met that my job here is to help things go right. And give a little nudge in the right direction when necessary."

"You mean by rigging the election?"

"Those are strong words," Owen cautioned.

"Then how would you describe it?"

"Counterbalancing. Making sure there's a level playing field."

"You're full of shit." Louie didn't bother trying to hide his disgust.

"Please, listen to me. I don't think you appreciate the potential danger of Emanuel Sekibo running this country."

"That's not for me to decide. The people have a choice. If that's what they want, then we'll all have to live with it. That's how the system is supposed to work. Isn't it?"

"Of course, in theory, you're right," Owen conceded. "But we're less than two weeks from the second round. I think we're all better off accepting things as they are and trying to move forward. We're not going to get anywhere if we spend all our time arguing about how we got here."

"My answer hasn't changed."

"Were you paying attention to what happened yesterday?"

"You mean the bombing at the university? Yes, I'm well aware," Louie said, his voice dripping with sarcasm.

"But did you hear what Sekibo's campaign said after the attack?" Owen pressed. "He promised a new offensive against the GLA on his first day in office."

"That isn't any different than what he's said before. Besides, isn't that what your third force is already doing out there?" Louie said.

"I've told you before, I don't know anything about a third force. Your reporter friend has an overly active imagination."

"I think she has good instincts," Louie said. "And I certainly trust her more than I do you."

Owen sniffed indignantly and looked away, ready to change the topic. "By the way, how was your lunch meeting yesterday?" he asked casually.

"I have no idea what you're talking about," Louie replied, struggling to keep a straight face to hide his surprise.

"There's no need to pretend it didn't happen," Owen said. "Rumors travel quickly in this town. I'm assuming he offered you something in return for pulling out of the race?"

"If you already know what happened, why bother asking?"

"Well, I don't know *everything*," Owen said. "Such as how you responded to his offer."

"I told him I couldn't accept it."

Owen nodded, appearing relieved at the answer. "Out of curiosity, what did he offer?"

"The Ministry of Defense. My uncle's old job."

Owen chuckled. "I've got to give the guy credit for sheer audacity. Not only would he get rid of you as a rival, but he'd also be able to pin the blame on you for anything that goes wrong with the offensive. I can't believe he thought you'd accept the offer."

"He seemed put out when I declined."

"No doubt. I think it's safe to say that you won't be getting another lunch invitation from Sekibo anytime soon."

"That's the least of my worries right now," Louie hinted.

Owen waited for him to continue.

"Something happened after I left the lunch. I'm hesitant to tell you, but I think I need help."

"That's what I'm here for," Owen reassured him.

Louie rolled his eyes but left the comment alone. "Yesterday, after the bombing at the university, Anna disappeared."

"Your wife?"

Louie nodded. "She was teaching a class when the attack happened. I went straight to the university to see if she was all right. When I got there, I found her handbag on her desk and her cell phone missing. She never came home last night and hasn't answered her phone since yesterday morning."

"Who else knows about this?"

"I called the embassy and filed a report. Other than that, just an old friend of mine who works at Police Intelligence. Sorry, I mean DSPO," Louie corrected himself.

Owen raised an eyebrow. "Are you sure it was a good idea to tell this person? DSPO is filled with Sekibo's cronies."

"My friend isn't one of them. He's probably the only person I can trust."

Owen rubbed his chin. "It's good that you told me," he said. "I know we got off to a rocky start. But please believe me when I tell you that I'm on your side. I may have some contacts who can help locate Anna."

"I would appreciate it."

"I hate to ask this," Owen said. "But are you sure that this wasn't about something else? I mean, you guys aren't having any problems or anything?"

"You're the second person to ask me that."

Owen shrugged and waited.

"No. It's not her style," Louie clarified.

"Sorry. I just needed to rule that out. Let me make a few calls and get some people on it. I'm assuming that the embassy will have already checked with the local hospitals and the police, so I won't bother covering that ground again." Owen paused. "You know, this won't stay a secret for long. Once word gets out, it could have some impact on the election."

"I don't give a damn about the election," Louie said. "I just want Anna back safely."

Owen nodded and got up from the chair.

"I'll do my best," he said, heading for the door.

+++

Louie was getting ready to leave the office for the evening when his phone buzzed with a text message. He grabbed the phone, hoping it might be Anna, but it was an unlisted number. The text contained five words: *gas station near airport roundabout.* Louie guessed that the cryptic message could only have come from Patrick. He was one of the few people who knew the route of Louie's commute home and that it took him past that gas station.

He quickly packed up his things and headed for the door. Fifteen minutes later, Louie pulled into the gas station. He didn't see any sign of Patrick, so he decided to fill his tank. After getting gas, Louie paid the attendant and parked around the back of the station. He sat there pretending to be involved in a phone conversation while keeping an eye out for Patrick.

Eventually, Louie grew tired of the ruse and went to use the bathroom. He got the key from the station attendant and was just about to unlock the door when he heard a whistle coming from a nearby grove of trees. Louie walked toward the sound, crossing a dusty field littered with old car parts and trash. When he neared the grove, Patrick stepped out from behind a tree and waved.

"You picked a scenic spot," Louie joked.

"I needed to see you right away, but I didn't want to risk going to your house."

"Probably a good idea. I'm starting to share your paranoia," Louie admitted. "I had an interesting meeting this morning with Owen Smith."

"The CIA guy pretending to be an election advisor?"

Louie nodded. "He knew about my lunch meeting with Sekibo."

"I'm telling you, people are watching your every move," Patrick warned. "You can't afford to make mistakes. What did this Owen guy want?"

"I'm not exactly sure. I bet he was worried that I would cut some deal with Sekibo. The Americans think he'll start a war if he gets into Green House."

"They're probably right. But there's something else going on," Patrick said. "This morning, I was going back through all the telephone metadata from the bombing, and I found something interesting."

"You mean from the SIM card that triggered the bombs?"

Patrick nodded. "I ran a check of all the other calls on the network around the same time and place."

"And?"

"There was different SIM card that received a call at the same time and location, just before the bombings. It was a similar pattern each time. The second number would receive a short incoming call. Then, about a minute later, the other SIM card would show up on the network and make the call to detonate the explosive. Then both of the SIMs would disappear from the network. Neither number became active again until right before the next attack."

"What about yesterday's bombing at the university?" Louie asked.

"The same pattern."

Louie took a moment to think through the scenario. "So, you're saying that the bomber always carries two phones, one to receive instructions and the other to set off the explosive?"

Patrick nodded. "There's no other explanation for the correlation of time and place. The calls always happen in the same sequence, using the same SIM cards."

"This is big," Louie said, glancing over his shoulder at the gas station.

"I haven't told you the important part," Patrick said.

The hair stood up on Louie's neck, and he leaned forward, eager to hear the rest.

"I was able to run a trace on the number sending instructions to the bomber," Patrick said. "Each of the calls came from the same landline."

"You know who was making those calls?" Louie blurted out.

"No," Patrick said, shaking his head. "But I know where the calls came from. It was a phone line registered to somewhere inside the DSPO headquarters building."

Louie felt himself go weak in the knees as he pondered the implications of Patrick's revelation. "You mean that someone inside DSPO headquarters has been giving instructions to the bomber?"

"I can't say that for sure since I don't have voice intercepts. But I can tell you without a doubt that someone inside my building has been calling a cell phone number co-located with the bomber just before each attack. There's no way that's a coincidence."

"Can you pinpoint where the calls are coming from inside the building?"

"Not precisely," Patrick said. "For the landline number, I had to map all the individual lines coming from the main trunk into the building. But I was able to trace it back to a group of offices on the top floor."

"Could you get inside to see whose desk the phone was on?"

"No. It's inside a limited access area. I'm not authorized to enter that section of the building."

"How is that possible?" Louie asked. "You have one of the highest security clearances in DSPO. How many offices can't you get into?"

"Just one," Patrick said. "The GLA fusion cell's."

"So you think that someone inside the fusion cell has been ordering the bombings, even though the GLA claimed them?" Louie asked, needing to say it out loud to make sense of it all.

Patrick looked grim. "I can't prove that, but it's the only explanation I can think of."

Louie struggled to untangle the web of contradictions, finding it difficult to make sense of what he was hearing. "Does anyone else know about this?"

"Only you. I can't risk telling anyone at work. This is too close to the top. The GLA fusion cell reports directly to the director of DSPO."

"What are you going to do?"

Patrick shrugged. "I guess I'll try to figure out who has been making those calls."

"Then what?"

Patrick was quiet, considering the question. "I don't know," he finally confessed.

"Can I do anything to help?"

"Take this," Patrick said, handing Louie a small notebook. "These are my notes on everything I've found so far. Keep it somewhere safe."

Louie nodded and stuffed it in his pocket. "Anything else?"

"Just watch your back. Someone is trying very hard to keep this a secret, and they've already shown how far they're willing to go."

"Do you think there's a connection to what's happened to Anna?" Louie asked, uncertain if he wanted to hear the answer.

Patrick took a deep breath. "I think it's possible," he confirmed. "I ran a trace on Anna's cell phone number. It was active on the network all day yesterday. Even when she wasn't answering your calls."

"Was it somewhere at the university?"

"No. It was moving all day. I was able to follow the signal as it switched between cell phone towers. I tracked it moving along the main road going out of town toward Kiskow."

Louie tried to understand what Patrick was telling him. "You're…you're saying that she's in Kiskow?"

"I don't know that. But that's where her cell phone signal was coming from last night. Then it started moving again early this morning."

"Where?"

"Toward the border. The last ping on the network was from a cell tower located near the border. That was late this morning. After that, nothing else."

"What does that mean?" Louie asked, feeling sick to his stomach.

"There's no way to know for sure. Her cell phone battery could have died. Or maybe someone turned it off. The other possibility is that the phone crossed over the border. Our systems can't track signals on the other side, only on the national network."

Louie closed his eyes and rubbed his forehead, feeling the beginnings of a migraine.

"I'm sorry," Patrick said, putting a hand on Louie's shoulder. "I put in an alert for Anna's number. If her phone comes back up on the network, I'll know right away. You'll be the first to know after I do."

Louie nodded. "I appreciate it," he said, forcing a smile. "I know you're taking a big risk for me."

"You'd do the same for me," Patrick insisted. "Why don't you go home and get some rest? I'll be in touch if I find out anything."

"All right, but please, be careful," Louie urged.

Patrick turned to leave and disappeared back into the grove of trees. Louie waited until he was gone, then headed back toward the gas station. As he was walking to his car, he sensed someone watching him.

He saw a man coming straight at him from the parking lot of the gas station. He was between Louie and his car and moving quickly, with a determined look on his face. Louie tried to alter his path, but the man shifted in response, blocking his way. Louie thought about yelling for help but realized no one would hear him over the noise from the nearby road.

Louie stopped in the middle of the field, tensing as the man approached. The sun was low on the horizon, shining in Louie's eyes, making it difficult to see the man's face. His hands were stuffed into the pockets of his windbreaker. When he was a few feet away, he slowly drew out a clenched fist. Louie dropped into a crouch, preparing to fight for his life.

The man took one last step and turned up his open palm, staring a Louie with a stern grimace.

"You got the bathroom key?" he asked.

Louie stumbled backward, nearly tripping over a rock. "What?"

"The guy in the station said you took the key and didn't bring it back. I gotta go, man. I can't wait," he pleaded.

Louie's heart was racing as he searched his pockets, found the key, and handed it over.

"Thanks," the man said. He grabbed the key from Louie, turned on his heel, and trotted off toward the bathroom.

+++

Louie drove home in a daze, trying to comprehend everything that Patrick had revealed behind the gas station. It was dark by the time he arrived. He sat in the driveway, not wanting to go into an empty house. Louie stayed in the car until he became worried that his neighbors might see him still sitting there and think he had gone mad.

Once inside, he got undressed and took a cold shower, hoping to clear his head. He wasn't in a mood to cook but knew that he needed to eat. He rummaged through the fridge and found a leftover bowl of fried rice. He took it to the couch, thinking he would watch something on TV to distract him from thinking about Anna.

At some point, his body gave in to exhaustion, and he nodded off in front of the television. After two nights without sleep, he had no reserves left. Sometime later, he heard the buzzing of his cell phone. Groggy and confused, he fumbled for the phone, hoping it was Anna. The number didn't come up on caller ID, but he answered anyway, thinking that it might be Patrick or the embassy calling with an update.

"Is this Colonel Bigombe?" the caller asked. It was a man's voice, and one Louie didn't recognize.

"Yes. To whom am I speaking?"

"Anna is with us," the man said. "Please, listen carefully."

"Why should I believe you?" Louie blurted out, ignoring the instructions. "If she's there, let me talk to her."

The line went quiet. Louie wondered if he had made a terrible mistake by issuing demands, perhaps throwing away his only connection to Anna, but a moment later, the voice returned.

"You may speak with her," the man said. "But she won't sound like herself. She's had a sedative to help her sleep."

Louie heard a door open and footsteps across a wooden floor, then Anna's voice.

"Louie, is that you?" she said, sounding tired and frightened.

"I'm here, Anna. Are you all right? Where are you?" he stammered, relieved to hear her voice but racked with guilt, blaming himself for what she was going through.

"I don't know. It's dark. There's dust everywhere, and it smells bad. I think someone is burning matches," Anna mumbled. "Where are you?"

"I'm at home," he said. "Who are the people holding you?"

"I don't know."

"Did they tell you what they want?"

"I'm sorry, Louie. I don't know what happened. They evacuated my building after the bomb went off. I was going to my car, and someone grabbed me from the street. I don't remember anything else."

Louie could hear her crying.

"It's not your fault," he said, trying to reassure her. "This is because of me. Don't blame yourself."

He could hear someone talking to Anna but couldn't make out the words. When the person stopped speaking, she came back on the line.

"They say if you leave the race, I get to come home."

"Did they say why they want me to quit?"

The next voice on the line was the man's. "Colonel Bigombe, do you understand what needs to happen?"

"Yes. You want me to drop out of the race."

"Once that happens, your wife will be returned. Is that clear?"

"Who do you work for?" Louie asked. "Why do you want me out of the race?"

"I work for someone you once tried to kill. You have three days," the man said. "Do you understand the expectation?"

"I understand. But how do I contact you when it's done?"

"You will be judged by actions, not words. There is no need for you to contact us. Your wife will be safe as long as you fulfill your end of the bargain."

"Can I speak with her again?"

Louie pressed the phone to his ear, waiting for the response.

"No. We're done for now. You know what you must do."

The next thing Louie heard was a dial tone. In frustration, he threw his phone against the wall. He had no idea what to do next, so after a few moments, he got up and started searching in the darkness for his phone. Miraculously, it was still working. His fingers hovered over the keys as he wondered whether contacting Patrick was worth the risk. He decided there was no choice and began typing out a message.

Are u there? he texted.

A moment later, Patrick replied with *y?*

Got a call from the people holding Anna. She's OK but scared, he texted back.

Did u get a number?

Nothing on caller ID, Louie quickly typed. *Can u trace it?*

Maybe. I will try.

Thanks. Be careful, Louie replied.

After sending the last text, Louie scrolled back through his phone log. He found the call from Anna's captor. The entire conversation had lasted less than two minutes. It was his only evidence that Anna was still alive.

He turned off the television. The room was dark except for the faint glow from a streetlight outside. Louie felt guilty for wanting sleep but knew he needed rest to have any chance of functioning in the morning. With the cell phone cradled in his hands, he lay down on the couch and closed his eyes.

+++

Anna awoke on a wooden floor. The room was dark, but she could hear the sounds of trucks passing by on the road outside. There was a single window, covered by metal shutters and locked from the outside. A ceiling fan spun overhead, making a clicking noise with each rotation. Sometime during the night, she got a chill and crawled around the room looking for something to keep her warm. The search yielded a thin foam mattress and wool blanket that smelled of gasoline. Otherwise, the room seemed to be empty.

By morning, she felt more herself; her body had purged the drugs her captors had given her during the drive. The last thing she remembered was walking toward her car after the campus was evacuated. Someone had grabbed her from behind and pushed her into a van while jabbing a needle into her arm. Her final thought as consciousness faded had been wondering whether her captors had properly sanitized the syringe before giving her the injection.

Anna had no idea where they had driven or for how long. She had no other recollection of anything before waking up in the darkened room with a terrible headache. During the night, she had heard someone moving around outside the door—footsteps over wooden floorboards and shadows interrupting the light through the cracks.

Her throat was parched from dust and her nostrils filled with the rancid smell of sulfur. Someone had taken her watch, so she didn't know the time or even the day. She thought about Louie and her colleagues at work, wondering when they had realized she was missing. She had a vague recollection of her phone conversation with Louie but wasn't confident it was real, perhaps just a hallucination conjured by the sedative.

Morning turned to afternoon, and the room became stifling. The rickety ceiling fan barely moved the air. Anna pushed the mattress closer to the window, hoping to get some fresh air from between the cracks in the shutters.

Anna guessed that it was early afternoon when she heard footsteps outside the door. The latch opened, and a man entered the room. He set down a folding chair just inside the doorway. In the darkness, Anna couldn't see his face.

"Are you feeling better?" the man asked, his voice muffled behind a scarf.

"I need water."

"The guard will bring you some shortly," he said.

"Why am I here?"

"You know that already. We need something from your husband. Your presence will ensure that we get it."

"If you want him out of the race, I'm assuming you must work for Emanuel Sekibo. Is that what this is about? Winning the election?"

"Your husband is an American stooge," the man spat. "We don't need the CIA running Green House."

"That's ridiculous. Louie never asked for any of this," Anna argued. "Did Sekibo order you to pick me up?"

"Emanuel Sekibo will be dealt with when the time comes," the man said. "For now, Colonel Bigombe is the more dangerous threat."

"My husband loves his country. You're making a mistake if you believe otherwise. How can you think that he's dangerous?"

"A fire must be put out while it's still small. That's why he will be dealt with first."

"If you're not working for Sekibo, then who?"

"Someone your husband will remember. Daniel Odoki. The commander of the GLA."

"That's ridiculous," Anna laughed defiantly in the darkness. "This is like a script from a bad James Bond movie. Odoki is dead. That is, if he ever even existed."

"Your husband tried to kill him," the man said without emotion. "He was the one who pulled the trigger on the drone strike."

"The entire thing was a hoax. No one was alive in that compound when Louie launched the missile. There was nothing there but ghosts."

"Ghosts don't wage wars," the man insisted.

"I'm not so sure anymore."

He stood up and grabbed the chair, then knocked once on the door. Someone outside slid the latch and opened the door.

"They will bring you water," the man said, turning into the light.

"Are you going to kill me?" Anna called out before he could shut the door.

Her captor hesitated in the doorway but didn't turn around. "Not if your husband cooperates," he said, and closed the door behind him.

CHAPTER NINE

As soon as Louie arrived at the office in the morning, he called the American embassy, hoping for news about Anna. He spoke to the same consular officer as before. The man was sympathetic but had little to offer. They had checked with the local police and the immigration office, but there was no record of her passport being used at the airport or border checkpoints. Without sounding either discouraging or hopeful, the man promised to keep trying and call back if they received any new information.

Work proved to be ineffective as a distraction. Louie struggled for an hour to draft a simple memorandum. Most of the time, he sat despondently at his desk, staring at the phone, waiting for it to ring. Louie reminded himself to be hopeful but feared the worst and couldn't help but blame himself for everything that had happened. He was about to give up and go for a walk to clear his head when his cell phone buzzed with a text. It was an unlisted number, and the message read: *I think I found something. Meet 1hr at the usual place?*

Louie glanced at his watch and sent a reply confirming the rendezvous. For the first time in two days, he felt hopeful. He grabbed his keys and headed for the door. As he was about to leave, Louie realized that he was still in uniform. After the meeting behind the gas station, he knew that Patrick wouldn't want to attract attention.

Louie quickly took off his jungle-patterned camouflage and put on a set of civilian clothes that he kept stored in his wall locker. For good measure, he stuffed a pair of sunglasses and a baseball cap into a backpack. It was a poor excuse for a disguise but the only option available on short notice. He discreetly slipped out of the office through the back door, avoiding anyone who might inquire why he was out of uniform and leaving work in the middle of the day.

When he arrived downtown, instead of going straight to the cafe, Louie circled the block in his car, keeping an eye out for Patrick. When he didn't see any sign of his friend, Louie parked in a spot where he could watch the tables in front of the cafe. Slumped down in the car seat, wearing his pathetic disguise, Louie looked conspicuously like someone trying not to be conspicuous.

After a few minutes, Louie spotted Patrick driving down the street, searching for a parking spot. Louie got out of his car and started down the sidewalk. He was about fifty meters from the cafe when he saw Patrick get out of his car. At first, Patrick didn't recognize Louie in the makeshift disguise; then his distinctive military gait gave him away. Patrick nodded and smiled when he spotted Louie across the road from the cafe.

Louie stepped off the curb between two parked cars at the exact moment an explosion tore through the street. The force of the blast knocked him backward, sending him crashing to the ground, the hat and sunglasses flying. When Louie tried to get up, he felt a sharp pain in his torso where he had slammed against one of the cars' bumpers.

He got to his knees and turned toward the cafe. The explosion had overturned all the plastic tables along the sidewalk. Shards of broken glass from shattered storefront windows covered the ground. Bystanders were screaming and running down the street. Louie spotted at two bodies on the ground, neither of them moving.

A surge of adrenaline flooded his system, helping him get to his feet. Louie stepped out into the street, looking for the spot where Patrick's car was parked, but the scene was unrecognizable. Nothing was left but a pile of smoldering debris where his car had been, the metal frame charred and mangled from the heat of the explosion. Thick black smoke from burning tires and gasoline swirled into the sky.

The sound of approaching sirens filled his ears. Gawkers gathered at the far end of the street, keeping a safe distance from the chaos. Louie saw the cafe owner venture outside, climbing through the splintered remains of his storefront. A bystander comforted a man lying on the ground. The man was missing an arm below the elbow and looked as if he was not far from death. Louie guessed that he must have been sitting at the cafe when the bomb went off.

Louie tried to approach the remnants of Patrick's car, but choking smoke drove him back. Something lying in the middle of the road caught his eye. It was one of Patrick's shoes among charred bits of metal and glass. The explosion had scorched the fabric, but the laces were still neatly tied, as if Patrick had just put the shoe on. Louie stood there staring at it until it dawned upon him that there was no need to look any further.

+++

The sun was setting when Louie left the emergency room. The doctors said that he had several cracked ribs and told him to go home and rest. After finishing the discharge paperwork, Louie passed through the waiting area where friends and relatives of the other victims awaited news. He attracted a few curious glances of recognition as he walked out the door, but most everyone was preoccupied with other worries and didn't notice him.

Standing outside in the humid air, Louie remembered that his car was still downtown, parked near the demolished cafe. The last thing he wanted to do was to go back there, but he didn't have a choice. While searching for a taxi, Louie noticed a parked car flashing its headlights at him, but he couldn't see who was behind the wheel. His heart began to race as it pulled into the road and drove in his direction.

Louie turned around and started walking, hoping to put some distance between himself and the car. He sensed it getting closer but was in no condition to run. He quickened his pace, wincing in pain from his injured ribs. As the car pulled up beside him, he glanced nervously over his shoulder at his pursuer, then stopped, recognizing Janet in the driver's seat.

"How are you feeling?" she asked through the open window.

"I've been better," Louie said, breathless and sweating from the bout of exertion. "Were you waiting for me?"

Janet nodded. "I heard a rumor you were at the scene of the bombing. You seem to be making a habit of this."

"I wasn't the target," Louie said flatly.

"How do you know?"

"I just do."

"One of my contacts said that an officer from DSPO was killed," she said.

"I don't want to talk about it," Louie muttered, avoiding her eyes. "If you're looking for a quote, I suggest you call someone over at police headquarters."

"I'm not looking for a quote. There's something I need to tell you."

Louie stood there, saying nothing, waiting for her to continue.

"There's a big story coming out tomorrow," Janet said. "It's something I've been working on for a while."

"Why are you telling me? Is my name in it?"

"No. It's about Emanuel Sekibo. But given the situation, I wanted you to hear about it from me rather than being surprised when you read it in the paper."

She gestured for him to get into the passenger seat where they could speak privately. Reluctantly, Louie got in the car.

"So, what's the big story?" he asked.

"It's an expose about Sekibo's S3 Corp. How he built the company and made a fortune from overcharging the government on security contracts."

"I doubt anyone will be surprised by that," Louie observed. "Everyone knows that Sekibo got those contracts from his connections in Green House. I don't think it's much of scoop to be rehashing old rumors."

"But there are some things that people don't know. I have a source inside S3 Corp," Janet confided. "He gave me copies of all the government invoices from the last years of the Namono administration. At the time, S3 Corp was providing security for almost every government facility in the country."

Louie shrugged, unimpressed by the revelation. "Everyone knows that's how Sekibo made his money after retiring as head of Police Intelligence. That was about the same time the government began privatizing all its security. Sekibo knew the players and was able to steer all the contracts to his new company. There's nothing new there."

"But there's a difference between rumors and actual billing records," Janet argued. "What I have is proof. The invoices show a clear pattern of fraud and abuse. The company was consistently overcharging the government for employees who weren't on the job. I've got people on the record alleging that Sekibo was running a kickback scheme, paying off senior officials inside of Police Intelligence to look the other way while he billed the government for imaginary security details. This went on until the day that President Namono fled the country. That's when the contract work dried up."

"Why are you surprised by any of this?" Louie said. "The Namono regime was rotten to the core. I could tell you dozens of stories like that."

"The difference now is that Sekibo is running for president. People deserve to know what's at stake if he wins," Janet argued.

"And what would that be?" Louie asked skeptically.

"Most likely, a return to S3 Corp defrauding the country. Do you remember our discussion about the Mining Reform

Act?" Janet asked. "If that bill gets approved, it will open up the entire western region to foreign investors. S3 Corp is almost certain to get a huge chunk of that security business. It will institutionalize his corruption."

"Yes, I understand," Louie said, nodding. "I promise I'll read your story in the morning. But none of this involves me."

"You aren't exactly a neutral observer," Janet reminded him. "We're less than two weeks away from the second round of the election. My story could affect the outcome of the runoff."

"People here are less concerned about corruption than you think," Louie pointed out. "We've lived with it so long that it's just part of the background noise. Right now, bombs are going off in the streets. People are scared. What they care about is having someone in Green House who can stop it. Some people seem convinced that Sekibo is the one."

Janet looked thoughtful. "Sekibo has a lot to gain by defeating the GLA. Investors won't take the risk of putting their money into this country until the security situation improves."

"I don't blame them. But I told you, it's not my concern."

"When are you going to stop pretending that you're not part of this?"

Louie glared at her. "I'm more a part of this than you'll ever know. That officer from DSPO killed today was a close friend, and I'm the reason he's dead. He was there trying to help me find Anna."

Janet turned away from Louie's glare and stared through the windshield. "I'm sorry. I didn't know," she whispered.

"It's not your fault. There's no reason you would have known."

For a while, they sat in the car, saying nothing, until Louie broke the silence. "I need to ask a favor," he said.

"I'm not pulling the story," Janet said immediately, assuming that's what he was thinking.

"No, it's not that. I'm giving you a different headline. I'm dropping out of the race. Anna and I decided to leave the country right after the election," Louie revealed. "I need you to put that in the paper."

"I can't just run a story based on a rumor," Janet said, incredulous at the suggestion. "Who's my source? How do I even know that's true?"

"What do you mean, who's the source?" Louie asked, astonished that she was challenging his assertion. "I'm telling you that I'm dropping out. I'm not running for president. What other source do you need?"

Janet shook her head. "I'm sorry, but that's not the way it works. I'm not putting my byline on something like that without some additional verification. Especially on the same day that I'm breaking a major story about corruption by Sekibo's company. What if it turned out not to be true? It would undermine my credibility."

"How can it not be true?" Louie shot back. "I'm *the* primary source. Who else needs to verify the story?"

"Why should I believe you?" Janet said stubbornly. "What about some kind of statement from the Electoral Commission? For all I know, it could be some kind of campaign stunt."

Louie closed his eyes and took a deep breath, thinking

through his next move. "Someone has kidnapped Anna," he revealed.

"What do you mean? When?"

"Two days ago. After the bombing at the university."

Janet gave him a suspicious look. "Why haven't I heard anything about this? There hasn't been anything reported in the media."

"The authorities are aware, but no one else knows."

"Then it's only a matter of time until word gets out. Do you have any idea who's involved?" she asked.

"Someone who is claiming to be from the GLA. He called yesterday and said they would hold her until I dropped out of the race."

"That makes no sense," Janet protested. "Why would the GLA want you out of the race? It's Sekibo who's promising to take the war across the border into their territory."

"I have no idea. None of this makes any sense," Louie said miserably. "But I'm not in a position to argue with them. If they promise to let her go, I'll give them whatever they ask for."

"What makes you think that will be enough? If they're willing to set off bombs and kill innocent people, why do you think they would keep their word about Anna?"

"What choice do I have?"

"If I run this story about the election, I'll need to include the part about Anna's abduction and the GLA's possible involvement," Janet said. "I can't pick and choose which parts of the story to tell."

"No way," Louie insisted. "That could jeopardize her life."

"I'm sorry, but that's the way it works. I'm a journalist. I report facts. All of them."

"What if they kill her? That will be on your hands."

"You're asking me to become personally involved in a story and compromise my objectivity. I can't report that you are dropping out of the race while ignoring the minor detail of kidnapping and extortion." Janet sighed. "Can't you see why I'm hesitant to become involved? It's going to look bad no matter what I do."

"Please," Louie begged. "Once Anna is back, you can report whatever you want. I'm not asking you to lie."

"We're splitting hairs here," Janet argued.

"Please. I just need a few days. The man who died this morning was bringing me information about Anna. That was my best chance to find her. Now, I don't know what else to do except give the kidnappers what they want."

"What you're asking me to do goes against all my professional ethics. Not to mention common sense," Janet said.

"I know it's asking a lot."

"The story about Sekibo and S3 Corp is running tomorrow, no matter what. I'm not pulling back on that," she said firmly.

"I wouldn't ask you to."

"What's your plan to find Anna, now that your friend is gone? I'm sorry," Janet murmured. "I don't even know his name."

"Patrick," Louie answered. "We've been friends since grammar school. This wasn't the first time he took risks to help me."

"He sounds like a good friend."

"He was," Louie whispered.

"So where does that leave you?"

"Patrick was the only one who had all the details. Now that he's gone, probably the only person who can get me out of this mess is the one who got me into it."

"Well…good luck," Janet said, sensing that Louie wasn't going to reveal any more. "You've got my secure phone number," she reminded him.

"Thank you," Louie said as he spotted a taxi coming down the road. He got out of Janet's car and waved the driver down.

+++

On his way into the office the following day, Louie stopped by a newsstand for copies of the local dailies and the international papers. He bought one of each, threw them into a pile on the front seat, and then raced toward the base. He went straight up to his office and closed the door behind him. True to her word, Janet had filed a short article, and the wire services had picked it up. A single blurb cited an unnamed source close to the campaign hinting that Louie intended to withdraw from the election.

After going through all the papers, he grabbed his phone and checked social media. Louie discovered a few trending threads speculating on the end of his noncampaign. However, most of the digital chatter was dominated by Janet's expose on S3 Corp and Emanuel Sekibo's financial links to the Namono administration. Louie had just started reading Janet's story when Owen Smith burst into his office without knocking, breathless from sprinting up the stairs.

"What the hell is this?" Owen gasped, waving a copy of a local newspaper over his head.

"I have no idea you're talking about."

"Don't play dumb!" he insisted. "This story about the campaign."

"You mean Sekibo and S3 Corp?" Louie asked innocently.

"Stop it! You know what I'm talking about," Owen yelled. "This rumor about you pulling out of the race. Where the hell did that come from?"

Louie picked up one of the newspapers from his desk and pretended to read the story. "It says the report came from an anonymous source inside the campaign," he said. "But since there isn't actually a campaign, I suppose it could only have come from you or me."

"Very funny. For your information, the second I leave this office, I'm calling that reporter and issuing an anonymous retraction, denying that you're leaving the race."

"You wouldn't dare," Louie threatened.

"Of course I would," Owen insisted. "You'd be crazy to drop out now. We've got Sekibo on the ropes. That expose is a bombshell. It couldn't have been better if I had written it myself."

"Do you even care if it's true?"

"Sure I do. That makes it even better. And that's precisely why I'm concerned about these anonymous rumors of you dropping out. The gap is closing. This story about S3 Corp could seal the deal and put you into Green House," Owen argued.

Louie threw up his hands in frustration. "How many times do I need to tell you? I'm not running for president.

I'm not going to Green House. The only thing I care about is getting Anna back."

"And give the election over to Sekibo? He very well could start a war resulting in thousands of unnecessary deaths. Are you willing to live with that?"

"You don't know what's going to happen," Louie countered. "Besides, why is what you're doing any better? This little charade of yours is just as corrupt as what Sekibo does."

"Don't be so naïve," Owen said. "We're fighting fire with fire. We know all about Sekibo's men stuffing the ballot boxes during the first round. If you hadn't been in the race, he already would have stolen it and be sitting in Green House right now."

Louie bit his tongue, wondering how much more Owen knew that he wasn't revealing. After a moment, he said, "If you've known all along that Sekibo was cheating, why not call him on it and show the world the evidence? Wouldn't it be easier that way?"

"If only it were that simple," Owen sniffed. "We can't afford to poison the well. What if we make that accusation and he still wins? Then we've got to work with the guy for the next twenty years."

"And running a fake campaign was your next best option?" Louie sighed.

Owen shrugged. "It is what it is. The point is, you're not pulling out of this race."

"Yes, I am."

"No, you're not."

"The only thing I care about is getting Anna back," Louie repeated. "If that means Sekibo wins, then so be it."

"May I?" Owen asked, gesturing at the chair in front of Louie's desk and sitting down without waiting for an answer. "I realize that we've put you in a difficult situation," he conceded. "But I hope you understand that this was all done with good intentions."

"Whose good intentions?"

Owen ignored the question and continued. "It's in nobody's interest to let Sekibo steal this election. However, if you drop out, that's exactly what's going to happen."

"This entire thing is a sham. I never asked to be a part of this," Louie said.

"I understand that, and I want you to know that I feel genuinely sorry for getting you involved. Nevertheless, you need to appreciate our situation. Other actors were making moves. We couldn't afford to sit this one out. Too much is at stake. I'll be the first to admit that putting your name on the ballot was a Hail Mary pass. To be honest, we were all taken a bit by surprise when your campaign took off as it did."

"What if I walked out this door, went to the newspaper, and told them everything you just said?"

Owen appeared to be untroubled by this scenario. "Naturally, I'd deny it. It might make you feel better in the short term, but it wouldn't solve any problems. Sekibo would win the election, and you would probably never see Anna again. How is that good for anyone?"

Louie closed his eyes, again feeling a headache coming on. He rubbed his temples, staring across the desk at Owen. "Do you know where she is?"

"Not exactly," Owen admitted. "We were tracking the same cell phone data as your friend over at DSPO. We know that the signal disappeared somewhere around the border. That was the last time we saw it on the network."

Louie wondered how Owen knew that Patrick had been tracking Anna's cell signal but decided not to ask.

"But if you're willing to keep your name on the ballot, I think we can help you find her," Owen offered.

"Why should I trust you? You're the reason they came after her in the first place."

"With your friend gone, I may be the only person left who can help you find her. We have reason to believe that Anna is somewhere across the border, possibly being held in the GLA's sanctuary zone. We have some assets in the area who may be able to help."

"The third force?" Louie asked.

"*Assets*," Owen answered impatiently.

"There's something else I want."

Owen waited for Louie to continue.

"I need to see my father's dossier."

"I have no idea what you're talking about," Owen insisted, straight-faced.

"You're lying. I know my father was working for the agency during the border wars. One of your colleagues told me so on the day Green House burned. He said there was a file. I want to see it. Unredacted."

Owen leaned back in his chair, staring at Louie as if they were playing a hand of poker. "That kind of thing is way above my pay grade," he said, hoping he was calling a bluff.

"In that case, this meeting is over," Louie said. "I'm going straight to the press and telling them everything I know. If that doesn't convince them to let Anna go, nothing will."

He got up to leave. He had crossed the room and was reaching for the door when Owen panicked.

"OK! Please, sit down," he begged. "I'll see what I can do about files."

"It's non-negotiable," Louie said firmly.

"I said I'll do my best. In the meantime, we need to act fast if we're going to find Anna."

"What about the campaign?"

"No need to fiddle with success," Owen said with a shrug. "It's been going fine without you so far. That article on Sekibo will keep people distracted for a few days. That should buy us some time to figure out where Anna is."

"What do you want me to do?"

Owen glanced at his watch, taking a moment to develop a plan. "Tell your boss that you're not feeling well," he instructed. "Go home and pack a travel bag. Be sure to throw in a few camo uniforms. Then meet me on the far end of the airfield around sunset."

"Where are we going?"

"You'll find out once we get there," Owen said. "I need to make a few phone calls and set things up."

He stood up and headed for the door. He reached for the handle and was about to leave, then paused and looked back at Louie. "Hey, I'm sorry about your friend," he said. "He seemed like one of the good guys."

"He was," Louie said.

Owen nodded, turned, and left the room.

+++

Anna pressed her face against the shutters, her only connection to the outside world. The light between the slats was her reference point for marking the passage of time. She could hear trucks driving nearby during the day, occasionally punctuated by the sound of men's voices yelling over the engines. At night, it was mostly quiet, except for the dull rumbling of machinery in the distance.

From the angle of the light, Anna guessed that it was late morning. She heard footsteps in the hallway. A guard opened the door and left a plate of food and a water bottle on the floor. It was beans and rice for the third meal in a row. Anna felt her stomach tighten. She took a drink of the water but left the food. The cap on the bottle was loose. Anna assumed that the guard had been refilling it from the tap, probably the source of her intestinal distress. However, she had no choice but to drink it.

The guard returned about an hour later to collect the dishes. Anna asked if she could use the restroom. As was the routine, he blindfolded her, then led her down the hall to a cramped washroom. She found the remnants of a soap bar in the sink and washed her face for the first time in days. When she returned to the room, the man in charge was waiting. He was sitting in a chair by the door, wearing a scarf to conceal his face. This time, he had brought in another chair, and he motioned for her to sit in it.

"There is a story in the paper about your husband leaving the race," he said.

"You must be pleased. Isn't that what you wanted?" Anna replied.

"It means nothing. His name is still on the ballot."

"Nothing you've been saying makes sense," Anna said, ignoring his comment. "If you represent the GLA, why do you want Emanuel Sekibo to win the race? He's promised to launch an offensive against GLA territory as soon as he's elected. He should be the last person you want to see in Green House."

"I've told you, Sekibo will be dealt with when the time comes," the man said. "For now, Colonel Bigombe is the greater threat. He's an American stooge, just like his father. He cannot be allowed to occupy Green House."

"And the people you represent have a better plan for the country?" Anna questioned.

"We'll take back what rightfully belongs to us. This land is fertile, with many resources, but only a few have benefited from it. We should all be wealthy, but not because we invite outsiders to take the best fruit, leaving us to fight over what remains."

"Louie has nothing to do with any of this. You're looking in the wrong place to find your villain."

"They're all a part of it."

"I assume that you're not going to let me go home, no matter what Louie does," Anna speculated.

"The election is just over a week away. If your husband acts in good faith, we will know by then," the man said, rising from the chair. "Until then, you will remain as our guest."

He turned and walked out the door. Once he was gone, the guard came inside and took his chair. He nodded at the one Anna was still sitting in. "A gift for you," he said, slamming the door behind him and leaving her alone in the darkness.

CHAPTER TEN

Louie parked on the far side of the airport, near the American camp, as Owen had instructed. He wore civilian clothes and had a duffel bag slung over his shoulder, as if he was heading off on a short holiday. Louie approached an American soldier standing guard at the gate leading to the military part of the airfield. He presented his identification, unsure what to expect. The guard didn't seem surprised to see him. He checked Louie's name off an access roster, then waved him through the gate.

Louie walked out to the runway as the sun dipped low on the horizon. Against the backdrop of a blood-red sky, he saw a group of men exiting an aircraft hangar. Louie recognized Owen Smith among them, but he didn't know the others. Owen stopped to talk to Louie while the other men continued walking toward a line of helicopters parked on the runway.

"Are you ready for the trip?" Owen asked, reaching out to shake Louie's hand.

"Where are we going?"

"First stop, Kiskow. After that, we're heading across the border."

"I forgot my passport," Louie said calmly, trying to conceal his surprise. "Is that going to be a problem?"

Owen chuckled. "Don't worry. We have an understanding with our friends at the border. A passport isn't necessary. Everybody will be sanitized before we leave Kiskow."

"Sanitized?"

"No identifying documents," Owen explained. "Once we cross over to the other side, we're no longer on official business. If you get separated and picked up by the local authorities, we'll deny that we know you, and you'll be on your own. Do you understand?"

Louie nodded but didn't understand at all. The crews on the flight line were going through preflight checks of the helicopters. Louie heard the engines purring and saw the rotor blades slowly turning as they prepared for departure.

"Shall we?" Owen asked, waving Louie toward the lead helicopter.

+++

The flight to Kiskow was uneventful, with clear skies and smooth air the entire way. A crescent moon hung on the horizon as they traversed a featureless landscape. When Louie heard the pilots announce the initial approach into Kiskow, he peered out the window. The camp was a glowing island of artificial light powered by massive diesel generators. Beyond the perimeter fence, the adjacent village was a sea of darkness, with a few lights flickering in the night.

The landing zone was on the parade field in the middle of the camp, the exact spot where Louie had been wounded by mortar fire during the GLA attack. His heart pounded in his chest as the pilot circled above the field. The helicopter's wheels touched the earth a few meters from where Louie had watched the wounded soldier die.

It was nearly midnight when they unloaded the helicopters. The pilots shut down the engines, and the camp returned to silence. In the moonlight, Louie saw a row of jeeps lined up along the edge of the parade field. Several drivers and an armed security detachment were waiting for them. Owen had moved beyond earshot and was speaking with someone on a satellite phone. After a brief conversation, he rejoined Louie on the parade field.

"Sorry for the delay," he said, putting away the satellite phone. "I was just coordinating the second part of our trip. As you may imagine, cross-border logistics can be complicated. A team on the other side is expecting us and will make sure that we don't run into any problems along the way."

"I suppose they don't get many guests," Louie speculated.

"You could say that. But don't worry, the General is taking care of everything."

"The General? Is that who's in charge of the third force?"

"Why does everyone keep calling it that?" Owen said through clenched teeth.

"When you deny that something exists, I think you relinquish any prerogative over naming it. Don't you think?" Louie chided.

Owen sniffed but didn't argue.

"Is that where we're going? To the base camp of the third force?" Louie pressed.

"Our final destination is an undisclosed forward operating base. What goes on there is considered classified. You can't discuss this with anyone. Do you understand?"

"Is it an American base?"

"No!" Owen insisted. "The forces operating there are entirely indigenous and virtually indistinguishable from the people they're fighting. They know the environment. They speak the dialect. They even wear similar uniforms to the GLA's. If you saw them out in the jungle, you wouldn't be able to tell them from any other militia group operating in the area."

"Except that they answer to you," Louie observed.

"Only indirectly," Owen clarified. "The United States provides limited logistical and technical support; however, there's no formal tasking mechanism. This is a fully independent force. The General exercises complete autonomy over his operations. Nevertheless, we share common goals and offer strategic guidance when needed, helping to achieve a mutually beneficial end-state."

"This General is American?"

"Technically, yes. He's a naturalized citizen, but he was born and raised here in DRoG. He knows the territory and the players. We couldn't have asked for a better leader to be running the show."

"On whose authority does he operate?" Louie asked, still not entirely understanding what Owen was describing.

"The General is responsible for tactical decision-making; however, we closely monitor all activities," Owen explained. "I can assure you, this isn't some unaccountable rogue army out there fighting a shadow war. They're working in the best interest of your country, operating in a very rough neighborhood."

"But doing so without any oversight by our political

authorities," Louie pointed out. "It sounds to me like you've just created another militia force. What makes them any different from the GLA?"

"On the contrary," Owen snapped, losing patience with the discussion. "This is a highly trained and professional fighting force tasked with bringing stability to an ungoverned space. Until the General arrived, it was like the Wild West out there. No rule of law, complete chaos. That's why the GLA was able to reorganize so quickly after Operation Brushfire. No one was there to check their ambitions."

"That's why you created the third force? To defeat the GLA?"

"Perhaps not defeat, but at least contain. We needed to provide your new government with some breathing room after President Namono's sudden departure. Quite frankly, we never viewed the GLA as an existential threat. They're a ragtag bunch of undisciplined fighters."

"Then why bother waging a covert war across the border?" Louie asked. "It seems like an unnecessary risk for a group that doesn't pose a major threat."

"Well, that was true until Emanuel Sekibo started threatening to kick off a new border war. He's making the GLA out to be ten feet tall, using them to justify a military buildup along the border. If that happens, it could upset the entire geopolitical balance of the region. Certainly you can appreciate the logic of having a buffer to mitigate the danger of miscalculation?" Owen asked. "It's a stitch in time that saves nine."

"You're tinkering with an election while running a proxy army across the border. *That's* your plan for stabilizing the country?" Louie asked, disbelieving what he was hearing.

"You're oversimplifying the situation," Owen protested.

"What is it about you Americans? You think that there's an easy fix to any problem you stumble across."

"We're a can-do people," Owen said with a shrug.

"I think the world would do fine with a bit less of that," Louie said, and sighed.

"That's one opinion," Owen snapped, glancing impatiently at his watch. "We need to get moving. It's a long drive to the border. I told the General that we'd be there before noon tomorrow."

Owen turned and began walking toward the vehicles. Louie hesitated, debating whether to follow, sensing he was falling deeper into something beyond his control. He watched Owen climb into the lead jeep. The driver revved the engine and flashed the running lights, signaling that it was time for them to go. Louie cringed at the thought of getting in the jeep and joining the madness, but he also understood that there was no choice if he wanted to find Anna. He picked up his duffel bag and followed Owen to the jeep.

+++

The convoy drove straight through the night. Louie tried to sleep, but the road was rutted and bumpy, making it all but impossible. They arrived at the border crossing just after sunrise. When the jeeps stopped at the checkpoint, several armed soldiers came out of the guardhouse to greet them. Despite Owen's assurances, Louie had butterflies in his stomach, anxious about crossing an international boundary without a passport or identification.

Owen got out of the jeep and followed one of the guards

to a dilapidated shack that served as the customs office. The officer in charge was waiting for them out front. He seemed to recognize Owen and reached out to shake his hand before inviting him inside the shack. Owen emerged a few minutes later and returned to the jeep.

The driver started the engine, and Owen instructed him to pull forward to the crossing point. The jeep nosed up to the gate, and one of the guards lifted the metal arm, waving them forward into the no-man's-land between the two border posts. The guard made a show of looking in the other direction as the convoy passed through. Louie assumed that the officials on the opposite side must have been partners in the scheme, because as the jeeps approached, they raised their side of the gate and played out a similar charade.

"See how easy it is for everyone to get along when we all speak a common language?" Owen said.

He was grinning behind his sunglasses and making a show of stuffing a large stack of euro notes into a hidden pocket of his safari jacket. Louie shook his head but said nothing, realizing the pointlessness of debating Owen's world view.

The convoy continued driving for several more hours. To Louie's surprise, the roads were even worse than on the Gisawian side. At various points along the way, the drivers stopped the vehicles to plumb the depth of water-filled potholes, concerned that the jeeps might disappear beneath the muck.

The region was sparsely populated. Occasionally, they passed through a small farming village or encountered a broken-down car abandoned by the roadside. Otherwise, there was little evidence of civilization. A few times, Louie thought he caught a glimpse of people hiding in the bushes along the road, but neither the driver nor Owen seemed to notice. Louie chalked the visions up to hallucinations, guessing that his mind was playing tricks from lack of sleep.

In the early afternoon, the convoy pulled off the main road onto an unmarked dirt path. They drove a few more kilometers until they came to a makeshift metal barrier blocking the way. A man in a camouflage uniform, carrying an assault rifle, approached the passenger side of the lead jeep. He peered through the passenger window, his eyes concealed behind mirrored sunglasses. Louie saw the guard's finger dancing on the trigger of his weapon, as if he was looking for a reason to respond with force.

"We're here to see the General," Owen said through the open window.

The guard looked into the back of the jeep, glaring suspiciously at Louie.

"He's cleared to be here," Owen explained, nodding back at Louie. "The General is expecting him."

"Did anyone follow you from the main road?" the guard asked.

"No. We haven't seen anyone since we left the border," Owen reassured him.

The guard nodded, seeming satisfied. He gave a birdlike whistle over his shoulder, and three more armed men emerged from the trees. Together, they lifted the barrier and pulled back a strip of tire spikes concealed underneath some leaves.

With the hazards removed, the convoy continued down the road, eventually arriving in an open clearing surrounded by dense jungle. The scene reminded Louie of a B-grade Hollywood movie set. A dozen open-air wooden huts sat in a semicircle around the clearing. They had roofs made of dried palm fronds and mosquito netting for windows, and appeared to serve as barracks and office space. One hut contained a field kitchen and some tables: a makeshift mess hall.

In the center of the compound was an exercise area featuring pull-up bars and free weights rusting in the subtropical air. Beyond the perimeter, Louie could see an improvised shooting range, a bayonet training course, and climbing ropes strung between the trees. Overlooking the compound was a three-story watchtower made of bamboo scaffolding. Inside the observation post, two guards armed with long rifles and binoculars were standing watch.

"I didn't realize the CIA had a sense of humor," Louie said to Owen as the jeeps rolled to a stop.

"The General decides on the decor, not us," Owen said, unamused.

"Do I get to meet him?"

"That's why I brought you here. If anyone can help find your wife, he's the one."

"You have a lot of confidence in this guy," Louie observed.

"You'll understand when you meet him. He's one of the best operators I've ever seen. Nothing gets by him. All right, it's showtime," Owen announced dramatically, exiting the jeep and stepping into the movie set.

He led Louie across the compound toward the most prominent structure, what appeared to be the headquarters building. It was an open-air bungalow with a wraparound veranda. Two armed guards dressed in jungle camouflage and black berets stood at the entrance. When they saw Owen approaching with Louie in tow, the men stepped in front of the door, blocking access into the building.

"He's with me," Owen explained. "The General is expecting us."

One of the guards stepped forward and motioned for Louie to raise his arms. Louie reluctantly complied, and the man frisked him from head to toe.

"Sorry," Owen shrugged sheepishly. "They can't take any unnecessary risks. The General is a high-value target. The GLA would love nothing more than to take him out."

After the guard finished patting down Louie, he opened the door and led them into the bungalow. There were several desks clustered in the main room. Behind one, a clerk sat behind an ancient-looking typewriter, hunting and pecking over the keys. Another soldier was in front of a table covered with electronic equipment. He wore a set of bulky headphones and was listening to radio transmissions, oblivious to everyone else in the room.

The guard led them to a door at the far end of the room. Attached to the wall above the door was a polished rank insignia showing two stars, hinting at who was inside.

"The General is in a meeting with his commanders," the guard said, reaching for the doorknob. "You may go in, but please, do not disturb them."

Owen glanced at Louie. "Are you ready?"

"I guess so," Louie said, though he was uncertain what he was supposed to be ready for.

The guard opened the door and motioned for them to go inside. Owen led the way, followed by Louie. Across the room, a group of men in camouflage fatigues huddled around a table covered with maps. One of the men was describing the outline of a reconnaissance operation, motioning at the map with a wooden chopstick.

The speaker was addressing a shorter man with his back turned to the door. Louie could see a glint of light reflecting off the stars pinned to his uniform's shoulder boards. He carried a pistol in an old-fashioned leather shoulder holster and wore a pair of highly polished riding boots. The General's attention was focused on the map, and he was nodding approvingly as the taller man continued his briefing.

Louie and Owen lingered in the background, not wanting to disturb them. When the briefing was over, the commanders waited in silence while the General traced his finger over the map, weighing the options. He mumbled a few words of instruction to the man who had presented the plan. At the sound of his voice, Louie felt a powerful sense of déjà vu. He couldn't place the voice precisely but was confident that he had heard it somewhere before.

Louie inched forward, trying to hear the conversation at the table. When he tried to catch a glimpse of the General's face, one of the soldiers shifted position and blocked his view. Louie leaned in the other direction, and the General looked up from the map, perfectly silhouetting him in the light.

Louie only needed one peek to fit the pieces together. Without a word, he turned and moved for the door. Owen hissed through clenched teeth when he realized what was happening, but Louie kept on marching out the door. By the time Owen caught him, Louie was already in the courtyard, heading for the jeeps.

"What the hell are you doing?" Owen screamed, racing to catch up. Louie refused to stop until Owen seized him by the arm and spun him around.

"Are you fucking crazy?" Owen yelled in Louie's face. "What do you think you're doing? You just walked out on the General!"

"He's not a general," Louie said, tearing his arm free of Owen's grip.

"What are you talking about? Of course he is. He's running this entire operation."

"I know him," Louie said. "His name is Sammy. He was a barista on the American base during Operation Brushfire. After that, he ran a chain of coffee shops in the capital. He disappeared on the day Green House burned down. I don't know how the hell he got back here or why you're calling him general, but there's one thing I can tell you for sure: this entire thing is a sham, and I'm not taking part in it." Louie opened the front door of the nearest jeep.

"Stop!" Owen ordered. "Let me explain. Then, if you still want to leave, I'll have one of the drivers take you back across the border."

Louie stood with his back to Owen, debating what to do. He took a deep breath, thinking of Anna, knowing that he was trapped. With Patrick gone, there was no one he could trust. No one else could help him.

"You've got two minutes," Louie said, turning around to face Owen.

Owen leaned closer, lowering his voice so none of the soldiers around the yard could overhear their conversation.

"Here's the deal," he whispered. "I don't know who you

think this guy is, but I'm telling you, he's a military genius. He's been leading operations here for the last three months. For the first time since this started, we're finally making progress. Before the General got here, the entire mission was floundering on the edge of failure. The GLA had a free hand. They were crossing the border and launching attacks almost every day. It's a damn miracle they didn't overrun Kiskow when they had the chance. But since the General came in, everything's changed. He revamped our entire operation and single-handedly turned things around. These men would follow him anywhere. He's thrown the GLA off balance and got them running scared."

"Jesus," Louie muttered, rubbing his forehead. "I can't believe this is happening." He looked up and pointed accusingly at the headquarters building. "Do you realize that your so-called general has no military training whatsoever?"

"I'm not in charge of paramilitary recruiting," Owen protested. "That's a completely different department."

"You're telling me that the CIA knowingly hired a barista to lead a top-secret covert military force?"

"This stuff is harder than it looks," Owen countered. "You can't just put an ad in the newspaper to hire these guys."

"You might give it a try next time," Louie hissed.

"I sense that you're skeptical," Owen said, softening his tone.

"Really? That's very perceptive. I can see why the agency hired you."

"At least go back in there and talk to him," Owen pleaded. "You've got to give him a chance."

"Why?"

Owen reached out and put a hand on Louie's shoulder. "I know you're worried about Anna," he said. "Believe it or not, I am too. I feel awful that she got sucked into this. That was never part of the plan. But things got crazy once your campaign took off. I suppose we didn't anticipate all the second-order effects," he offered apologetically. "Anyway, here's the bottom line. The General is the best chance we've got of getting her back."

"If Sammy is my best chance, then I'm ready to give up."

"Please, at least talk to him," Owen begged. "I don't know what he was like back when you knew him. But since coming here, he's been a game-changer. I'm telling you, we've got the GLA on the ropes. Besides, we don't have a plan B."

"I can't believe this," Louie muttered, staring at the ground and kicking the dirt with the toe of his boot. "It's all come full circle: me, Anna, and Sammy, even someone claiming to be Daniel Odoki. We're right back to where it started. It's like nothing changed."

"I have no idea what you're talking about. But maybe someday, once this is all over, you can tell me about it over a beer."

Louie snorted. "You wouldn't believe me if I told you."

"Those stories are usually the best kind," Owen said, pausing and glancing over his shoulder at the headquarters. "Will you please come back inside and talk to the General?"

Louie rubbed his eyes, exhausted from lack of sleep. Finally, he nodded and followed Owen back to the cabana.

By the time they returned to the headquarters building,

the meeting had ended. The General was alone in his office, sitting at his desk, reading a stack of papers. Owen knocked on the door and stuck his head inside.

"Sir, I have Colonel Bigombe here with me. Amazingly, I just discovered that you two already know each other. I guess that saves me the trouble of introductions."

Louie walked past Owen toward the desk as the General rose from his seat. The men stood there staring at each other until Louie reached out his hand.

"It's good to see you again, Sammy," he said.

The General broke into a broad smile, seizing Louie's hand and shaking it vigorously. "Mr. Louie, it's been so long," he said, tears welling in his eyes. "I can't tell you how happy I am."

"I wish it were better circumstances," Louie said. "Anna's in trouble. I need your help."

The smile faded from Sammy's face as he nodded gravely. "I understand, Mr. Louie. I promise I'll do everything I can to get her back."

"Thank you," Louie said. "I know she would be happy that you were here."

"Let's have a coffee and discuss our plan," Sammy suggested, waving Louie to one of the chairs in front of his desk.

He glanced at Owen, who was still standing by the door. "Mr. Smith, if you don't mind, I'd like to speak privately with Colonel Bigombe."

Owen cocked his head as if confused about the General's intention. He seemed on the verge of protesting, then changed his mind. He was turning toward the door when the General called out to him.

"If you wouldn't mind, Mr. Smith, please have the clerk bring us an espresso, a tea, and some soda water."

Owen looked as if he was about to say something but hesitated, then continued out the door.

+++

The next morning, Louie walked over to the camp's primitive field kitchen, hoping to find some hot water for his cup of tea. He peeked through the mosquito net walls and saw that it was empty; he had missed the breakfast hour. The soldiers had already moved out on their patrols or were doing training around the camp.

The door was unlocked, so Louie went inside. In the dining area were some rickety-looking tables and chairs. Gas lanterns dangled from the wooden rafters. Louie heard someone in the kitchen and stuck his head inside. One of the cooks was cleaning up from breakfast. Louie asked him for hot water, holding up a tea bag by way of explanation. The cook gestured at a metal vat of steaming water sitting on top of the gas burner.

The vat was filled with rusty brown water that must have been drawn from a local stream. The cook was using it to clean the breakfast dishes. Having no other option, Louie grabbed a metal spoon and scooped hot water into a mug, dropping in the tea bag from the small supply he had brought with him across the border. He thanked the cook for the water and went out to the dining area, where he sat down at a table while his tea was steeping.

The cook came out a few minutes later with a bowl of leftover porridge and some milk and sugar for Louie's tea. He apologized for the meager offering, explaining that nothing else remained from breakfast. Louie smiled and thanked him again before the man wandered back to the kitchen.

Louie added milk to his tea, trying not to speculate on its origin. As he took a sip, Owen appeared in the doorway, looking as if he had just woken up.

"Mind if I join you?" he asked.

Louie glanced around at all the empty tables, then reluctantly nodded at the empty chair across from him.

"That trip yesterday wiped me out," Owen said, flopping into the chair. "I must have slept straight through breakfast."

"Help yourself," Louie said, pushing the bowl of cold porridge across the table.

Owen examined the contents and shrugged, then added a generous amount of sugar and milk. "Did you have a good meeting with the General?" he asked, digging into the porridge. "You guys were in there quite a while."

"We had some catching up to do," Louie explained. "It's been a few years since we've seen each other."

"Anything interesting?" Owen asked, obviously curious about what had transpired.

"You might say that. I got the full story about how he got mixed up with you guys."

"Really?" Owen said, eyebrows raised.

"Before he left DRoG, Sammy had been moonlighting as an informant while running his cafes. Something went wrong, and he was exposed," Louie explained. "The agency decided to exfiltrate him out of the country on the day Green House fell. They gave him a new identity and a green card, then got him set up running a cafe in a northern Virginia strip mall. He did that for a few years but was having trouble with the business. About six months ago, someone from the agency called him about a job. The next thing he knew, he was at a secret camp, training as a paramilitary."

"I don't know much about his backstory," Owen mumbled, staring into his porridge, clearly lying.

"I suppose I don't blame him for leaving here when he did," Louie mused. "If he had stayed after the regime collapsed, his business would have fallen apart, just like everything else in the country. It would have been foolish for him to turn down a golden parachute and the chance to leave when he could. Sammy is nothing if not enterprising."

"I know you're skeptical, but he's done wonders since showing up here," Owen insisted. "Did you talk about anything else?"

Louie took a sip of his tea, letting Owen stew for a moment before answering. "Mostly, we talked about a plan to find Anna."

"Does the General have any ideas?"

Louie shook his head. "There isn't much to go on. We know where she might have crossed the border based on the last signal from her cell phone. But the GLA controls a large area. She could be almost anywhere."

"Where does he plan to start?"

"Over the last few weeks, Sammy's patrols have captured several GLA fighters. During interrogations, they provided some information about the GLA's logistical system. Sammy thinks they're using a hub-and-spoke system to supply a series of remote camps. If we can figure out how they rotate around the camps, it might give us a general idea of where they have their headquarters. That may be our only chance to find Anna."

"It seems like kind of a long shot," Owen said.

"It is. But that's all we've got," Louie replied. "A patrol brought in two GLA fighters a few days ago. They seemed to know something about the procedures for resupplying the camps. We're going to talk to them this morning and see if there's anything we can exploit."

Owen put down his spoon and pushed aside his porridge. "I doubt you'll get anything useful out of them," he said. "We've debriefed all the detainees several times. They're mostly low-level foot soldiers. They don't have a clue about the big picture."

"We've got to start somewhere," Louie argued, confused about Owen's hesitancy.

"Sure, but we're running out of time."

Louie shot Owen a quizzical look. "What do you mean, running out of time? There is no timeline. We came here to find Anna."

"Yeah, of course," Owen conceded. "But we can't just forget about the election. We're less than a week away from the second round. It wouldn't do us any good to have you sitting out here in the jungle when things are coming down to the wire back in the capital."

Louie shrugged indifferently. "If they can't find me, then maybe people will finally realize that I'm not running."

Owen straightened in his chair, agitated by the turn of the conversation. "Have you forgotten our deal? he asked. "I told you that I would help find Anna. In return, you promised to stay in the race."

"I don't see you doing much to help," Louie said, pointing accusingly at Owen from across the table. "Sammy is the one coming up with ideas. He's also the one sending his soldiers out looking for her. And by the way, I haven't forgotten about the other part of our deal," he warned.

Owen stared at him blankly, feigning ignorance.

"My father's personnel file," Louie reminded him.

Owen thrust his chair away from the table, throwing his arms up into the air with indignation. "You act like I haven't done anything for you!"

"I'm not getting into this again," Louie shot back, getting up from the table and preparing to leave. "I trust Sammy a hell of a lot more than I do you."

"Where are you going?" Owen called out as Louie headed for the door.

"To the detention facility. I'm going to see what I can get out of the detainees," he shouted over his shoulder.

"Not without me, you're not!" Owen yelled after him, leaving his breakfast on the table and racing out the door after Louie.

+++

Owen followed Sammy and Louie down an overgrown path leading away from the main camp. They came to an open clearing and a cinderblock structure with a roof made of corrugated metal. Two armed guards were posted outside the door, sitting in the shade under an awning. The soldiers leapt to attention and saluted when they saw Sammy approaching.

"This is our temporary holding facility," Sammy explained. "When our patrols capture GLA fighters in the field, we bring them here for their initial debriefing."

"What happens after that?" Louie asked.

Owen interrupted before Sammy could answer. "We have a special arrangement with the authorities on this side of the border. We turn the low-level fighters over to them for adjudication."

"What do they do with them?"

"There's a process for demobilizing former militia members. If they can be rehabilitated, eventually they'll return to their villages and go on with their lives."

"And if they can't?"

"It's not our country," Owen said, avoiding the question. "We can't accommodate long-term detainees. There's no choice but to let the locals sort it out."

"What about the high-level prisoners?"

Owen glanced at Sammy, waiting for him to respond.

"We haven't got any yet," Sammy explained. "We've had challenges pinpointing the location of the GLA's senior leadership."

One of the guards lifted a latch and opened the exterior door. Sammy led them all inside. It took a moment for Louie's eyes to adjust to the light. They were in a small room that smelled of urine and sweat, with a bare concrete floor. The interior walls were made of reinforced plywood lined with mesh wire. Against the far wall, Louie saw three doors. The two rooms on either end were holding cells. The middle room was used for questioning.

"We only have two detainees at the moment," Sammy explained. "One of our patrols picked them up a few days ago. They didn't put up a fight and have been willing to talk."

"Can I go in and see them?" Louie asked.

Sammy nodded. "The guards will bring them into the room once we're ready."

"I should be there too," Owen interjected.

"No," Sammy said unequivocally. "We can't risk having them see a white man here at the camp. It will raise too many questions. You can listen from the observation area." He pointed at a mesh screen built into the wall. "Besides, they don't speak English. You wouldn't understand them anyway."

Owen appeared to be pouting but didn't press the issue. Sammy opened the door and led Louie into the room while Owen waited outside. They spoke with the detainees for over an hour. Sammy served as the interpreter, since Louie struggled with the dialect. Owen was pacing outside the door when they finally finished and came outside.

"That seemed like a waste of time," he said when they came through the door.

"There could be more there than it seemed," Louie hinted.

"How's that? From what I heard of the translation, it didn't sound like these guys know much of anything about the recent GLA attacks," Owen said, challenging Louie's assertion.

"That's because they aren't fighters," Louie explained. "But that doesn't mean that they don't have useful information. They're middlemen in a protection racket. They make their money overseeing artisanal mining operations out in the jungle."

"You mean these jokers aren't even GLA?" Owen asked, confused.

Sammy shook his head. "They call themselves that to

intimidate the locals. It helps scare away the competition."

"Then you just wasted an hour interviewing two low-level criminals? How is that going to help you find your wife?" Owen asked.

"They still work for someone. But they don't know who," Louie explained. "Every week, a truck comes to their camp and picks up what these guys collect from the miners. In exchange for the minerals, the men in the truck leave money, food, and guns. That's all they know. These guys are at the very bottom of the food chain, but it must lead somewhere."

"If that's all you got out of them, then we're wasting our time," Owen said. "They aren't going to help you find Anna. We're better off going back to the capital and waiting for her captors to call back. I can bring in a trained negotiating team to run the show. They'll have a much better chance of getting Anna back safely instead of relying on those clowns in there."

Louie looked at Sammy, who offered a nod of encouragement. "We made a deal with them," he told Owen.

"What on earth are you talking about?" Owen said, throwing his hands in the air in frustration. "What kind of deal?"

"Their next exchange is scheduled to happen tomorrow. They agreed to lead us to the drop point so we can see how it all works. If everything goes as planned, I told them that we would let them go once we see what we need to see."

"Are you crazy?" Owen exploded. "We're less than a week away from the election, and you want to spend two days following these guys into the jungle on some wild goose chase?"

"We're leaving now," Sammy interrupted. "Otherwise, we won't get to their camp in time for the exchange."

"This is ridiculous. It's a complete waste of time," Owen blustered.

"Have you got a better idea?" Louie challenged. "You said yourself, the best chance we had to find Anna was coming here and working with Sammy. For once, you may have been right."

Owen paced the room, fidgety with frustration. "I can't allow this," he muttered, turning back to Louie. "You're putting everything at risk. Including your wife. There's no guarantee they won't lead you into the jungle, shoot you in the head, and leave you there to rot."

"I don't think that's going to happen," Louie replied calmly. "We're taking a squad of Sammy's soldiers for backup."

"In that case, I'm going too. I'm responsible for getting you back to the capital in one piece. So you're not going anywhere unless I'm with you."

Sammy frowned with disapproval at Owen's declaration. "That would be unwise," he said. "There isn't another white man within fifty miles of here. Your presence would compromise the entire mission. This is our one chance. We cannot afford any mistakes."

"You expect me to sit here at the camp, twiddling my thumbs, while you guys head off into the jungle following two small-time mineral smugglers?"

Louie glanced at his watch, then back at Owen. "We're leaving in fifteen minutes," he said, answering Owen's question. "We'll have radios and a satellite phone so that we can check back with you every few hours. You can monitor everything from the headquarters hut."

Louie nodded at Sammy, indicating that the plan was

settled. Sammy instructed the guards to escort the prisoners to the headquarters building. Owen stood defiantly, arms crossed, a scowl on his face, but he was unable to stop what was happening.

Twenty minutes later, Louie and Sammy were outside the headquarters, preparing to leave. A group of soldiers was busy loading the jeeps with food, water, and equipment, while the detainees were standing off to the side waiting for instructions. Sammy glanced at his watch and turned to Louie.

"We should go," he said.

Louie nodded in silent assent. Sammy whistled to his men, signaling for everyone to load the jeeps. One of the detainees sat in the front seat of the lead jeep, tasked with leading them to the meeting point. Owen stood silently on the veranda of the headquarters building, watching as the convoy rolled away.

They drove for nearly two hours, eventually stopping near where the men had been captured the week before. From there, the group moved by foot through the jungle, guided by the detainees to their encampment. When they entered the compound, Louie was shocked by what he saw. It was a crude shanty village of tin-roofed lean-tos and primitive tents made from tattered plastic tarps.

A dozen or so teenagers and young men milled around the camp, dressed in filthy jeans, rancid T-shirts, and flip-flops. The clothing hung loosely from their sinewy limbs, suggesting they got just enough food to keep them alive. No one seemed to pay any attention when their patrol moved into the camp. Apparently, they were accustomed to armed men suddenly appearing from the jungle.

Louie watched several of the young men carrying burlap sacks of rocks down into a shallow ravine where a stream snaked through the camp. At the water's edge, they busied themselves dumping the contents of the bags into wooden sieves. Then they poured buckets of water over the deposits to separate the valuable minerals from worthless rock and soil.

The detainees led Sammy and Louie over to the sturdiest-looking of the buildings. It had a raised floor made of wooden planks and was fenced off with chicken wire for security. A man armed with a rusted AK-47 was guarding the entrance. He nodded at his compatriots when they approached.

They exchanged a few words with the guard, presumably explaining the presence of the entourage. Then the guard stepped aside to let them enter. Sammy and Louie joined them in the building, which was piled high with heavy burlap sacks. One of the men tore open a bag and reached inside, pulling out a grayish-green chunk of rock. He handed it over to Sammy, who held it up to the light for Louie to see.

"Cobalt," Sammy murmured.

The detainee was chattering at Sammy in bursts of impenetrable dialect. Louie had trouble following the conversation and waited for a translation.

"He said that the truck comes once a week to pick up the bags of ore," Sammy explained. "That's when they get their payment."

"Do they know what happens to the shipments after that?" Louie asked.

Sammy translated the question. The man shook his head, leaving no doubt about his answer.

"Ask him if they work with anyone else," Louie instructed.

After the man gave what seemed like an overly complicated explanation, Sammy turned back to Louie. "He says that there are more camps like this one all over the area. The men who come each week to collect the ore claim to work for Daniel Odoki. But these guys swear that they've never seen him."

"But they believe that Daniel Odoki is alive?" Louie asked, incredulous.

The men understood what Louie was asking without translation. With a look of fear in their eyes, both of them nodded.

"When does the truck arrive for the next pickup?" Louie asked.

"Early tomorrow morning," Sammy said.

Louie stared at the bags of ore, thinking through their plan, then turned to Sammy. "Make sure that it's a normal delivery tomorrow, just like they always make. Remind them not to say anything about being captured or bringing us here to the camp. Tell them we won't interfere but that we'll be watching everything from nearby. If we see anything suspicious, we'll shut down the camp and take them back to the holding cells. But if everything goes without problems, they'll be free to go and carry on their business."

Sammy spoke to the men, reminding them about the terms of the deal. When he finished, they both looked at Louie and nodded.

"They understand," Sammy said. "There won't be any problems. This one said he would show us a safe place where we can watch without being seen."

"Good," Louie said. "We'll make camp here tonight and wait for the truck in the morning."

+++

The following day, Sammy's soldiers woke before daylight and moved away from the camp. In the twilight, they made breakfast over an open fire. Louie was too nervous to eat but gladly accepted a cup of tea offered in a tin mug. He had been awake most of the night, worried that they were wasting precious time by chasing leads that wouldn't take them to Anna. Louie tried his best to suppress the thought as he sat on a log, sipping his tea and watching the sunrise.

"It's time to move into position," Sammy said, joining him on the log and holding a fragrant mug of coffee.

"Do you trust them to go through with the plan?" Louie asked with worry.

Sammy nodded. "They have no loyalty to the GLA. For them, it's just a name. Something used to frighten the people. This is only about survival. They'll do whatever we ask if it means they can go back to business as usual."

"I hope it works," Louie said with a sigh. "Otherwise, it's been a waste of two days."

"Have faith, Mr. Louie," Sammy urged. "I promise we'll find Anna."

Louie could only hope his friend was right. He glanced at his watch and realized there wasn't time to finish his tea. He dumped it on the ground and followed Sammy through the woods in the direction of the camp. They came to a patch of dense vegetation on the edge of the compound and crawled into a shallow ditch that offered a good vantage point on the camp. Sammy nodded at the spot where the exchange would happen.

"The men said the workers will transfer the bags from the storage building once the truck arrives," he whispered.

"Then what happens?"

"The drivers inspect the samples and estimate the load's weight. They pay based on the quality and quantity of the ore."

"How do the miners know if they're getting a fair price?" Louie asked.

"Out here, they don't have much of a choice. The GLA control the entire network and set the prices without negotiation. It's a take it or leave it offer."

Louie and Sammy had been hiding in the bushes for nearly an hour when they heard the sound of a truck's engine through the trees. Louie flattened himself to the earth, his heart racing. When the vehicle appeared, the two men went out to greet it. Someone dressed in jungle fatigues and carrying a notebook jumped out of the truck's passenger side. Meanwhile, the driver backed the truck up to where the ore was stored. As soon as it stopped moving, the workers began loading heavy sacks into the back. The man with the notebook stopped one of the workers and ordered him to empty the bag onto the ground.

Louie glanced at Sammy, who was watching the entire scene unfold through a pair of mini-binoculars. Sammy saw the man from the truck sift through the pile of rock, picking out a few pieces and inspecting them. He said a few words to the other men, but Louie was too far away to hear the exchange. After their brief conversation, it seemed that everything was in order, and the workers continued loading the rest of the ore onto the truck.

Louie tried to remain calm as they slowly filled it to the top, finishing about thirty minutes later. The man with the notebook had been sitting in the cab of the truck, writing down figures. When he returned to the group, he handed over a dirty envelope to the men who ran the camp. The driver was already back in the truck, preparing to leave.

Louie and Sammy remained hidden until the sound of the truck's engine faded, then got up and rejoined the rest of the patrol. Sammy found the team's communications expert and told him to power up a satellite phone attached to a small laptop computer.

Louie watched impatiently as the soldier established a connection to the satellite. Next, he opened an application on the computer showing a map on the screen. Sammy was standing next to Louie, watching without a word. Both of them held their breath, waiting for something to happen.

A few seconds later, a single blue dot appeared on the map, moving slowly across the digital landscape. The soldier operating the computer looked up at Sammy and grinned.

"Sir, we've got a good signal. The transmitter is working," he announced.

Louie breathed a sigh of relief and smiled at Sammy.

"Let's get back to camp and see where they end up," Sammy told the team.

"General, what about the detainees?" one of the soldiers asked. "Should we bring them back with us?"

"No," Sammy said. "They held up their end of the deal. We'll do the same."

+++

They arrived back at the camp just before dinnertime. The soldiers began unloading the jeeps while Louie and Sammy went straight to the headquarters building. Owen was already there, waiting for them.

"Where the hell have you guys been?" he asked impatiently.

"What do you mean?" Louie shot back, already annoyed with him. "You know exactly where we've been. The communications team was sending back updates the entire time."

"You were gone almost fifteen hours," he grumbled. "I hope it was a good use of our time."

Louie ignored Owen and walked across the room to where the communications officer was hooking up the laptop to the satellite terminal. As the digital map came up on the screen, Louie held his breath, waiting for the blue dot to reappear. His mind raced with possible scenarios that might cause them to lose the signal, but then the transmitter's location appeared at the edge of the map.

Louie bent over the laptop, studying the map closely and thinking that he wasn't reading it correctly. "This can't be right," he muttered. "It looks like they've crossed the border back into DRoG."

"What are we looking at?" Owen interrupted, joining Louie and Sammy at the laptop.

"We hid a GPS tracker inside the shipment of ore," Louie explained.

"Where are the two detainees?" Owen asked.

"We let them go," Sammy muttered, also perplexed as he watched the blue dot slowly moving away from the border, deeper into DRoG.

"What the hell?" Owen said, staring at Sammy. "They were GLA fighters. We should have turned them over to the local authorities, per our standard operating procedure."

"They aren't GLA," Louie interjected. "They're low-level thugs running a protection racket. They don't know anything about the GLA or Daniel Odoki. They're just middlemen who shake down the local artisan miners and take a service fee for moving their product to market. Holding those guys doesn't do us any good. If we're going to find out who's at the top, we need to follow the product upstream."

"And what exactly is the product?" Owen asked.

"Copper-cobalt ore. But there aren't any processing facilities anywhere near the mining sites. They must be transporting the ore across the border then refining it somewhere inside DRoG," Louie speculated.

Sammy pointed to the area on the map where the truck had crossed the border back into DRoG. "Mr. Louie, there isn't an official border crossing in that area. They must be using roads that aren't on the map."

"Gentlemen," Owen interrupted. "This is all very interesting, but we don't have time to be researching a smuggling operation. The election is a few days away. If we aren't any closer to finding Anna, then our best option is getting back to the capital ASAP."

Louie looked at Sammy, waiting for his reaction. Sammy stared at the screen, ignoring Owen's suggestion.

"We're not going anywhere until we see where that truck stops," Louie said, once it was clear that Sammy was deferring to him. "It's our best chance of finding Anna."

"I just want to be sure that we understand each other," Owen said, staring straight at Louie. "I'm under strict orders to have you back across the border no less than twenty-four hours before the election. That's a firm time. No negotiation. If you insist on wasting your last few hours pursuing this goose chase, that's your decision. However, our timeline is final."

Louie ignored him and addressed the soldier monitoring the truck's location on the computer. "I'm going to clean up and grab something to eat," he said. "Please let me know when the truck stops moving."

The soldier nodded and turned back to the computer, his eyes following the blue dot as it continued across the map.

+++

Louie was the first to arrive in the dining hall, even before the sun crested the horizon. He didn't want to bother the cook, so he went back into the kitchen to heat water for his tea. While he was waiting for it to boil, Sammy appeared at the door.

"Good morning," Sammy said.

Louie nodded hello. "Cup of tea?" he offered.

Sammy smiled and chuckled. "You still don't have a taste for coffee, Mr. Louie?"

"Nothing personal, Sammy," Louie said, offering a smile in return.

"Did the communications officer wake you when the truck stopped moving?"

Louie nodded.

"What do you think?"

Louie poured some boiling water into a canteen and added the tea bag. "I think there's something that our friend isn't telling us," he answered.

"Mr. Owen?" Sammy asked, seeming unsurprised.

"He knows more about those shipments of ore crossing the border than he's letting on. That truck stopped at a processing plant a few hours outside the capital. The facility is probably a legitimate business; however, they are only permitted to process minerals extracted from inside the country."

"What are you suggesting, Mr. Louie?" Sammy asked, not seeing the connection.

"The people claiming to be GLA are not what they seem to be. It's not an insurgency. It's a cover for moving illegally mined cobalt across the border. I'm guessing that it's being processed and exported from DRoG under a legitimate license."

"Can you prove it?"

"Perhaps. May I use your satellite phone?" Louie asked. "I have a friend who may be able to help." Sammy handed over the phone as Louie glanced at his watch. "It's early, but we don't have time to waste."

Louie walked outside and pulled Janet's business card from his pocket. He dialed her secure phone number and waited. When he heard her sleepy voice, he could tell that he had woken her up.

"It's Louie Bigombe. I'm sorry for calling so early, but I need your help."

"Where are you?" Janet asked, still groggy. "Do you know that people are looking for you? Rumors are going around that you were kidnapped."

"I'm fine," Louie assured her. "I can't go into all the details right now. I'm at a camp across the border."

"The third force?" Janet asked, now wide awake, reaching for a notepad on her nightstand.

"Call it what you want."

"Are you with Owen Smith?"

"How else would I end up here?"

"Why did you agree to go with him?"

"It was the only way to find Anna," Louie replied.

"I think you're probably better off on your own," Janet warned.

"You may be right. But I met an old friend here at the camp. Someone I can trust."

"What do you want from me? And I'm assuming this is all off the record?"

"I need you to check on something for me," Louie said. "An industrial facility a few hours outside of the capital."

"You're kidding, right? We're less than a week from the election, and you expect me to waste an entire day driving out into the countryside to look at a factory?" Janet asked incredulously.

"I know it sounds like a wild goose chase, but it's urgent. I need you to go out there this morning," Louie explained.

"Oh, sure, I'll just drop everything and head right out there," Janet said, chuckling into the phone. "Do you have any idea how busy I've been since breaking the story on S3 Corp? I've hardly slept in days. Sekibo is on the defensive. He's dropping in the polls and refusing to do interviews. I'm in the middle of a huge story and you want me to disappear out into the boondocks?"

"Please," Louie begged. "This may be the only chance to find Anna."

"What on earth does this factory have to do with finding your wife?"

"I think something is going on there that may be linked to the people who kidnapped her. I can't explain it just yet, but I don't think the GLA is what it claims to be."

"Then what are they?" Janet asked skeptically.

"I don't know what to call them. A crime syndicate, I suppose." Louie paused, then explained, "Yesterday, we tracked a truckload of copper-cobalt ore from an illegal mining camp moving back across the border into DRoG. The shipment ended up at this factory."

"Minerals are smuggled across that border all the time," Janet argued. "That story is not going to be news to anyone."

"But this isn't some small-time operation. It's being co-ordinated at a higher level, operating throughout the GLA's sanctuary area. I also think Owen Smith knows more about it than he's letting on."

"Without knowing any details, I would say that's a safe assumption," Janet agreed. "But I still can't just drop everything and drive out there. I don't even know what I'm supposed to be looking for."

"Please!" Louie begged. "I just need to know what's going on there and who's running it. If I'm right about this, it could turn into a big story. You'll have the scoop."

"What are you going to be doing while I'm driving out to this factory?"

"We'll keep looking for Anna on this side of the border. We have patrols searching the area where we got the last signal from her cell phone."

Janet went quiet. Louie waited, giving her time to respond.

"Send me the coordinates for the factory," she finally said.

"I just sent a text with what you need," he replied as soon as she said the words.

Louie heard Janet sigh on the other end of the line. "I'll do my best," she said. "But I'm not staying out there all night. I'll get my driver to take me out this morning for a quick look, but that's it. In the meantime, I can have my local stringer do some digging through the public records to find out who owns the factory."

"Thank you," Louie whispered, feeling not only grateful but also somewhat surprised that she had agreed.

"How do I contact you if I find something?" Janet asked.

"I'm calling on a satellite phone. I'll send you the number, and you can call me on this line."

"Good luck," she said.

"Same to you."

CHAPTER ELEVEN

After hanging up with Janet, Louie started walking back to the headquarters building. He was halfway across the yard when his cell phone began vibrating. He glanced at the screen and felt a chill run up his spine. It was Anna's number on the caller ID. Louie fumbled with the phone, almost dropping it in his haste to answer.

"Anna!" he yelled.

"Your wife is still with us," a man's voice answered. "But there's no need for her to speak."

Louie recognized the voice as belonging to the same man who had called after Anna's disappearance.

"Put her on the phone, or I'm hanging up," he demanded.

"Colonel Bigombe, you are in no position to dictate the terms of our discussion. We have something you want. Therefore, we are the ones who make the rules."

"Who are you working for?"

"You are wasting precious time. We are the GLA, and we answer to our commander, Daniel Odoki."

"That's nonsense. The GLA doesn't exist, and Daniel Odoki is dead. Tell me who you are," Louie pressed.

"You are playing games with her life," the man warned.

"If you want to see your wife again, listen very closely. You failed to meet our demands. Your name is still on the ballot."

"I told you, I can't get it off. The entire election is a sham. I never wanted to run in the first place," Louie insisted. "There's nothing more I can do."

"It's too late for excuses," the man said sternly. "You have twenty-four hours. If your name is not off the ballot by then, you'll never see her again. Do you understand?"

"I told you, there's nothing more I can do."

"Then what happens to her is your responsibility," the man said before the line went dead.

Louie held the phone to his ear, not believing the call had ended. When he realized what had happened, he threw his phone and screamed in anger. A few soldiers standing nearby witnessed the outburst and exchanged nervous glances before quickly moving on. Louie was standing there, not knowing what to do, when Owen came rushing out of the headquarters building.

"We got it," he yelled, waving a sheet of paper in the air.

"What are you talking about?" Louie called back, worried, annoyed, and in no mood to deal with him.

"A trace on the call. It came from a village less than an hour from here."

"You've been intercepting my phone calls all this time?"

"You're kidding, right? Of course we listen to your calls. Who the hell do you think I work for?" Owen asked rhetorically.

"I should have listened to Patrick," Louie muttered, angry at himself for forgetting his friend's advice.

"The important thing is that we got a fix on the signal from Anna's phone. I'm putting a drone up now. We should have eyes over the target in less than thirty minutes."

"Then what?"

"We'll assess the situation before making a move. Go find Sammy and meet me in the command center," Owen said, turning on his heel and heading back into the building.

A few minutes later, the three of them were huddled around a computer screen, watching a live video feed from a small drone flying toward the coordinates.

"What if the drone tips them off?" Louie asked, suddenly worried that things were moving too quickly.

"No way," Owen assured him. "It's a tactical drone, small and quiet. We're flying high enough that no one on the ground will have any idea we're overhead."

A soldier at a different computer called for Owen's attention. He was monitoring the data feeds from the drone's onboard sensors and pointed at something on the screen.

"What is it?" Louie asked.

"We picked up a ping from Anna's cell phone," Owen explained. "Someone must have left it turned on after making the call. We should be able to get a good location from the signal."

A few minutes later, the drone passed over a clearing in the forest. A few scattered huts were located at a crossroads, virtually indistinguishable from any other settlement in the area. The flight controller put the drone into a circular pattern over the target. Down below, they could see two jeeps parked under some trees but no other signs of activity. The soldier at the computer turned to Owen and motioned at the screen.

"Sir, that building is where the phone signal is coming from," he said, pointing to a hut on the far edge of the clearing.

Owen glanced over at Sammy. "General, what do make of this? Is it actionable?"

Sammy studied the image on the screen as the drone circled above the camp. "Maybe," he said. "But we need time to plan an operation. It's too dangerous to go in during daylight. The earliest we could move on the target would be after sundown. But I want to know who's down there first. The camp looks empty, but there could be GLA nearby."

"We have three small drones, each with about three to four hours of endurance," Owen said. "We'll put them into a rotation over the target until you're ready to move. That should give us an idea of what we're up against." He turned to Louie. "It's your wife down there. We won't make a move unless you're comfortable with the decision. You get the final call if you think something looks fishy."

Louie looked at Sammy. "Is this something your men can handle?" he asked his old friend.

Sammy nodded.

Louie took a deep breath. "Let's get the team into position. We'll wait until sundown, then reassess the situation. I only have one condition."

Owen was quiet, waiting to hear the terms.

"If Anna's down there, I want to be with the team when they go through the door."

It was clear from Owen's expression that he didn't like the idea, but he reluctantly assented, knowing that Louie wouldn't change his mind.

"I'll get the men ready," Sammy said, heading for the door.

"Thank you," Louie said, grateful to have his old friend there.

"I'll stay here with the drone team to monitor the situation on the ground," Owen said. "We'll give you an update on the target before you leave."

Louie nodded and followed Sammy outside to gather their team for the mission.

+++

As twilight fell, Louie lay flat on his stomach, hidden inside a dense thicket of vegetation. He scanned the horizon with a night-vision scope that cast everything in an eerie greenish tint. Sammy lay a few inches away, watching his soldiers move into position around the edge of the clearing. The conditions for the operation were nearly perfect: a moonless night with a thin layer of clouds overhead.

They had been watching the settlement for over an hour without seeing any sign of activity. Louie focused on the building where the cell phone signal was coming from. Through cracks in the window shutters, they could see a dim light inside the hut. Earlier, the drone had spotted several armed men wandering around the camp, but they had left in the jeeps and now were nowhere to be seen.

Louie pushed the button on his radio and whispered into the microphone, "Command base, this is patrol leader. Do you see anything from overhead?"

He had the radio volume turned low and was using an

earpiece to ensure that the sound wouldn't tip off anyone nearby.

"Negative, patrol leader," Owen's voice came back over the radio. "Nothing since the jeeps left. We can see your men around the perimeter on the infrared camera, but no other signs of activity around the target. We've still got a good signal on Anna's cell phone, as well as a heat source coming from inside the building."

"Can you estimate the number of occupants based on the heat source?" Louie asked.

"Negative. All we can tell is that there's something warm inside."

Louie glanced at Sammy, who had been listening to the conversation on his radio. "What do you think?" he whispered.

"We need to try," Sammy said. "We've come too far to go without knowing if she's there."

Louie nodded his agreement but felt his stomach tighten at the thought of what would happen next. For the first time, he questioned his decision to join the patrol, uncertain if he was ready for what they might find inside. He took a deep breath, trying to calm his nerves, then locked eyes with Sammy.

"Let's do it," he whispered.

Sammy signaled his squad leaders to advance into the final positions from which they would launch the raid. Once he received confirmation that they were in place, he turned back to Louie.

"The teams are ready," he said. "We move on your command."

Louie took one last look through his night-vision scope, hoping for some sign that they were making the right decision, but nothing had changed. Nothing reassured him that things would turn out all right. Louie put down the scope and pressed the transmit button on his radio.

"Command base, this is the patrol leader. The teams are in position and prepared to initiate the operation."

There was a moment of silence, followed by the sound of Owen's voice. "Affirmative, patrol leader. We'll be watching from overhead. Good luck."

Louie gave Sammy a thumbs-up, letting him know that it was time to move. Sammy passed the signal on to his team leaders. On either side of the line, the men rose like ghosts from the jungle floor. They advanced to the edge of the clearing without a sound, their feet seeming to float above the ground. At the edge of the woods, they stopped, just as they had rehearsed. Advancing any further would expose them to observation by anyone inside the settlement.

The men held their places, looking and listening. It was a final chance to detect unexpected danger before crossing the point of no return. The jungle sounds were amplified in Louie's ears. He could hear every creature creeping through the leaves and the sound of bats' wings flapping overhead, as if the entire forest had exploded in a cacophony of activity.

With no sign of activity inside the camp, Sammy ordered his men forward. The fire teams moved quickly into the open clearing, alternating positions and providing cover while the other teams advanced. Within seconds, they had crossed the empty yard and surrounded the target, waiting for the final command to move inside.

Sammy glanced at Louie, giving him one last chance to call off the mission. Both of them knew that once the order was delivered, there was no turning back. Louie closed his eyes and told himself that there was no other option. He nodded at his friend. Sammy pressed the transmit button on his radio twice in quick succession. Seconds later, two soldiers charged at the door with a handheld battering ram, tearing it from its hinges. Four more men rushed through the gap, weapons at the ready.

Louie held his breath, waiting for staccato bursts of automatic gunfire, but there was only silence. The next thing they heard was the voice of the assault team leader on the radio reporting that the building was secure. The other squad quickly established a perimeter around the clearing's edge while a third assault team searched the other buildings in the compound.

Louie and Sammy sprinted through the clearing toward the hut. The soldiers were still searching the room when they stepped through the door. The team leader spotted them and went straight to Louie with an update.

"I'm sorry, sir. She's not here. This was all we found," he said, handing Louie a cell phone. "The heat signature we picked up from the drone was from some old coals in the fire pit," he explained, pointing to a hole dug into the dirt floor filled with hot rocks and smoldering embers.

Louie stared at the phone, realizing what must have happened. He punched in Anna's security code to unlock the device. Someone had set the forwarding option to send incoming calls to Louie's cell phone. He checked the phone's call log and saw that the last call had come through at the same time that Anna's captor had called him that morning.

"They wanted us to come here," Louie muttered, staring at Anna's phone. "They must have known we would trace the call."

As Louie spoke, Anna's phone began vibrating. Sammy's eyes grew wide as he too stared at the phone and figured out what had happened. Someone had been observing their entire operation from the start. Louie let the phone ring several times before answering.

"You've proven that you can't be trusted," the now-familiar voice said.

"I want my wife back."

"The terms of our deal were clear. You were instructed to withdraw from the election. After that, she would have been returned unharmed. But your actions have invalidated our agreement. We're no longer playing games."

"I've told you, there's no way I can give you what you want," Louie pleaded. "If I could, I would."

"The time for negotiation is over. If you want your wife back, there is only one way."

"Tell me what you want."

"An exchange. Your wife in return for you," the man said.

"Where and when?"

"You will receive a call with instructions. She will be released once you have fulfilled your end of the bargain."

"How do I know you'll do it?"

"You should have thought about that before going to your American friends for help. Now we are the ones setting the rules. If you comply, your wife will be released."

"When will you call?"

"You will receive instructions soon. Goodbye, Colonel Bigombe."

The line went dead. Sammy had overheard the entire conversation and put his hand on Louie's shoulder. "Don't worry, Mr. Louie. I know we'll get her back."

Louie shook his head, unable to share his friend's confidence. "If I don't come back, promise me that you'll find her."

Sammy nodded.

"Let's get back to camp," Louie said, feeling defeated. "There's nothing more we can do here."

+++

It was after midnight when the patrol returned to base. Louie was wide awake, still riding the adrenaline rush from earlier in the evening. He went straight to the mess hall, hoping that a cup of decaf tea would calm his nerves. The kitchen was closed, so he turned on the lights and lit the butane stove to heat some water. When his tea was ready, Louie sat down at a table and stared through the mosquito netting into the darkness. He had just taken his first sip when he heard someone outside. Owen came through the door and joined Louie at the table.

"I saw the light on and figured it was you," Owen said.

"I needed to something to settle my stomach."

"I'm sorry you didn't find her."

"Are you?" Louie snapped.

Owen sighed and shook his head. "I'm not as bad as you think. Believe it or not, I didn't come here to ruin your life."

"Maybe that's not what you intended, but you're sure doing a fine job of it. I suppose I'm just collateral damage in your big plan."

"I was sent here to do a job. That's what I'm doing," Owen said without emotion. "However, that doesn't mean I'm not sorry about what happened to Anna. I know you didn't ask for any of this. But you need to understand that what's going on here is bigger than you and me."

"Do you guys ever think about the people who get caught up in your schemes?" Louie asked.

"Of course we do. But sometimes, it's a matter of the greatest good for the greatest number. But given our present situation, I can understand why it's hard to focus on that calculation. I'm still confident that we're doing the right thing. If Emanuel Sekibo comes to power, everyone will pay the price."

"It's interesting that you're so intent on keeping him out of Green House, yet you didn't seem to mind the thirty years that President Namono was sitting there," Louie pointed out. "Things were bad then too, but you went along with whatever he did."

"Mistakes were made. But you need to put it into context," Owen argued.

"You're telling *me* to put it into context?" Louie exploded. "This isn't even your country. You weren't even born when Namono came to power. Precisely what context do you think that I'm overlooking?"

"I'm talking about the larger geopolitical environment. The Cold War was still going on when Namono came to power. We were dealing with an existential threat to the global order."

"You think that propping up Namono for all those years made a difference in the end?" Louie asked incredulously.

"The Cold War was won on the margins. DRoG played a vital role in slowing the expansion of Soviet-backed communism," Owen said defensively.

"And my father dying for the cause was a critical element in that historic victory?" Louie asked, dismissing Owen's interpretation of history.

Owen didn't reply. Instead, he reached into his backpack and pulled out a heavy-duty document bag. He unlocked the zipper and placed the contents on the table: a thick manila envelope double-taped around the seams. Owen pushed it across the table and gestured for Louie to open it.

"What's that?"

"Your father's file," Owen said.

Louie stared at it, uncertain whether he should believe anything Owen was saying.

"Let me tell you, it was a pain in the ass getting authorization to release this. But after everything that's happened, we felt we owed it to you."

"How generous," Louie said, rolling his eyes.

"Of course, you'll find that some of the names have been redacted. Several individuals are still in public life. Revelations of their previous activities and associations with the agency could be damaging for them and us. However, I think you can read between the lines and guess most of the players."

Louie narrowed his eyes. "Why should I believe anything you say? How do I know this isn't another elaborate hoax, just like my campaign?"

"You're right," Owen conceded. "It could all be fake. I have no way of proving it to you. But I think what's in there may confirm some things that you've already suspected. However, I need to warn you, some of it isn't pretty."

Louie took the envelope, unsealed the tape, and pulled out the files. There was a thick stack of scanned records, copies of handwritten notes, and a few photographs. On the inside flap was a picture of his father: an official photo from his Army personnel file. Louie had never seen it before, and his heart was pounding as he held it in his hands. He fought back tears, overcome with emotion at seeing his father as a young man. He was tall and strong, dressed in a pair of starched combat fatigues, just as Louie remembered him.

"I'll leave it here for you to read," Owen said. "Unfortunately, I'll need to have it back. I can give you an hour."

He rose from his seat and turned to leave. At the door, he stopped and looked back. "I don't suppose I can convince you not to go forward with the exchange?"

Louie looked up from the file and glared at Owen.

"I'll take that as a no," Owen said. "I'll be back in an hour for the file."

He headed for the door, leaving Louie alone with his reading.

CHAPTER TWELVE

Louie fell asleep with his phone propped against the pillow, afraid of missing the call from Anna's captors. He had tried staying awake but had eventually given in to exhaustion. When the call came, he shot up in bed and grabbed the phone. The unlisted number on the screen left Louie with no doubt about who was calling.

"Listen carefully," the familiar voice instructed.

"Go ahead."

"There's an abandoned village a few miles from where you were last night. The locals can tell you how to find it. You need to be there at nine o'clock this morning."

"That's not much time," Louie said, glancing at his watch.

"This is not a negotiation. You need to be there, or the deal is off. When you arrive, you'll find a clearing and some old huts. At the north end of the village is a grove of palm trees. Go there and wait for instructions."

"Who do I look for?"

"You'll receive instructions when you arrive. You must come alone. If we see anyone else, we'll consider the deal broken, and your wife stays with us. No cell phone, no trackers, and no tricks. Do you understand?"

"Yes," Louie whispered. "But how do I know you'll keep your end of the bargain? What guarantee do I have that Anna will be released?"

"Your decisions have brought us to this point," the man said. "You have no one to blame but yourself. This is the only option left. You may take it or leave it. The choice is yours."

Louie took a deep breath, knowing there was nothing to be gained by arguing. "I'll be there."

"Nine o'clock. Come alone," the man reminded him before hanging up.

Louie dropped the phone and fell into his bunk. He lay there, staring up into the mosquito netting. Outside the window, he saw the first glow of sunrise on the horizon. It was too early to call Janet, but Louie realized that he might not have another chance. He reached into his backpack for the satellite phone and dialed Janet's number. She sounded groggy when she answered.

"It's Louie. I'm sorry to call so early, but I don't have much time," he explained.

"I didn't get back until after midnight from the errand you sent me on," she said, sounding grumpy.

"Did you find anything out?"

"There wasn't much to see. It's a big factory surrounded by fences and armed guards. I couldn't get close without attracting attention."

"Was there anything unusual about it?"

"I didn't think so until I got back home and exchanged notes with my stringer," Janet said. "While I was on the road, he was digging into the company's financial records. I think he found some discrepancies."

"What do you mean, discrepancies?"

"To begin with, it's not clear how the factory makes a profit. It processes raw ore, extracts the mineral concentrates, then exports them out of the country for refining. But that stuff is the low-margin part of the business. The real money comes up the supply chain when they refine the concentrates into high-grade chemicals and alloys."

"But you said that the factory is turning a profit?" Louie asked, confused by Janet's explanation.

"Yes. Far more than it should, given the small amount of raw ore mined inside DRoG. Three years ago, the company was on the verge of bankruptcy. But starting last year, there was a big uptick in their numbers."

"Did mineral prices go up?"

"Yes, but not enough to explain the sudden spike in profits. The company's most recent financial reporting statement showed a significant increase in exports, even though there haven't been any new mines opened anywhere in DRoG. It's almost as if the stuff has been falling from the sky."

"Or being moved illegally across the border," Louie said, seeing the connection. "That explains what we saw inside that camp. The GLA has been smuggling raw cobalt into DRoG and processing it for export. But where's it going?"

"That's no secret," Janet said. "Over the last few years, China has locked up the entire supply chain coming out of DRoG. They have exclusive contracts with all the major extractors. They can't make smartphones and electric cars without batteries, and that means a huge demand for cobalt."

"You sound like an expert," Louie said, impressed by her command of the information.

"Hardly," Janet snorted. "What I just told you represents the entirety of what I learned about cobalt mining during a long taxi ride back home last night."

"Anything else?"

"Just a few other things. The holding company that owns the factory is also a partner in the deal to rebuild the railroad line out to Kiskow."

"What do you make of that?"

"I don't know yet, but there's a connection between all the projects," Janet hinted.

"Emanuel Sekibo," Louie guessed.

"All of these schemes are under contract with S3 Corp for security," she said, confirming his suspicion. "Sekibo has locked up the protection racket for every single project."

"In that case, Sekibo must know that the minerals going to that factory have been smuggled across the border."

"I would assume so," Janet said.

"Can you keep digging into this?"

"Don't worry; I intend to. But since we seem to be working collaboratively, do you mind telling me where you are and what you're doing?"

Louie hesitated. "I'm sorry, I can't go into the details."

"When are you coming back to the capital?"

"I don't know."

"What do you mean, you don't know?" Janet asked, flabbergasted. "The election is less than forty-eight hours away! Have you seen the recent polling?"

"No. I've been busy."

"Then let me fill you in. You're neck and neck with Sekibo."

"This is crazy," Louie muttered.

"Your noncampaign has turned into the real thing."

"I'm about to see my campaign manager. I'll be sure to congratulate him on the numbers," Louie said sarcastically. "I'm sorry I can't tell you more about what's going on, but if you find out anything more about the factory, will you let me know right away?"

"I'll do my best. Just don't ask me to drive out there again. That place stinks to high heaven."

"What do you mean?" Louie asked, surprised that she hadn't mentioned it before.

"I mean the place *stinks*, like sulfur or something. It must be from processing the ore. Why?"

"Anna said the same thing when I spoke with her right after the kidnapping. She was sedated and not making sense, so I didn't think about it at the time. But I remember her saying something about burning matches."

"Yeah, that's exactly what it smelled like. Do you think you've been looking for her in the wrong place?"

"I'm starting to think so," Louie said. He glanced at his watch and saw that he was running out of time. "I've got to go, but I need you to do one last thing. I'm going to text you instructions to find something that I buried in my backyard."

"Now you're sending me on a treasure hunt?" Janet sounded amused.

"Please, this is serious. It's information that Patrick gave me before he was killed. There are some notes inside explaining everything he told me. It may help you make connections between Sekibo, the bombings, and the election. I don't have time to explain, but I'm the only one who knows where it is. I'd feel better if you had it."

"OK, I'll get it. I know you aren't going to tell me what you're doing, but please be careful anyway," Janet said, sensing the anxiety in his voice.

"You too," Louie replied, and ended the call.

+++

After hanging up with Janet, Louie walked over to the command center. Owen was sitting at the table and tapping at his watch as if scolding a tardy pupil.

"Please, sit down. We don't have much time, and we need to go over the plan," he said.

"First, I have some questions," Louie said, ignoring the empty chair, preferring to stand.

"Your call." Owen shrugged. "I'm just trying to help you get your wife back. Trust me, none of these distractions are making my job any easier."

"Really?" Louie snapped. "I suppose I should be grateful for all you've done. For orchestrating the bogus election campaign. For getting my best friend killed and my wife kidnapped."

"You can't blame all that on me," Owen said, straight-faced. "Sekibo would have gotten to you sooner or later."

"Why? You mean because of what was in my father's file?"

"That's part of it. But there's more you don't know."

Louie snorted. "Why should I believe anything you say? You haven't told the truth from the first day I met you. This was never about defeating the GLA. You knew all along that it was nothing but a hoax."

"That's true, but only to a point," Owen argued. "The

GLA may not be what they claim to be, but that doesn't make the threat any less real. General B- and the rest of them don't see the big picture. They're too busy fighting the last war, seeing terrorists lurking around every corner. Meanwhile, they've missed the real danger right in front of their faces."

"So, your job is fighting the real war while your army is busy fighting a fake one? Is that what this third force was all about? An excuse to keep an eye on the Chinese? If it weren't for them, would you even give a damn who wins this election?" Louie asked.

"You should care about who wins as much as we do," Owen said, jabbing a finger accusingly at Louie. "Sekibo has been in bed with Beijing from the start. If he wins the election, they'll be the ones calling the shots in Green House."

"Is that any different than what your side was doing all those years with President Namono?"

"Don't be naive! The Chinese don't give a damn about anyone in this country."

"And you do?"

Owen shook his head and chuckled. "China wants nothing more from DRoG than to suck out every last resource from under your feet: lithium, cobalt, copper, rare earth elements. You name it, and Beijing is trying to corner the market on it. For the last twenty years, the US has been wasting blood and treasure fighting endless wars against two-bit jihadis. Meanwhile, all that time, Beijing has kept its eye on the real prize. We've got to get back in the game before it's too late."

"Even if what you say is true, there's no way you're going to stop it," Louie argued.

"That's where you're wrong," Owen said, slapping his hand on the table. "Emanuel Sekibo can't be allowed to come to power."

"What if that's what the people decide?"

"He's not what he seems," Owen insisted, ignoring Louie's question. "His campaign is a Trojan horse. Once you let Beijing in through the gate, there's no going back."

"I assume that's what you told my father during the border wars. That the world's fate depended on him holding some arbitrary line drawn through an empty jungle. How is this any different? In the end, it's the people here who suffer."

"We don't have time to debate ancient history," Owen said, tapping his watch again to emphasize the point. "If you want your wife back, we need to move now. I've got two vehicles waiting outside. Sammy will drive you to a drop point near the village. From there, you can walk the rest of the way. We'll have eyes on you the entire time."

"The man said no cell phones or trackers," Louie said, then realized that Owen probably already knew that from listening in on the phone call.

"Don't worry. You'll go in clean. But we'll have surveillance overhead. They'll be high enough that you won't even know they're around."

"Then what?"

"Hopefully, you'll lead us to Daniel Odoki."

Louie rolled his eyes. "You know as well as I do that there's no Daniel Odoki. Why is it so important for you to find whoever's claiming his identity?"

"Because Sekibo has something planned, and we're running out of time to figure it out. We know that someone calling himself Daniel Odoki has been working for Sekibo. He's been running the GLA as a false flag operation. The reincarnation of Odoki was the perfect foil for Sekibo's campaign."

"But that doesn't explain why I became a target," Louie observed.

"At first, we didn't see the connection either," Owen admitted. "But then we came across something that helped put it all together and explain why this person pretending to be Daniel Odoki had a personal interest in your campaign."

Owen pushed a red folder across the table.

"What is it?" Louie asked, hesitant to touch it.

"It's a voice analysis from the GLA's shortwave radio broadcasts. The person claiming to be Odoki has been communicating with his followers using a series of mobile radio stations," Owen explained. "When he first appeared on the scene last year, we started getting suspicious, since we knew that the real Daniel Odoki has been dead for years."

"Even before the drone strike during Operation Brushfire," Louie pointed out.

"We don't need to get into that; however, you are correct," Owen confirmed. "The real Daniel Odoki has been gone for a very long time. But that hasn't stopped warlord wannabes from co-opting his legend when advantageous. That was true during Operation Brushfire, and it seems to be the case now."

"Why bring a dead man back to life?"

Owen shrugged. "Odoki's name carries a certain mystique. If people believe he's still alive, that's a useful fiction."

"That makes no sense," Louie protested. "Why would

Sekibo need to bring back the ghost of Odoki to get what he wants?”

“Everyone needs a foil. When Sekibo decided to run for president, he needed something to run against. Nothing wins votes like fear.”

“But I still don’t see how this relates to me.”

“It’s all in there,” Owen said, tapping his finger on the folder.

Louie reluctantly reached for the folder and opened it to the cover page. He skimmed over the technical data, going straight to the analytical summary at the bottom of the page. After reading it twice, he took a deep breath and closed the report.

“Why didn’t you tell me before?” he asked.

“Would it have made a difference?”

Louie shrugged, uncertain he knew the answer.

“Of course, it’s obvious once you think about it,” Owen continued. “Daniel Odoki reemerged around the same time that your uncle disappeared. After the failed coup attempt, Mugaba was a wanted man. All his assets were frozen, and he was on a worldwide travel watchlist. If he had gotten onto a plane or fled to another country, he would have been arrested. It’s not surprising that he would want a new identity.”

“But why Odoki?” Louie asked. “Pretending to be a famous warlord is not the way to avoid attention. Besides, my uncle was never close to Sekibo. Why would he agree to work with him?”

“Maybe you can ask him that when you see him. I’m guessing Mugaba saw it as his only chance to reclaim his old life. If Sekibo wins the election, he will have the power to pardon your uncle. Mugaba could return home a free man instead of living out the rest of his days in exile, hiding in the jungle."

Louie closed his eyes and massaged his temples, dismayed to feel yet another headache coming on. "None of this makes sense," he mumbled. "Would you have told me the truth about this if it hadn't come to this point?"

"Would it have changed your feelings about running against Sekibo?" Owen countered. "Your uncle tried to frame you for the attempted assassination of President Namono. I don't think he has your best interests in mind."

"He's still my uncle. I deserved to know the truth."

"Was the last time you saw him on the day Green House burned?"

Louie nodded.

"In that case, I'm guessing that the two of you probably have some unfinished business to discuss."

"Was this the plan from the start? To get me here to confront him?"

"You're kidding, right?" Owen chuckled. "There was no plan. This has been a pickup game from the start. I've been making this up as I go along."

"How reassuring."

"It's my first field assignment," Owen said with a shrug. He glanced at his watch, then back at Louie. "We're running out of time. Are you in or out?"

"Do I have a choice?"

"Probably not," Owen said, seeming almost apologetic. "The General is waiting outside. I'll be here at the command center monitoring the operation."

"What am I supposed to do?"

"Find your uncle. Figure out what Sekibo has planned. Then convince Mugaba to turn against his boss. Piece of cake."

Louie shook his head in disgust. "I'm starting to see why China is eating your lunch," he said, sneering at Owen.

"Just do your best," Owen shot back, pointing at the door.

+++

Out in the yard, the convoy of jeeps was waiting with their engines running. A squad of camouflaged soldiers was in the first two vehicles, and Sammy was in the driver's seat of the trailing jeep. Louie walked over to it and climbed into the empty passenger seat. Sammy smiled at him.

"Are you ready, Mr. Louie?"

"I suppose so," Louie said without conviction.

Sammy gave a thumbs-up out the window, signaling to the lead vehicle that it was time to go. The convoy disappeared down the road in a cloud of dust. They drove for a while in silence. Louie was exhausted and needed sleep, but the rutted road made it impossible. After an hour, they came to an intersection. Sammy turned to Louie and nodded at the spot.

"The place we'll leave you is just ahead. From there, it's a short walk to the village," he explained.

"What will you do?"

"Go back to the headquarters. Don't worry, Mr. Louie, the drone is already watching," Sammy said, pointing up at the roof.

"I'm not worried about me," Louie replied. After a moment of silence, he said, "Can I ask you a question?"

"Of course."

"Why did you come back?"

Sammy's eyes remained fixed on the road as he thought before answering. Finally, he said,

"It was too hard to do business with all the rules and inspections—lots of taxes and complications. The spoiled American teenagers were always showing up late for work, then asking to leave early. Oh, and the traffic in America!" Sammy griped. "Everyone is in a hurry but going nowhere. I spent all of my time sitting in the car."

Louie detected ambivalence in Sammy's voice. "Was that the only reason?"

Sammy chuckled, embarrassed that he was so transparent. "I was homesick," he admitted. "Then, one day, a man came into the cafe and said he had a job for me back here, offering me a chance to do something good for our country."

"Did he tell you what that was?"

"No. They never tell you the whole story," Sammy said.

"Was it worth it, coming back?"

Sammy stared through the window into the cloud of dust from the other jeeps. "I don't know yet," he said. "But I do know that Sekibo is a bad man. If I can help stop him, then I've done what I can do."

"Do you trust Owen?"

Sammy smiled and gave Louie a conspiratorial wink, with no need for words.

"Me neither," Louie said. "I don't know what's going to happen after you drop me off. But there's something I need you to do."

"Of course, Mr. Louie. Anything."

Louie pulled an envelope from inside his jacket and placed it on the dashboard. "If they don't let Anna go, promise me that you'll keep trying to find her."

"If they have you, why would they need to keep her?"

"I don't know. But I have a bad feeling about this. Inside the envelope are the coordinates for the factory back across the border in DRoG. I think that's where they're holding her. But don't tell Owen. I need you to do this on your own."

Sammy nodded. "Anything else?"

"There's also a letter in the envelope. If I don't come back, please give it to Anna."

Sammy nodded again.

Five minutes later, the convoy pulled over to the side of the road.

"This is the place," Sammy said, pointing at a dirt path leading off into the jungle. "It's about a ten-minute walk from here to the village."

Louie placed his cell phone on the dashboard and went through his pockets one last time, making sure he wasn't carrying anything that could be deemed suspicious. Then he reached out for Sammy's hand.

"Thank you for your help," he said. "You're the only one left I can trust."

They shook hands, and Louie got out of the jeep. He closed the door behind him and waited until the convoy disappeared down the road. Once the dust settled, Louie broke into a jog, following the path toward the village.

CHAPTER THIRTEEN

Louie had jogged just under a mile when the trail opened up into a clearing. Ahead was the abandoned village. He paused before stepping into the open, glancing reflexively at the sky and wondering if they could see him back at the headquarters. As soon as he had done it, Louie realized his mistake and scolded himself for being so foolish. He prayed that no one had been watching, then stepped beyond the trees into the open.

The village was nothing more than a few dilapidated huts, a collapsed water well, and some vegetable gardens overgrown with weeds. Feral chickens pecked around the yard, ruling over the remains of the settlement. At the far end of the clearing, Louie spotted the palm grove that the caller had described.

Louie checked his watch and saw that there were only a few minutes until the deadline. He stood in the shade of the palm grove and soon heard the sound of an engine through the trees. A white Toyota Hilux sped down the road in his direction and skidded to a stop nearby. Two men dressed in jungle camouflage and ski masks exited the cab.

One man was waving a pistol in the air and moved straight for Louie. When he was a few feet away, he motioned for Louie to turn around and spread his arms and legs. Louie complied as the man patted him down and searched his pockets, even feeling down inside his boots. All that he found was a few sheets of paper in one of Louie's pockets. The man briefly glanced over the pages, then stuffed them into his fatigues.

Once he was satisfied that Louie was clean, the man removed Louie's watch and slipped some plastic zip-tie restraints over his wrists. He tightened them down until they pinched Louie's skin, then pointed to the back of the truck. A burlap tarp covered the bed. The man yanked it off, revealing a dirty blanket spread out over the metal floorboards.

Louie climbed inside, and the man pulled the tarp back over the truck bed, then tied it down. Gaps around the edge let in a little bit of light and air to breathe. Louie heard the man get back inside the truck while the driver started the engine, but they didn't move. Louie lay on the hard metal, wondering what would happen next.

+++

Back at the headquarters building, Owen studied the video feed from the drone's camera as it circled high above the abandoned village. He could see the pickup truck idling on the edge of the palm grove and had just watched Louie climb inside. Sammy came through the door and joined Owen at the video screen.

"Any problems with the drop?" Owen asked him.

Sammy shook his head. "What's happening?"

"Louie is handcuffed and lying under a tarp in the back of that truck," Owen said calmly.

"What are they doing?"

"I have no idea," Owen admitted. "They've been sitting there for almost twenty minutes."

As he spoke, the truck started moving. Owen turned to the soldier operating the drone. "They're on the move," he said, unnecessarily. "Keep on them."

The soldier was already making the necessary adjustments to the drone's track, keeping the truck in the center of the picture. Owen and Sammy watched as the vehicle began driving in a slow circular pattern around the village. The tires rolling over the dry dirt created a cloud of dust that obscured the view from the drone's camera.

"Damn it," Owen mumbled. "They know we're watching."

"Are we going to lose them?" Sammy asked, worry in his voice.

"There's a radar sensor on the drone. We should be able to track them through the dust even if we lose visibility on the electro-optical camera," Owen reassured him.

On the edge of the video frame, another truck suddenly entered the village. It was a white Toyota Hilux, identical to the first, with the same black tarp covering the bed.

"Is that a second vehicle?" Owen asked, confirming what he was seeing with the soldier at the drone's controls.

The man nodded, keeping his eyes fixed on the screen, trying to keep track of the original vehicle with Louie in the back. As the trucks sped in a circle, the dust cloud enveloped the entire village. Owen and Sammy were also fixated on the action, trying to follow Louie's truck.

"Sir, two more vehicles are coming into the village. Now there are four," said the drone's operator, an edge of panic in his voice, before correcting himself. "Wait! Now there are five."

The dust thickened as the swarm of identical trucks raced in a circle around the clearing.

"Zoom out," Owen ordered. "I need to see what's around that village."

The drone's operator toggled the switch controlling the camera's focal length. The view changed to a wide-angle shot showing the area surrounding the village. As soon as it came into focus, Owen realized what was about to happen. A network of roads led away from the clearing, radiating out like the spokes of a bicycle tire.

"Stay on the one with Colonel Bigombe in the back," Owen yelled. "They're going to split up."

Seconds later, a truck emerged from the dust cloud and sped down a road away from the village. At the same time, another vehicle disappeared down a different path.

"Were either one of those Colonel Bigombe?" Owen asked, trying to remain calm.

"I don't think so, sir," the soldier mumbled, keeping his eyes glued to the screen.

A third truck left the circle.

"What about that one?" Owen shouted.

The soldier shook his head, still waiting. The drone's radar showed two trucks still circling inside the cloud of dust. One split off and started moving for the road.

"I think that's the one!" the soldier exclaimed.

"You better be right," Owen threatened.

The drone arched from its orbit, following the truck as it raced down the road. Sammy pulled up a chair and sat down next to Owen. He was in a trance, still fixated on the images from the drone's camera.

"How long until the drone runs out of power?" he asked.

Owen glanced at his watch. "About two hours."

Sammy nodded. "What should we do?"

"There's nothing we can do but wait and see where it goes."

They sat there in silence while the drone operator kept the aircraft in a perfect position above the truck. When it was a few miles away from the village, the driver turned onto the main road and slowed down, either unaware of being observed or having no reason for evasive driving. They watched for nearly thirty minutes as the truck drove through the countryside until the soldier at the controls called for Owen's attention.

"Sir, there's a town about three miles ahead. It's the only major settlement within an hour of that location."

"Stay on him," Owen urged needlessly.

It was a busy market day in the town. Most of the traffic was pedestrians and motorcycles, making it easy to pick out the truck. After maneuvering through the central square, it parked near a row of produce shacks. The driver got out and greeted a man who emerged from one of the huts.

"Can you zoom in?" Owen asked.

The soldier focused the camera on the truck, and they could see the men talking and the driver gesturing at the back of the vehicle. After a brief conversation, they exchanged what looked like a small package. Then both men walked to the tailgate and began untying the black tarp over the truck's bed.

Owen turned to Sammy. "That town is about forty minutes from here. Are your men ready to move?"

Sammy nodded and held his breath as the men yanked back the tarp, revealing the precious cargo.

"What the hell is that?" Owen muttered.

Sammy shook his head in frustration. "Mangoes," he answered. "We got the wrong truck."

Owen slammed his fist on the table as the camera showed the men unloading plastic buckets of fruit and setting them on the roadside.

"What now?" Sammy asked.

Owen slumped in his chair. "We'll wait and hope for the best," he finally answered, then got up and left the room.

+++

It felt to Louie as if they had been driving for about an hour, but it could have been longer—or shorter. He had no way of judging from underneath the tarp and without his watch or phone. It was a battering ride over unforgiving roads. At one point, Louie feared that the truck might overturn as the driver maneuvered through deep, water-filled potholes. The plastic restraints on Louie's wrists cut his skin as he braced himself against the driver's erratic maneuvers.

When they finally stopped, Louie heard the men exit the truck and other voices greeting them. Someone yanked back the burlap tarp. Louie was lying on his back, staring into the bright sun. After his eyes adjusted to the light, he saw the men who had picked him up at the village. One of them threw Louie a bottle of water told him to drink it. Louie gratefully guzzled the water. Then the man tossed Louie a cloth bag and motioned for him to pull it over his head. Louie did as instructed, then waited until the men grabbed him by either arm and yanked him from the truck.

They led him a short distance into a building. Once inside, he was pushed into a chair and left alone. A little later, he heard the door open, followed by footsteps across the floor. Someone sat in a chair, close enough that Louie could feel his breath.

"You made this more difficult than was necessary," the voice said.

"Who are you?"

"Someone you once tried to kill," he replied.

"You're a liar," Louie spat. "Daniel Odoki is dead and has been for a long time. I want to speak to the man in charge. Not some make-believe imposter."

"You're in no position to make demands," the man said.

"Then we have nothing to discuss. There's only one person I'm speaking to, and it's not you. Ask him why he won't face me. What is he scared of?"

There was no reply. Louie heard the scrape of the chair legs across the floor, followed by footsteps leaving the room. The door shut, and he was alone again. A few minutes later, someone else entered. Louie could tell by the fall of his footsteps that it was a different person. He sat down in the chair but didn't speak.

"Is this another imposter, or have you sent me the real Daniel Odoki this time?" Louie taunted.

The man shifted in the chair but didn't reply.

"I asked to speak with the man in charge. Is that you?" Louie pressed, goading him to respond.

"I am the one you asked to see," he finally replied.

As soon as Louie heard the voice, there was no doubt.

"Uncle, why have you done this?" he asked.

Louie heard him rise from the chair and step closer. Without warning, he grabbed the hood and tore it from Louie's head. The shock of seeing his uncle set Louie's heart racing. At first, he seemed a different man. His eyes were tired and bloodshot, hair thinner and graying. Mugaba had lost so much weight that Louie wondered how he had survived his time in exile.

Mugaba tossed the bag to the ground and glared at his nephew. He pulled a knife from his belt. Louie's eyes followed the blade as his uncle's grip tightened on it. Mugaba stepped closer and motioned toward the plastic cuffs. Louie hesitated, then presented his hands in front of his face. With a stroke of the razor-sharp blade, his uncle cut through the plastic, letting the cuffs fall to the floor. Then he sat back down in the chair, which was across a table from Louie.

"Do you need food or water?" Mugaba asked.

Louie shook his head and looked around the room. It was sparsely furnished, with the feel of a police interrogation room. There was the table and the two chairs. A single door led outside, and there were no windows. In one corner of the room, Louie noticed a video camera mounted to the wall near the ceiling. A red blinking light indicated that the power was on. He stared into the camera, wondering who else was watching their reunion. On the table between them were the papers Louie had in his pocket when he was picked up.

"You haven't answered my question," Louie repeated.

"How is my sister?" Mugaba asked, ignoring Louie's query, letting him know that he was not the interrogator.

"She left after you disappeared," Louie explained. "She's been in New Jersey with my brother. It broke her heart when you went away without saying goodbye. She couldn't understand why you never tried to call."

"And what did you tell her?"

"What could I say to make it better? She'd already been through enough. I was not going to invent excuses for why you did what you did."

"I suppose you expect me to thank you," Mugaba growled.

"No, of course not. But I would expect you to take responsibility for what you did," Louie replied calmly.

Mugaba tensed in his chair. "My only crime was loving my country. We had a chance to set things right, and you let that opportunity slip away."

"You tried to kill the president."

Mugaba chuckled. "Lutalo, you have always been naive. Do you think that President Namono would have let go of Green House without a fight? You must think that you did some noble act, letting it all burn down, but you're mistaken. When you defied me, you invited chaos and misery."

"If that was true, you could have stayed and tried to fix things," Louie challenged. "Instead, you ran away and broke your sister's heart. First she loses her husband, then her brother. Didn't you think of her when you decided to leave?"

"You know the old saying, Lutalo. Pretend you are dead and see who loves you. Did anyone else care besides my sister? If I had stayed, I'd be in jail now. And for what crime? Trying to save my country from collapse?"

"There could have been another way," Louie argued. "Is that why you brought me here? Is this some kind of revenge for not helping you take Green House that day?"

"I don't need revenge. I simply want back what's mine."

"You think you can get that by pretending to be a dead warlord and helping Emanuel Sekibo get into Green House? How will that get back your old life?" Louie asked incredulously.

"I will not live out my years hiding in this godforsaken jungle!" his uncle swore.

"You think he'll let you come back? Sekibo has no loyalty to you. Do you know that he offered me your old job as minister if I dropped out of the race?"

Mugaba stared at his nephew, unsure whether to believe him.

"It's true, Uncle. You're a fool if you think he'll let you come back across that border and reclaim your old life. I remember an old saying you told me once: Even friendly dogs can't share a bone. Sekibo will turn on you the moment he gets what he wants."

"I have known him since we were young men, back during the border wars. He was always a snake," Mugaba mused. Then his face hardened. "But the snake you see is not the one who bites. I'd rather take my chances with Emanuel Sekibo than live my remaining days out here like an animal."

"Why do you believe he'll protect you?" Louie asked.

"What choice do I have?"

"Did you read that?" Louie asked, nodding at the papers he had brought with him.

"What is it?"

"An intelligence report about my father's death. It's from the Americans."

Mugaba took the pages and read through them. His eyes widened with surprise as he reached the end.

"You knew that my father was working with the CIA during the border wars, but you never told me," Louie said.

Mugaba put the pages on the table and stared at his nephew.

"Why does it matter now? Would it be any less of a tragedy if you knew that he died fighting someone else's war?"

"I would have wanted the truth," Louie whispered.

"Truth is the first victim of war."

"What do you know about the mission he was on when he died?"

Mugaba shook his head. "Why does it matter? It was a long time ago."

"It matters more than you realize," Louie insisted.

Mugaba stared at the wall, lost in thought. "His unit was sent on an impossible mission," he finally said. "It never should have happened. I was working at army headquarters at the time. There had been bloody fights in that sector during the previous weeks. They sent your father's unit in to break the stalemate. He was the best commander in the army, but even that didn't matter. In the end, it was a suicide mission."

"Why was it so important to take the area?"

"We were under pressure to show progress. We had been losing ground the entire year. The Americans were threatening to cut support for the army. Our commanders had to prove that we could hold the line."

"Why was my father selected for that mission?" Louie pressed.

"I told you. He was the best we had. A rising star. If anyone could have pulled victory from defeat, it was him."

"Was the CIA trying to get him promoted?"

"There were rumors, of course," Mugaba said. "The Americans had great hopes for your father. They saw him as someone who could turn everything around. But naturally, there were rivals. Men were jealous of his success and his closeness with the Americans."

"Were you among them, Uncle?"

"Yes. Maybe," Mugaba chuckled. "But of course, he was married to my sister. So I was happy for him as well. Don't forget, I was the one who introduced them."

"Look again at the last page of the report," Louie instructed. "It's the CIA's assessment of the battle where my father died. It says that his commander knew he was sending my father into a death trap but did it anyway."

Mugaba read the final page of the report again. When he had finished, he sighed and looked at Louie.

"All the names were redacted," Louie said. "Including the identity of my father's commander. The man who approved that mission. But I think you can probably guess who gave that order."

His uncle nodded, confirming what Louie had suspected. "Emanuel Sekibo was your father's commanding officer," Mugaba revealed. "He was the one who sent him on that mission."

"He must have known that the Americans were pushing for my father to lead the army," Louie said. "That's why

Sekibo sent him. It wasn't about winning the war. It was about eliminating a rival."

Mugaba didn't respond.

"Yet you still believe that you can trust him? After everything that's happened, why wouldn't he turn on you as well?"

"We're wasting time," Mugaba said impatiently.

"Uncle, listen to what I'm telling you," Louie pleaded. "Sekibo has no intention of giving you your old life back. He's only using you to get what he wants. Is this how you wish to be remembered? As a lackey for Emanuel Sekibo and the one who helped get him into Green House?"

"We're finished here," Mugaba announced. He threw the papers onto the table and got up from his chair. "There's nothing more to discuss."

"What about Anna?" Louie called out before his uncle reached the door. "At least tell me where Sekibo took her."

Mugaba froze.

"You didn't know about Anna, did you?" Louie said, confirming his suspicion. "Sekibo had her kidnapped. That's how he got me to come here, but you had no idea. What else about his plan don't you know? He's keeping you in the dark and using you, just like he does everyone else."

Mugaba pushed a button on the wall, signaling for the guard to open the door. He waited, but no one came. Mugaba pressed it again without any response. In frustration, he tried the door handle and was surprised to find it unlocked. He pushed the door open and looked out into the empty hallway. The guards who had let him inside were gone. Louie caught a glimpse of his uncle's expression, seeing confusion turn to worry.

"Wait here," Mugaba ordered and continued outside into the hallway.

He was gone for several minutes, leaving the door wide open. Louie realized nothing was stopping him from getting up and leaving, but he didn't know where he'd go or what he'd do. Instead, he sat there waiting for his uncle's return. Louie heard footsteps in the hallway, then saw Mugaba standing in the doorway, looking shaken.

"We're alone," he revealed.

"What do you mean, alone?"

"Everyone's gone. All the guards. The drivers. The entire camp is empty. We're the only ones left," he muttered. "I don't understand."

Louie remembered the camera in the corner of the room. He looked up and saw the red light flashing.

"Uncle, do you have a satellite phone?" he asked.

Mugaba nodded and pulled a phone from one of the pockets in his fatigues. He walked across the room and handed it to his nephew. Louie dialed Janet's secure number and waited for her to pick up.

"It's Louie," he said when she answered.

"Where are you? Janet asked, surprised to hear his voice. "Do you have any idea what's going on?"

"No. I'm still across the border, and you'll never believe who I'm with."

"Hmmm, let me guess. Perhaps your uncle, the disgraced former defense minister," she replied.

"How did you know?" Louie gasped, trying to understand what was happening.

"Pictures of you and Mugaba just popped up on social

media. They show the two of you sitting together at a table, having a little chat."

Louie looked at his uncle, then at the camera on the wall, realizing what had happened.

"What do the posts say?" he asked.

"Anonymous sources are claiming that you and your uncle have been behind the GLA attacks all along. It says that your uncle has been masquerading as Daniel Odoki and is rebuilding the GLA in secret camps across the border. They're accusing you of masterminding the bombing attacks against Francois Akua and Emanuel Sekibo as a way to win the election. They're saying it's all a conspiracy so that you can pardon your uncle once you become president."

"That's insane!" Louie said. "Why would anyone believe that?"

"Wait, there's more," Janet said. "There are also pictures of you leaving the restaurant on the night of the first bombing. And of you near the cafe when your friend Patrick was killed. The posts are accusing you of orchestrating Patrick's death, supposedly because he discovered the truth about your scheme."

"When did this come out?"

"Just a few minutes ago. But it must have been planned for a while. Whoever was behind this went to a lot of trouble to make sure that it would go viral right before the election."

"Are people are paying attention to this nonsense?" Louie asked.

"You're kidding, right?" Janet said. "We're two days away from the election, and one candidate is accusing the other of working for the enemy. Of course people are paying attention! Sekibo's campaign just released a statement calling for an investigation. He's demanding that you and your uncle be detained until they can clarify the truth behind the accusations."

"How convenient for him," Louie said sarcastically.

"Are you coming back?"

"Why? So I can end up sharing a jail cell with my uncle?

"I don't think we're at that point yet," Janet reassured him. "Sekibo's bluffing. Right now, there's no hard evidence, nothing but a conspiracy theory and some photos. Although those pictures of you and your uncle will take a bit of explaining, since no one has seen him in over two years."

"I'm not coming back until we find Anna," Louie insisted.

"What about your uncle? He's a wanted man. If you come back here without him, there will be questions about your motives."

"I can't worry about that now," Louie argued. "I'm sorry, I've got to go."

"Whatever you're doing, be careful," Janet warned.

Louie hung up and turned to his uncle. "Sekibo did it," he said, pointing at the camera on the wall. "You've been revealed as Daniel Odoki. And apparently, I'm your partner and the mastermind behind the GLA attacks across the border. It seems that Emanuel Sekibo is getting rid of us both with a single stroke."

"That's impossible!" Mugaba blurted out.

"There are already pictures of us posted on social media, sitting together at this table. Sekibo has called for an investigation. If either of us crosses the border, we'll probably be arrested."

Mugaba walked over and collapsed into a chair, holding his head in his hands.

"You were right, Lutalo," he muttered. "Just like the old village saying: By the time the fool has learned the game, all the players have gone. I've been that fool. Sekibo hasn't changed. He was playing me all along, and I let him do it."

"And me as well," Louie admitted. "Ever since my name appeared on the ballot, I became a threat to his plan, just like my father was once a threat. Now, it's our word against his. But those pictures mean nothing. He has no evidence. We can still fight back."

Mugaba stared at the ground between his boots, shaking his head. "No, he thought of that as well," he said.

"What do you mean?"

"Tomorrow morning, the GLA will launch an attack against the garrison at Kiskow. We've been planning it for months. It was scheduled to happen on the day before the election. Sekibo knew that a major GLA attack would help his chances of winning. But now I understand the other reason. They'll blame us for all of it, not him."

Louie's eyes grew wide as he realized how completely they had fallen into Sekibo's trap. Then he thought of something.

"It's not too late to stop it. If the fighters still believe that you are Daniel Odoki, then you can call off the attack."

"No, it is too late," Mugaba insisted. "The wheels are in motion. The fighters are already moving into their pre-attack positions. We designed the plan to be executed without direct supervision. They've been given orders to commence the assault just before sunrise."

"How many men?"

"I don't even know," Mugaba admitted. "Maybe several hundred. We've been moving weapons out to the fighters for weeks. Couriers hand-delivered the orders to each of the commanders. The entire operation is decentralized. Even if I wanted to contact them and call it off, there's no way of doing it."

"They won't be able to take the garrison," Louie said. "We've been reinforcing our positions there for weeks. It will be a suicide attack."

"It doesn't matter. Even if they die trying, it still achieves Sekibo's purpose," Mugaba said bitterly. "He knows that the news of a major GLA offensive against Kiskow will justify everything he's been saying during the campaign. If it turns into a bloodbath, that's all the better. Then no one will question his promise to take the war across the border once he's sitting in Green House. He intended it that way from the beginning. This was all part of his plan."

"We need to stop this!" Louie pleaded. "Uncle, please come back with me to our camp. There must be something we can do. But I'll need your help to convince them."

Mugaba slumped into his chair, defeated.

"You once told me that a man's deeds are his life," Louie pressed his uncle. "You still have a chance to fix this. Please, come with me and try."

Mugaba looked up at the camera and back at his nephew, weighing which fate would be worse. "I will try," he sighed, and followed Louie out the door.

+++

When they arrived at the third force camp, the guards

stopped them at the checkpoint. They approached the truck with their weapons at the ready. One of the guards peered through the window and did a double-take, recognizing Louie's passenger but not believing his eyes. Louie didn't bother to explain. Instead, he told the guard that Mugaba was there to meet with the General. The soldier fumbled with his radio and called headquarters for instructions.

A call came back instructing them to let Louie and his uncle pass through to the headquarters building. During the short drive to the compound, the rumor of Mugaba's capture spread quickly through the camp. By the time they pulled up outside the headquarters, a group of soldiers had gathered in the yard, eager to catch a glimpse of their infamous visitor.

Sammy and Owen were waiting outside on the veranda. Mugaba stared straight ahead, ignoring the soldiers gawking in the yard. He followed Louie into the operations center, with Owen and Sammy right behind him. Once they were in Sammy's office, there was an awkward interval of silence until Louie finally spoke.

"We don't have much time," he began, turning to his uncle for introductions. "This is Owen Smith. He's with the American government," Louie said, leaving volumes unspoken. Then he turned and gestured at Sammy. "The General is in charge of operations on this side of the border. All of the men here at the camp answer to him."

Mugaba nodded at the two men.

"I assume you've heard what's happening back in the capital?" Louie asked Sammy and Owen.

"Yes. I think Emanuel Sekibo just turned the two of you into his October surprise," Owen said.

"It's June," Louie felt compelled to point out.

"Same difference," Owen snapped. "The point is, he just blew this election wide open. We might as well throw out all the polling data. We're less than forty-eight hours away, and nobody has the slightest idea what's going to happen."

"There's more," Louie said, turning to his uncle, who hadn't yet said a word. They all waited for Mugaba to speak.

"Kiskow will be attacked tomorrow morning," Mugaba said without emotion.

"You've got to be fucking kidding me!" Owen blurted out. "This is not what we need right now."

"When is it going to happen?" Sammy asked.

"Just before dawn," Mugaba replied.

"How many fighters?"

"Several hundred, at least. They've already crossed the border and moved into assembly areas on the outskirts of town. They'll make a final movement into their assault positions tonight and commence the operation sometime before sunrise."

"You're their commander," Owen interrupted, pointing at Mugaba. "Get on the radio, turn on your best Daniel Odoki voice, and call off the attack."

"It's too late," Mugaba said. "It's been planned for weeks. The unit commanders already have their orders and will execute them regardless of what they hear on the radio."

"How many men are at the garrison in Kiskow?" Owen asked Louie.

"Around eight hundred in total. But not all are riflemen. That includes the support personnel as well."

"Is that enough to defend against the attack?" Owen asked.

"Probably. Especially if they know it's coming. But that's not the point. For Sekibo, those fighters attacking Kiskow are expendable. He doesn't care if it turns into a massacre," Louie explained. "In fact, he would probably prefer that. His only goal is to influence the election and justify sending the army across the border once he's in office. If the fighting starts, then he's already won, no matter what happens."

Owen looked at Sammy. "General, what options do we have? Can your men get between the GLA and Kiskow and somehow disrupt the attack?"

Sammy glanced at his watch and shook his head. "There isn't enough time," he said. "We don't know the locations of the GLA units. There's no way we could get across the border and move into position before tomorrow morning."

Owen was pacing the room, on the verge of panic. Meanwhile, Mugaba had walked over to the wall and was studying a large map of Kiskow.

"We need to call General B— and let him know that the garrison is at risk," Owen said, thinking out loud. "We still have time to fly in reinforcements from the capital. We can get a few more platoons out there tonight by helicopter."

"That doesn't solve the problem," Louie argued. "It might even make it worse. And don't forget, there's a village full of civilians outside the walls of the garrison. If we escalate, we run the risk of destroying Kiskow while trying to save it."

"I don't hear you coming up with any better ideas!" Owen yelled at Louie.

While they argued, Mugaba remained fixated on the map. "A fight between grasshoppers only brings joy to the crow," he muttered from across the room.

"What the hell does that mean?" Owen snapped.

Mugaba turned around. "For Sekibo, the battle itself is the victory. He wins, no matter what happens on the ground."

"So what's the alternative?" Owen demanded.

"We give it to them without a fight," Mugaba said calmly.

"You mean surrender the garrison?" Owen said, choking on the words.

"Not precisely. But we must deny him the battle. What if the garrison was empty when the attack happened?" Mugaba asked.

Everyone was silent as they considered the proposal.

"No fucking way," Owen finally said, crossing his arms defiantly. "Do you realize the blowback we'd get from DC if we abandoned the garrison? My government has staked its credibility on winning this counterinsurgency. Handing over Kiskow to the GLA would be utter humiliation. Not to mention the end of my career."

"The GLA isn't real," Louie reminded everyone. "Those men attacking Kiskow tomorrow aren't part of some global ideological battle. They're mostly poor miners fighting for survival. Emanuel Sekibo has been using them to smuggle minerals across the border. Now he's going to sacrifice them to win an election."

"It's true," Mugaba interjected. "They've been told that the Gisawian army is coming across the border to take their mining claims and give them to the Chinese. They think that following Daniel Odoki and attacking Kiskow will keep that from happening."

"But that's exactly what's going to happen if Sekibo wins," Owen insisted. "He's going to order the army across the border and declare a military exclusion zone, clearing the way for Chinese investors to move in and set up operations. It's nothing but an excuse to gain control over the mineral deposits across the border."

"That was always the plan," Mugaba confirmed. "He's turning the miners into agents of their own demise."

"There must be another way," Owen mumbled, resuming his pacing around the room.

"We're running out of time," Sammy interrupted. "We have less than twenty-four hours. If we're going to do something, it needs to be now."

"Damn it!" Owen yelled, spinning around and kicking a trash can, sending it clattering across the room. He grimaced in pain and limped toward a chair. "I can't believe it's come to this," he muttered, sitting down and massaging his foot. "I need to call General B— to let him know the situation. What is the exact timeline for the attack?" he asked Mugaba.

"The fighters will move into final positions sometime after midnight."

Owen grabbed a satellite phone from the table and dialed the general's number. He turned away from the others with a defeated look on his face.

"Give me a minute," he said, and limped out the door while they waited in the office.

CHAPTER FOURTEEN

Louie's alarm went off at three-thirty. He still felt half asleep as he made his way to the operations center. Owen was already there, sitting in front of a monitor and watching a live feed from a drone circling over Kiskow.

"There's coffee if you want some," Owen offered.

Louie nodded his thanks but didn't take any. "Did you sleep?"

"Maybe an hour or two," Owen replied. "I was here until midnight, waiting until they confirmed that the last few soldiers made it out of the garrison."

"Any problems?"

"Once the order came down, things moved quickly. They're on the road now and should be back in the capital sometime later today."

"I know you didn't like the plan, but there wasn't any other option," Louie said, trying to rationalize the decision to abandon the garrison.

Owen stared at the screen but didn't reply.

"If we left them there to fight, there would have been hundreds of needless casualties on both sides. It was the right thing to do," Louie continued.

"How can you say that?" Owen grumbled, glaring at Louie. "After all that work, we just gave it away."

"What did we give away? Those men out there don't even know why they're fighting. They're just pawns in a game run by Sekibo."

"That's not how they'll see it back in Washington," Owen argued. "Do you know what the newspapers will be saying tomorrow? America loses yet another war to a band of irregular misfits. And guess who's going to get hung out dry for letting it happen?"

"Is that what General B- told you on the phone?"

"He might as well have. The shit always rolls downhill and stops at the bottom. In this case, that's me."

"They say that America is the land of second chances. I'm sure you'll bounce back," Louie said, annoyed that Owen was unable to see anything beyond his stake in the drama. "Has there been any activity on the ground since the withdrawal?"

"We detected some movement around the perimeter during the night, but it's hard to tell what's going on," Owen said. "The camp is surrounded by dense jungle, and we can't see much from the air. There's been some chatter on the low-power radio frequencies, so someone down there must be doing something."

"If it's going to happen, they should be in their attack positions by now," Louie said.

Owen glanced at his watch and nodded. "Sunrise is less than an hour away. If your uncle is telling the truth about this, things should kick off pretty soon."

"You think he's lying about the attack?"

"I have no idea," Owen said dismissively. "But it doesn't matter. Either way, he's going to jail."

"You're turning him over to the authorities?"

"Did you think we wouldn't?" Owen asked, surprised by the question. "He's an international fugitive. We aren't going to let him go."

From across the room, the soldier at the controls of the drone called for Owen's attention. "Sir, we're detecting movement at several locations around the perimeter."

"I guess the show's about to start," Owen said, looking around the room, then back at Louie. "Where the hell is the General?"

Louie shrugged. He grabbed a chair and sat in front of the monitor, watching the live feed from the drone circling high over Kiskow. Occasionally, the infrared camera picked up a blob of heat moving among the trees, but there were few other signs of activity. A few minutes before sunrise, simultaneous flashes of bright light filled the screen.

"What was that?" Owen yelled to the soldier flying the drone.

"Mortars impacting inside the perimeter, sir," the man replied.

"Here we go," Owen mumbled, watching as a barrage of rounds peppered the camp.

The initial mortar attack lasted less than five minutes. When the explosions subsided, the drone's infrared sensors showed several buildings on fire. A fuel container next to the camp's generator had exploded and was burning brightly in the predawn twilight.

"Sir, we have movement on the perimeter," the soldier called out.

They could see pixilated figures advancing from the jungle's edge, probing the camp's defenses. Several assault teams approached the outer fence and quickly retreated. Owen watched helplessly, sensing what was coming next: simultaneous explosions tore open the perimeter fence.

"Sir, we've intercepted a radio transmission ordering the units to advance," the soldier reported.

GLA fighters began pouring through the gaps in the fence. Once inside the camp, they fanned out to occupy the empty guard towers. Without meeting any resistance, they moved quickly to seize their objectives. Meanwhile, the second wave of fighters began clearing the buildings.

"I guess that's it," Owen said grimly. "Kiskow has fallen without a fight."

He got up from his chair and crossed the room to the coffeepot. He refilled his mug and stood there staring at the wall in a daze. Louie joined him and took what remained of the coffee.

"I thought you were a tea guy?" Owen asked, watching Louie take a sip and wince at the bitterness.

"I ran out of my supply," Louie explained. "So, what now?"

Owen checked his watch. "It won't take long for this to hit the news. Once word of the attack gets out, the election is all but over. Sekibo will play this for all its worth."

"What happens to Sammy and the third force?"

"The third force!" Owen burst out laughing, spilling coffee from his mug. "What a fucking joke! That was never anything but a red herring. We planted the idea with some idiot congressman from Pennsylvania during an intelligence briefing, knowing that he'd blab about it at the first opportunity."

"I don't understand," Louie mumbled.

"*You* were the *real* third force," Owen sneered as if it should have been obvious to anyone paying attention. "The rest of this was nothing but a sideshow. A distraction." He waved his hand dismissively at the operations center. "Green House was the real prize, and now that's gone to Sekibo."

Louie felt numb as he tried to process what Owen had revealed. "So all of these men are expendable?" he asked, looking at the soldiers working around the headquarters.

"Don't worry about it," Owen said. "They'll be fine. Of course, we'll be shutting down the operation here. But the General and his men will be evacuated and well compensated for their trouble."

"What about me and my uncle?"

"Once Sekibo gets into Green House, I'm assuming he'll charge both of you with treason. I can't stop you from going back across the border, but I wouldn't recommend it. There's probably already a holding cell over at DSPO with your name on it."

"How reassuring," Louie sighed.

"But if you decide to leave, I'll make sure there's a spot for you on the plane. We'll drop you off in New Jersey or wherever you want to go."

"And my uncle?"

"I told you, Mugaba's a fugitive. I can't take him back to the US. I'm probably getting fired as it is. I don't think exfiltrating a warlord is going to make things any better."

"A *fake* warlord," Louie reminded him.

"It doesn't fucking matter!" Owen snapped. "He's not getting on the damn plane!"

"I'm not going anywhere without Anna," Louie insisted.

"Whatever," Owen said, shrugging indifferently. "That's your choice. However, I think you're making a big mistake. Emanuel Sekibo doesn't strike me as the forgiving type. My advice to you is get as far away from here as you can. But whatever you decide, we're shutting down this operation and pulling out of here ASAP. You've got a ticket if you want it."

Owen put down his coffee, unable to stomach the burnt remnants from the bottom of the pot. He was about to leave the operations center when one of the soldiers called out from across the room.

"Sir, something's happening on the ground," he said urgently.

Owen and Louie walked back to the screen. The video feed showed a dozen fires still burning inside the compound, but the fighters' movement seemed to be reversed. Small groups of men were fleeing the camp, slipping back through the gaps in the perimeter fence.

"What the hell's going on?" Owen demanded.

"I think they're retreating, sir," the soldier said. "We picked up some chatter on the radio. They were confused when they found the camp empty. They think it's a trap. The commanders ordered everyone to get out and pull back from Kiskow. They're retreating into the jungle."

Owen and Louie stared, dumbfounded, at the screen as the last few stragglers fled from the garrison. When there was no sign of movement anywhere on the ground, Owen pulled a satellite phone from his cargo pocket and began dialing.

"Who are you calling?" Louie asked.

"General B-."

"Why?"

"I'm getting that convoy turned around before they get to the capital. We're reoccupying Kiskow."

+++

Two men in camouflage fatigues and ski masks crept toward the guardhouse outside the front gate. A radio inside the building was playing music, muffling the sound of their advance. Their target was dozing in a plastic lawn chair, waiting for the morning shift change.

The men quickened their pace with the last few steps. One of them seized the guard's arms with fluid precision while the other wrapped a strip of duct tape over his mouth. They pulled a cloth bag over his head and secured it with another length of tape. Then they hogtied the guard, leaving him lying on his stomach, confused but unharmed.

With the guard neutralized, they opened the gate leading into the factory compound. One of them signaled with an infrared strobe light. It was followed by the sound of a truck moving toward the gate. When it rolled past the guard shack, it slowed enough for the two men to leap onto the tailgate.

There was a faint glow of sunrise on horizon as the truck pulled up to a two-story maintenance building. The upper-level windows were tightly sealed, and there were no signs of life inside. The driver turned off the engine and watched for activity around the building. Meanwhile, a dozen men quietly crept out of the back of the truck and fanned out around the target.

The driver watched through a pair of binoculars as the teams moved into position. Seeing no signs of danger, he flashed an infrared strobe, signaling for the teams to advance. The first man reached the exterior metal door and found it locked. He pulled out a set of tools out of his vest and began working the pin tumbler inside the keyhole. Seconds later, the door swung open, and he waved for the others to advance. With weapons at the ready, the team disappeared through the door.

Once the last man was inside, the driver got out of the truck. He chambered a round in his semiautomatic pistol and slid it back into his leather shoulder holster. The soldiers were crouched inside the building, waiting for the order to ascend the staircase. The driver made eye contact with the team leader and nodded for them to proceed. The squad crept silently up the stairwell, disappearing into the darkness. When the sound of the first shot echoed down the stairs, the driver could tell it wasn't one of their weapons, but the second and third rounds were.

The driver drew his pistol and bounded up the stairs, covering two steps at a time. At the far end of the hallway, one of the team members was lying in the corner, holding his bleeding arm. The team medic was already applying a hemostatic bandage to the wound. Beyond him, another man lay dead in pool of blood, having taken the second and third shots in the chest.

The team leader waited beside an unmarked door near the dead guard's body. Two other soldiers held a battering ram and waited for orders to breach the door. The driver gestured for them to proceed while the others readied themselves on either side of the door. The impact of the battering ram tore the door from its hinges. As it hit the floor, the assault team flooded through the gap. Red lasers from the aiming sights of their automatic weapons cut through the darkness.

The driver stepped through the splintered remains of the doorframe, one pace behind the assault team. The room was empty except for an overturned chair. The men took a knee, waiting for instructions. The driver noticed something in the far corner of the room. He walked over, knelt, and reached out, feeling the rough texture of a woolen blanket. Something underneath recoiled from his touch. He grabbed the edge of the fabric and gently drew it back.

"Miss Anna, you're safe now," he said.

She squinted into his headlamp, unable to see his face but recognizing his voice. "Sammy, is that you?" she gasped, not believing what she was hearing.

The General pulled off his facemask and smiled. "Mr. Louie sent me."

"Is he all right?"

"Yes. Don't worry. We'll take you to see him now."

Sammy turned to his team leader. "Get the men back to the truck. We need to move quickly, before the workers arrive for the morning shift."

The soldiers cleared the room while Sammy helped Anna to her feet. "We have food and water in the truck," he said.

"How about a coffee?" she asked with a tired smile. "Just like old times."

"Of course, Ms. Anna. I remember exactly how you like it."

By the time they passed back through the door, the

soldiers had removed the guard's body and cleaned up the shell casings and blood from the floor, leaving no evidence of what had happened. The soldiers helped Anna into the truck, laying her down on a padded stretcher. The medic made her comfortable and started an intravenous line for rehydration. As the truck pulled out the front gate, Anna caught a last glimpse of the factory in the morning light.

+++

Mugaba awoke in a cell less than a stone's throw from his old office at the Gisawian Ministry of Defense. When he had arrived there, the guards had taken his rancid clothing and given him a gray jumpsuit and sandals. After two nights of good sleep, undisturbed by the nocturnal sounds of the jungle, he was beginning to feel recovered. He had had his first proper bath in months, a haircut and shave, and was getting three full meals a day that were putting some of the weight back onto his frame.

The cell was sparsely furnished with a cot, a table, and two chairs. The walls were chalky white, without adornment. In the corner was a private toilet and sink hidden behind a retractable curtain. The only other notable feature was the large, two-way mirror built into the wall.

Mugaba was resting on his cot, staring at the ceiling, when he heard a knock on the door. A soldier entered the room with a tray of coffee, some bread, and fruit for his breakfast. Mugaba stayed on his bunk, watching the soldier put the tray on the table. The young man was about to leave when he glanced at Mugaba, inadvertently making eye contact. The flummoxed soldier straightened to attention and rendered a salute, uncertain of the protocol for serving food to the former minister of defense. He quickly dropped the salute, spun on his heels, and rushed for the door.

Once he was alone, Mugaba went to the table and poured himself a cup of coffee, pushing aside the bread and fruit. He sipped the coffee while staring into the two-way mirror, wondering who was on the other side. A few minutes later, someone slid open the lock and a guard opened the door. Louie appeared in the doorway and stepped inside. Mugaba sat there, expressionless, as his nephew joined him at the table.

"Are you comfortable?" Louie asked, uncertain how else to begin.

His uncle looked around the empty room and chuckled grimly. "You know the old saying: He who burns down his house knows why ashes cost a fortune."

"Do you believe this to be unjust?" Louie asked, surprised by his uncle's words.

"Corn cannot expect justice from a court of chickens," Mugaba answered.

"Uncle, enough with the village proverbs!" Louie exploded. "I'm asking you a serious question."

"Do you expect me to say that I deserve whatever comes?" Mugaba hissed angrily across the table. "If so, that's not the answer you will get. Some men reign as kings for doing far worse than I have done. Yet I sit here now as a common criminal. Tell me, what has become of Sekibo?"

"He will sit for judgment soon enough," Louie said calmly.

Mugaba sniffed and looked away. "I suppose he's in the next cell over?"

"No. Not yet," Louie said. "But the people are finally demanding answers. He will have difficulty explaining how S3 Corp profited all those years from its government contracts and all the rest of it. Someday, the truth will be known, and he will be held accountable."

Mugaba shook his head in disgust, pushing aside his coffee. "But for now, he is free, and I am here. What lesson should I take from this?"

"Would you have preferred that we left you in the jungle as a fugitive? Without Sekibo's men for protection, you might have fared much worse," Louie countered.

"Then I should be thanking you for your mercy?"

"No, Uncle. I don't expect your gratitude," Louie said tiredly. "However, you should know that I've asked the judge to consider your cooperation in thwarting the attack on Kiskow."

"I suppose they'll expect me to testify against Sekibo."

"Why wouldn't you? He had no loyalty to you. He tried to frame us both. If the attack on Kiskow had happened, we would have taken the blame for it. He wanted to turn us into fugitives for life."

"How is this any better?" Mugaba replied angrily, waving at the mirror and whoever was behind it.

"You did the right thing," Louie said. "It probably saved the lives of hundreds of men. They would have died for no reason, just like my father."

Mugaba frowned, unconvinced. "What happens now?"

"There will be an investigation."

"An investigation? By whom? Police Intelligence?" Mugaba huffed. "They're all loyal to Sekibo. It would be fixed from the start."

"No," Louie said. "The legislature will appoint an independent investigator. The process will be fair and open. The people deserve no less."

Mugaba chuckled at his nephew's confidence. "Even after all these years, you still don't understand how this place works, do you?"

Louie stared at his uncle across the table but said nothing. There was a knock on the door, and a man dressed in a suit nervously poked his head inside. "I'm sorry to disturb you, sir. But we must go soon to make the ceremony."

"Please, just one more moment," Louie requested.

The guard glanced at his watch and nodded, resigned to the delay. "Yes, Mr. President," he whispered, closing the door behind him.

When Louie turned back to his uncle, Mugaba's eyes were wide with understanding. "So, I see that you have realized your father's promise after all," he said, in amazement. "I shouldn't have underestimated you."

"This was never my plan," Louie said without emotion.

"It may not have been your plan, but it was your destiny. You remember the old village saying: The one nearest to the enemy is the real leader."

Louie got up from his chair and moved to the door. As he reached for the handle, he stopped and turned as something occurred to him. "My mother came back from New Jersey," he said. "Would you like to see her?"

Mugaba was staring down at the table, defeated. "Why would she want to see her brother like this?" he mumbled.

"Because she loves you. I can have someone bring her over if you like."

Mugaba nodded without looking up. "Thank you," he whispered.

Louie left without another word.

+++

Owen was waiting outside in the observation area, sitting behind the two-way mirror.

"He's a broken man," he said, almost gleefully. "You got to him out there in the jungle when he was vulnerable. That was a masterful bit of work. You know, you could have a great future in the agency if you ever want to come over to the other side. We could use guys like you."

"You consider this a success?" Louie asked incredulously.

"Arc you kidding?" Owen said, barely able to contain his excitement. "This is pretty much as good as things turn out at this latitude. I can assure you, the home office was very pleased with the outcome."

"Is that so?" Louie deadpanned.

"Absolutely. For once, the press is giving us a fair shake. They're spinning this as a great victory for our counterinsurgency strategy: a major attack on Kiskow thwarted by a plucky band of Gisawian soldiers, a notorious fugitive captured, and a corrupt government official facing justice. We're coming out of this looking like fucking heroes."

"Funny that no one bothered mentioning the fact that Emanuel Sekibo was on your payroll for years when he was head of Police Intelligence," Louie noted. "You created the monster that eventually turned on you."

"It was a different time and different circumstances," Owen protested. "There's nothing to be gained from rehashing ancient history. What's important now is the big picture. We stopped him from launching a senseless war and selling out your country to the Chinese. How can you not see this as a good thing?"

"I suppose they're declaring it a victory back in Washington?" Louie speculated.

"It's close enough for government work. We're chalking this one up as a win."

"A win for who? You manipulated an election and got my best friend killed," Louie hissed.

"Wait a second," Owen said, throwing up his hands. "We didn't push the button on the bomb that killed your friend. Sekibo's men were responsible for that. You know we had nothing to do with it."

"You knew all along that he was behind the attacks, but you never said a thing."

"We exercised our best available options under challenging circumstances," Owen pushed back. "Your friend's involvement was never part of the plan. He made himself a target when he started asking questions. Of all people, he should have known the risks of poking around in Sekibo's business."

Louie was having none of it. "He wouldn't have done it if I hadn't asked for his help. This all started because you put my name on that ballot."

"We didn't have a choice!" Owen insisted. "Your country and mine would have been far worse off if Sekibo had stolen the election."

"That's not for you to decide."

"There's no point arguing over this," Owen said in frustration. "But you better get used to it. That's how the game is played now. No one has the stomach for big wars anymore. Everybody's chasing tactical wins on the margins. These days, information and influence are the weapons of choice. It's just like I told you when we first met."

"More wisdom from Dr. Ziegler, I presume?" Louie asked sarcastically.

"Ignore him at your peril. Either you're the hammer or the nail. It's your choice."

The door opened, and the nervous man in the suit reappeared. "Sir, I beg you. We're running out of time," he pleaded.

"I'm sorry," Louie said. "I'll be right out."

The man closed the door, and Louie turned back to Owen. "I want you out of the country by the end of the day. Is that clear?" he demanded.

"Sure thing," Owen said, smiling smugly. "My work here is done. I've got to get back to Washington anyway. I'm starting a new assignment next week."

"And to be completely clear, you're not welcome back here. Ever."

"I'm sorry to hear you say that." Owen shrugged. "But I guess you're in charge now, so I'll respect your wishes."

Louie headed for the door and left Owen alone in the room.

+++

The soldier was pacing outside the building when Louie appeared. He ushered him straight to a waiting limousine, opening the door and bowing as Louie stepped inside. Anna was waiting in the back seat, wearing a blue dress, pillbox hat, and high heels. She smiled as Louie slid in beside her. He leaned over and kissed her cheek.

"You look nice," he said. "I don't think I've ever seen you in heels."

"It's not my style, but then again, one doesn't have many opportunities to attend an inauguration. I figured I should step it up a bit."

"I think you're more excited than I am," Louie chuckled.

"I didn't get invited to my high school prom. This is probably the best I'm going get," Anna said with a wink. "I hope you have something else to wear," she said, looking disapprovingly at his camouflage uniform.

"There's a suit in the trunk," Louie said as the limo pulled away. "I'll change once we get there."

Outside the Defense Ministry, they were met by an armed convoy, which escorted them to the ceremony. Gun jeeps from the presidential guard surrounded them while a swarm of police motorcycles raced ahead, clearing the route to Independence Square.

"How did things go with your uncle?" Anna asked, gazing out the window at the spectacle.

"As expected, I suppose. No matter what I say, he'll always believe that I betrayed him."

"Did you tell him about the election?"

"Sort of," Louie said. "But it only made things worse. I think it confirmed in his mind that I was planning this all along."

"If he thinks that, then he never really knew you," Anna reassured him. "Do you know what will happen to him?"

"That depends on how much he helps in the case against Sekibo."

"Will he cooperate?"

"I don't know. Perhaps if he sees it working to his advantage. But it will take more than my uncle's testimony to convict Sekibo. He still has powerful friends willing to protect him. And he knows where the skeletons are buried. If Sekibo ever decides to talk, he has enough dirt to take down half the government."

Anna was quiet, still staring out the window as the convoy raced through empty streets.

"Your father would be proud of you," she said, finally.

"Maybe. I don't know anymore. Nothing that I once believed seems to be true. Everyone always said that my father would have become president someday. But what does that say about him? Sekibo and my uncle were corrupted by power. Who's to say that my father wouldn't have been the same? I'm not sure that I knew him well enough to know the answer."

"I suppose that makes today even more ironic," Anna said.

"What do you mean?"

"Do you remember back when this all started? Nesi and Didier wouldn't believe me when I told them that you never registered for the election," she said.

Louie shook his head, having forgotten the conversation.

"I told you that the only person who can be trusted with power is someone who doesn't want it," Anna continued.

"That's what makes you different from people like your uncle and Sekibo. You never wanted any of this."

"People still don't believe it," Louie sighed.

"Have you made up your mind which speech to use?"

Louie reached into his breast pocket and pulled out two envelopes, identical except for a cryptic marking on the outside flap. He stared at them for a moment, then handed one over to Anna.

"This is the one I plan to use," he said, putting the other back into his pocket.

"Should I open it?"

Louie nodded.

"Has anyone else read them?" she asked, unsealing the envelope.

"No. I wrote both versions and sealed them right away. No one has seen them but you."

Anna pulled out the pages and began reading. When she came to the bottom of the second page, she turned and stared at him. "Are you sure?"

Louie nodded again.

Anna smiled and resumed gazing out the window as the convoy entered Independence Square. Thousands of people were streaming into the overflowing stadium. Louie caught a glimpse of the inaugural dais, adorned with streamers and Gisawian flags flapping in the wind. The limo raced past throngs of cheering crowds before disappearing into a service entrance under the stadium. It rolled to a stop at the entrance to a tunnel. Two armed guards were posted outside the door, waiting to escort Louie to the stage.

Anna was lost in a daydream, staring out the window.

"What are you thinking?" Louie asked.

"I was just wondering. Do I still get to call myself a former first lady when you resign from office at your inauguration?"

Louie smiled and reached for her hand.

"I'm not sure how that works," he admitted. "But if nothing else, maybe someone will finally get around to fixing the air conditioner in your office at the university."

Anna smiled. "In that case, it will all be worth it."

A soldier opened the limo door and waited for Louie to get out. Another one stood at attention, holding a pressed business suit and a pair of highly shined leather shoes.

"Mr. President, we only have a few minutes until the ceremony begins," the man said, urging Louie out of the limo.

Anna squeezed Louie's hand and gestured for him to go. "I'll see you on the stage," she said.

He got out and was about to walk away when Anna called after him. "Don't forget this," she said, handing him the envelope with his speech inside.

Louie smiled, grabbed the envelope, and disappeared down the tunnel.

ABOUT THE AUTHOR

Glenn Voelz served for twenty-five years in the Army as an intelligence officer and spent over a decade living and working in Asia, Europe, the Middle East, and Africa. He held in leadership positions at the Pentagon on the Joint Chiefs of Staff, in the White House Situation Room, and at NATO headquarters.

Voelz lives in Oregon with his family and has published over a dozen books and journal articles on various topics, including diplomatic history, government contracting, military innovation, and emergency management.

THE GISAWI CHRONICLES

War Under the Mango Tree

Operation Hermes

The Third Force

To learn more about the author visit
GlennVoelz.com